PRAISE FOR JOE HART

We Sang in the Dark

"Joe Hart is one of the most exciting and consistently entertaining horror writers to come along in years. If you haven't yet read his work, I'd advise you to rectify that oversight posthaste. Trust me, you'll be glad you did. Hart's is an old-school sensibility with a modern twist, and anything he writes is well worth reading."
—Kealan Patrick Burke, Bram Stoker Award–winning author of *The Turtle Boy* and *Kin*

Obscura

"Outstanding . . . Fans of Blake Crouch's Wayward Pines series, with its combination of mystery, horror, and science fiction, will find this right up their alley."
—*Publishers Weekly* (starred review)

"This gripping book will be a must-read for fans of SF-based mysteries such as John Scalzi's *Lock In* and Kristine Kathyrn Rusch's Retrieval Artist series, as well as aficionados of stories about science gone wrong, too far, or both."
—*Library Journal* (starred review)

"The pacing is excellent from beginning to end."
—*Los Angeles Times*

"Those seeking an off-planet sci-fi thriller with a haunting plotline will devour Joe Hart's *Obscura*, which reads quick and is ̶ ̶ ̶ ith terrifying surprises."

"For the reader who likes hard science fiction with some mystery and suspense thrown in, *Obscura* should hit the spot. It's not merely sci-fi, but a thriller wrapped in the deadly solitude of space with a determined heroine who refuses to give up."

—*New York Journal of Books*

"Joe Hart is a tremendous talent, and with *Obscura*, he has taken his storytelling to the next level. This is a genius work of science fiction, brimming with thrills, scares, and most importantly, heart. I devoured this book, and you will too."

—Blake Crouch, *New York Times* bestselling author of *Dark Matter* and the Wayward Pines series

The Last Girl

"What if there were only one thousand women left on the planet? This is the conceit of *The Last Girl*, and it's the kind of premise I live for. Part *Children of Men*, part *The Count of Monte Cristo* for the modern age, Joe Hart has written a rapturous, thought-provoking, impossible-to-put-down thriller that is destined to become the first BIG BOOK of 2016."

—Blake Crouch, *New York Times* bestselling author of *Dark Matter* and the Wayward Pines series

OR
ELSE

ALSO BY JOE HART

The Dominion Trilogy

The Last Girl
The Final Trade
The First City

The Liam Dempsey Mysteries

The River Is Dark
The Night Is Deep

Novels

Lineage
Singularity
EverFall
The Waiting
Widow Town
Cruel World
Obscura
I'll Bring You Back
We Sang in the Dark

Novellas

Leave the Living

Short Story Collections

Midnight Paths: A Collection of Dark Horror
Something Came Through: And Other Stories

Short Stories

"The Line Unseen"
"Outpost"
"And the Sea Called Her Name"
"The Exorcism of Sara May"

Comics

The Last Sacrifice

OR
ELSE

A THRILLER

JOE HART

THOMAS & MERCER

Text copyright © 2022 by Joe Hart
All rights reserved.

Published by Thomas & Mercer, Seattle

www.apub.com

Amazon, the Amazon logo, and Thomas & Mercer are trademarks of Amazon.com, Inc., or its affiliates.

ISBN-13: 9781542035125
ISBN-10: 1542035120

Cover design by M.S. Corley

Printed in the United States of America

For Jade

A wonderful fact to reflect upon, that every human creature is constituted to be that profound secret and mystery to every other.

—*Charles Dickens*

You're responsible. All of us are our choices, and yours are suddenly on fire and burning the ones you care about the most. You did this.

You are going to find her. You are going to find the boys. All of them alive and well. You are going to do this because you are the reason they're missing.

This is how you'll do it.

You're going to dig in and keep your head up. You're going to notice things. You're going to see what other people miss. You are going to think and reason and deduce better than any of the sleepy-eyed detectives you write about in your books. You are going to work harder than you ever have before, because you love her.

And you're going to do it in secret, because a secret is trust, and she trusted you.

1

Footsteps coming down the hall in the dark.

Dad was up again.

I woke, rubbing my eyes in the faint blue light of the still-glowing television. I was on the couch, neck hurting from falling asleep against the world's hardest pillow.

Dad emerged from the hall and skirted through the living room, barely a ghost in the light of whatever god-awful programming was on at . . . I checked my phone . . . two thirty in the morning. He passed out of view, slippers shuffling.

Tired. So tired. A few broken nights of sleep in a row will do that to a person. I thought back to days of yore, of flopping down at 10:00 p.m. and going somewhere else completely for a flawless eight or nine hours. That was the past; this was the now. Before and after. Like a diagnosis.

"Dad," I said, rising from the couch. He'd already disappeared into the main bath. I don't know why he always came out to use this one when he had an en suite in his bedroom. Just another mystery of what was happening to him, another quirk of the disease slowly lowering blinds and turning off lights in the corridors of his mind.

He was standing at the sink holding his razor, hot water beginning to steam up the mirror, obscuring his reflection. The writer in me thought of an overobvious metaphor about how soon he wouldn't be able to see himself in the mirror, and I stuffed a mental gag down the writer's throat.

"Hey, Dad, whatcha doin'?" I asked, rubbing the last of the sleep from my eyes.

"Hmm? Oh hey, forgot you were still here. I had to pee." He stopped, blinking a few times, then reached out and shut off the hot water. "Thought I had an early shift." He huffed a quiet laugh and shook his head.

"It's okay. Wanna try going back to bed?"

"No. I think I'll sit up a bit. Watch a little TV." I followed him back to the living room, helped him get comfortable in his recliner, made sure he had the remote, hugged him good night.

"Night, son."

How many of those did we have left? It's what I'd taken to wondering whenever he called me *son* or said my name. How many more times would I be Andy? How long before I became a stranger with a familiar face? Then just a stranger.

"Night, Dad."

I stood on his covered porch and took in the neighborhood, so dark and still and quiet at this hour. Long breath out, deep breath in of night air. The Loop, what we called the little development where our family had lived since my parents bought the lot the house stood on now, was dotted with a dozen or so homes—both sides of the long, curving street on the lower slope of a hill. Beyond the far side of the road, untouched wilderness met the edges of manicured lawns. Wildness and domesticity merged but didn't mingle. In the distance the Adirondacks were dark heaves against the night sky.

I took the steps down to the front walk, pausing for a second to glance at the house two doors up from Dad's. It was like all the others and different at the same time. I smiled at that. Knowing a secret was good. At least I'd always seen it that way. A secret was safety. A secret was trust.

Past the house the church rose at the pinnacle of the hill, lording over all below. Its steeple stabbed at the sky. I looked at the building, its shape still seeming much too large for its plot of land, a stomach spilling over a cinched beltline. The church was new—at least to our town it was. New fifteen years ago, when I was transitioning from high school to college out of state. The old church had been demolished, torn down and removed like something the community was ashamed of. They rebuilt on the foundations, though, the sprawling catacomb basement of my nightmares. My older brother, Cory, had lured me down there one day on the pretense he would let me fly his radio-controlled plane if I just explored with him for a while. Mom had been busy with whatever function she'd been overseeing in the parish hall above, and Cory and I were left to our own devices.

The basement door was a thousand feet tall. That's how I remember it. Constructed of gray steel from a time when things were built to last. It made such a heavy clunking sound when Cory locked it behind me. I can still hear it. Hours down there in the dark, pounding on the door, no one coming to help. Then stumbling through the dusty rooms, hands scrabbling for a light switch and never finding anything except cobwebs and doorways leading into more rooms. The basement and the dark were endless.

Mom found me eventually. She'd been angry from what I recall. Not at Cory so much, though I think he'd gotten a stern look. I shouldn't have been playing down there. Irresponsible. How had it looked to everyone when she couldn't find me? Her hand had been cold on my arm, clutching me all the way down the hill as she steered me home.

Deep breath in. Out.

I ignored the church and focused again on the house up the street before smiling at the stars glittering on their dark blanket. I crossed the drive to my house. It sat kitty-corner from Dad's place, a simple slab-on-grade with big windows in the living room I liked to read by when it was cold or rainy. They also gave me a good view, easy to look out and see if Dad was awake when he should've been sleeping or if he was finally starting the landscaping project my mother had hounded him about when she'd still been able to hound.

Up the stairs to the front door. I gave the neighborhood one last look. Perfect in the night. My problem is I'm a romantic—at least that's what my editor always says. *Happy endings are fine, Andy, but not every thriller should have so much closure. Less tied up with bows, more interpretation for the reader.* Yeah, okay, I guess. But I like to think things have a way of working out, a natural order sometimes disguised as chaos. For the most part I thought everything would be okay. Maybe that's why I'd be seriously searching for a new line of employment soon. Publishing wasn't a sure thing, so I had a distinct feeling bartending or perhaps pushing a broom at the paper mill in the center of town was in my near future if the latest story idea didn't pan out.

So be it. I was where I needed to be. That was the important thing.

I pulled open the storm door. Something drifted down and landed at my feet. A note. It had been folded neatly in half and tucked there sometime after I'd gone over to Dad's for the evening. I picked it up and stepped inside the house, flipping on the entry light. The note was typed, only two lines long:

> I know about you and Rachel. You will stop seeing her. Don't ruin her or her family's life.
>
> Do as I say or else.

Deep breath. In and out.

2

I read the note perhaps twenty times before walking to the nearest chair and sinking into it.

I'd turned on only the one light, and I sat partially in shadow near the dining room table. It's how I felt, half in reality, half in disbelief.

How? That was the first question. How did someone find out about Rachel and me? Just as quickly I thought, Does it matter? Not really. Someone knew despite how careful we'd been over the last six months. It didn't matter we'd left our houses at different times, met at different hotels, motels, parks where she'd climbed into my car or I'd climbed into hers. Someone knew, and now the best thing in my life was over.

———

Rachel August Worth.

A year younger than me in school. I'd seen her for the first time struggling to climb the jungle gym in fifth grade. Skinny, shy, fading freckles from summer. I'd always thought she was pretty in a delicate way. The way you might admire a statue behind glass.

We'd see each other in church. She sat in the frontmost pew with her mom and dad alongside David Barren and his parents. The two most powerful families in Sandford. More money between them than in any other ten households in town combined. The Worths owned two clothing stores and the movie theater. The Barrens had a hotel, a hardware store, and three restaurants. Prominent in the church. Active in the city council. Leaving their marks on the community one board meeting at a time.

It was no surprise to anyone that they maneuvered their children together just like any of the other projects they undertook. Thin, quiet, waifish, brittle Rachel nudged toward charismatic, loud, smug, handsome David. A match made in heaven, or as close as their parents could afford to it.

The last time I saw Rachel before moving back to look after Dad was at my sister's funeral. She'd whispered condolences to me in the receiving line. I'd barely heard her over the sound of my grief. My particular sorrow sounded like the rustling of plastic covering the hole in the side of the church where the stained glass had been before I'd put a rock through it in a drunken haze a few nights prior.

I'd thanked her in the same quiet volume, and then I hadn't seen her for fourteen years. It was like any other story about people you knew at one point. You went your separate ways, ships setting off for destinations across limitless seas, and you thought about them sometimes, maybe never, until one day you were living just down the street from them.

Rachel Worth, now Rachel Barren, had been standing at her mailbox the day I moved back to the Loop. I didn't recognize her at first; then she'd given me a wave, and all the memories returned. I'd watched her walk up her driveway to the sprawling split-level until my view was cut off by the moving truck hauling all my earthly belongings to the next stage of my life.

A stage beginning then and leading to the note left in my front door.

I made coffee. It's what I did whenever I needed to think. I drank coffee while I wrote my novels or short stories. Caffeine got the mind working. While it brewed, I weighed my options. The scales had tipped by the time the coffee hit the cup.

I had to quit seeing her.

It turned my stomach. Made me sick.

I took my coffee into the living room and sat by the big windows. I could see both Rachel's house and Dad's. Rachel's was still dark, but a light would come on in the kitchen soon. She was an early riser, organized, deeply committed to her boys. Asher was nine, and Joey was going to be six soon. She always packed their lunches. She'd told me this the first time we'd talked, really talked, not just the polite conversation of neighbors bumping into one another. That was a few days after the kiss in the kitchen and . . .

I stood up from the chair, staring into the dark.

God, how had I forgotten? Passed it off as nothing, I suppose. Told myself it was okay, that whoever it was hadn't seen anything from their vantage point on the lawn. They hadn't been paying attention. The angle was wrong. Sure.

But obviously it hadn't been.

Slowly I sat back down and watched the blue light dancing from Dad's TV. Maybe he was sleeping now. I hoped so. He seemed to be better when he got good rest. Less wandering of his thoughts, fewer memories being displaced and refiled in the wrong spots.

I should sleep too. Right.

The note was on the kitchen table, but I'd already memorized it. Pretty straightforward. *Do as I say or else.* Inelegant, but I guessed whoever had penned it didn't write notes demanding an end to affairs on a regular basis.

I wanted to take it all back.

I wanted to take it further than we had.

My coffee was cold.

I made her laugh. I guess that's what I can trace it back to. I'd been settled in my new place for a few days and was helping Dad with something in the backyard when his doorbell rang.

Rachel was as striking as I recalled, and for a second I didn't know what to say. Both of us just standing in Dad's front doorway, looking at each other. Her holding a loaf of banana bread, me holding my breath. Then I spit out some stupid line about not wanting anything from Schwan's and shut the door in her face. I pulled it open again right away, and she laughed.

That was it.

We saw each other around town. Most times she was with her boys. I said hi. They said hello, both very polite little gentlemen. We talked at any church functions I brought Dad to. She never commented on me not entering the sanctuary for Mass or how I'd wait outside the front doors if the weather was nice. She understood. We'd chat for a minute in the river of parishioners, two fish swimming momentarily side by side. Just a few "How are yous" and a joke here and there. I made it a point to try to make her laugh. It was a little selfish—I liked the sound of it. Sometimes she would look at me and I'd see something behind her eyes, some momentary flash that didn't remind me of a delicate glass sculpture. It brought to mind a summer storm on a beach, waves crashing in and a relentless tide pulling them back out.

I ran into David, her husband, one afternoon in midsummer. He'd walked down the street while I was mowing Dad's yard, a cold beer in each hand. I thought, Okay, now I'll feel like an ass for admiring this guy's wife, because he'll be different than he was in school. He'll have grown up and become a nice man with a nice family, and Andy Drake should go stick his head in the sand for being a total creep.

David was still a prick.

Loud. Overbearing. Uncomfortably charming by the sheer pressure of his gaze and smile. He chatted me up in the hot sun and left me with a hard slap on the shoulder and an invitation to stop by his lending agency if I ever needed anything. When he was gone, I poured out the beer he'd given me.

Skip forward three months.

A neighborhood get-together at the Barrens'. I got the impression David hosted them because it kept the image of his perfect suburban family freeze-framed in the community's collective mind. Mr. and Mrs. Barren, loving couple, handsome sons, successful business owners, church board members, pristine lawn.

I'd been clearing plates from the tables in the backyard near the tail end of the party. Dad and my sister Keli sat off to one side in the shade, sipping from paper cups. The house was wide open, doors and windows ajar, kids running in and out. I sidestepped my nieces as they raced after Rachel's two boys, calling out the obligatory warning for them to slow down. Rachel was upstairs in the kitchen crying into her hands.

I hadn't known what to do. No one else seemed to be in the house. There were the outside sounds of people talking faintly, the hum of a lawn mower somewhere else in the Loop, and her soft sobs hitting me right in the chest.

When she heard me step into the kitchen, she turned, tears trailing mascara down her cheeks. She saw me and huffed a laugh that turned into another sob, and then I was near enough to put a hand on her shoulder and ask what was wrong. She looked at my hand there on her shoulder, then so did I.

I pulled it away, saying, "Sorry, sorry, sorry." She shook her head, sniffling and grabbing a paper towel off the counter to dry her eyes. We stood there for a second, all the confines of suburban life muted outside the little bubble we were in, and I just watched her, waiting for her to talk. She didn't, only shook her head again before giving me the saddest smile I've ever seen.

In one of my books, my main character would've said something comforting, something profound to get the other person to open up. But I had nothing except a sense I'd invaded a very private moment with no idea how to extricate myself.

Rachel went to move past me, and I backed up out of her way until my hip touched the countertop. I was about to issue another apology when suddenly she was inches away, her face brushing mine.

She kissed me.

It was wonderful, and so fleeting. There and gone in a half second that seared itself into me. To a casual observer it could have just been Rachel reaching past me for an item on the counter or leaning close to say something discreet. But it had been a kiss. A secret.

Then she was gone. Out of the kitchen and down the hall to the bathroom. The faint clicking of a door being shut.

I turned, bracing myself against the counter, and looked out the window into the side yard just in time to see someone disappearing around the corner of the house.

3

I didn't sleep. Dawn came and backlit the mountains in hues of gray, then pink.

More coffee, bordering on the point of jitters. I tried to write but gave up after putting down a few dozen sentences, then deleting the last page I'd written. Not writer's block, writer's distraction. Writer's scatterbrain. Writer's world upending.

I used binoculars to look up the street as soon as it was light enough to see if there was a twin of my note poking from the Barrens' storm door. I felt dirty, like the bird lady next door. Mrs. Tross. Pushing eighty with a husband dead nearly ten years, probably killed by the point of his wife's sharp tongue. We called her the bird lady because at any point in the day, she could be seen at one of her windows, Swarovski binoculars glued to her face, looking like some kind of alien insect, gathering intel on the Loop, while claiming she was only watching the local avian species.

I couldn't see a note, but that didn't mean it wasn't there. I had to trust our observer wasn't going to be too overt. I hoped they were cautious. The chances of someone stumbling upon my note, especially in the middle of the night, were low. But I could see one of Rachel's kids, maybe Joey, opening up the door and finding her note. Not sure of all the words, he brings it to his dad to read. Christ on a bike.

That was, of course, if David himself hadn't written it.

No, if Rachel's husband had caught wind of us, I would've known right away. Probably in the form of catching one of his fists with my face. David was a lot of things, but he wasn't subtle.

Besides, the note itself felt like a warning, not a threat. Whoever wrote it wanted us to stop discreetly—otherwise they would've shouted it from a rooftop. Being the possessor of neighborhood gossip was tough to resist. My stomach turned, and something Rachel had said came rushing back. *My mother told me if I ever made a mistake again like I did that time with Joey, she and my dad would take David's side if he sought custody.*

I shoved away visions of our affair's fallout. It was all too much. I was used to being persona non grata in town after vandalizing everyone's precious church, but I didn't want that for Rachel or her kids, didn't want anything to happen to them if I could help it.

The air smelled like spring when I stepped outside a while later. The neighborhood was waking up. Garage doors opening, cars backing out. Kids trundling down the sidewalk, backpacks hoisted on shoulders, a few dog barks. I threw a couple of looks at Rachel's as I crossed to Dad's but didn't see anyone. I guess I'd eventually get used to not looking at her house, but it wouldn't be today. Not tomorrow either.

Dad was snoozing in his chair, white hair in disarray, hand on the remote. I turned off the TV and started breakfast. Eggs, bacon, toast, orange juice, more coffee. It was our routine for me to come over for breakfast and normally dinner. It wasn't that Dad couldn't look after himself—he could for the most part. Constant supervision was a ways off yet. The plan Keli and I had worked out was I'd move into my old room once things became more unmanageable. And when I couldn't give him the full care he needed, well, we'd stumble across that bridge when we came to it.

The smell must've woken him, because he shambled into the kitchen not long after the bacon hit the pan. "Morning," he said, pouring himself coffee. "Gonna be a beauty today."

"I think so."

"Who won last night?"

"Yanks."

He grunted. "Should go down for a game this summer. Be fun, wouldn't it?"

"Sure. You feel up to something like that, we'll do it. Maybe for your birthday? Only a couple weeks away."

"Don't remind me. Oof. Getting old sucks, but the alternative isn't any better." He thought for a moment. "Yeah, a game might be a good present. We could take Keli, Mark, and the girls."

"Don't think Mark will want to tag along, Dad."

As I transferred eggs and bacon to our plates, I watched the processing in his features. A slow realization that it wasn't three years ago and Keli and Mark were no longer bound in holy matrimony. "Oh right, Kel probably wouldn't want him to come."

"The girls and Kel would love it, though," I said. He nodded.

We ate in silence. The silence ate at me.

This house used to be loud. Four kids, two parents, a dog at one point. Always someone coming or going. Dad worked for twenty-five years as a security guard for the paper mill in town, the first fifteen of them night shifts. He'd come in around the time we were headed out to school, always a smile for us, a question about what was happening that day, before ambling off to bed. Our mother worked as a stenographer at the courthouse. She not only typed in shorthand but lived it too. Almost all her interactions were abbreviated, boiled down to the bones of what she needed out of a conversation. And beneath everything was the bedrock of her faith. Trust in the Lord, she'd say, and you'll never want for anything.

Our older brother, Cory, could quote scripture and turn his faux innocent gaze on our mom like a heat ray, while Kel and I could recite old episodes of *Teenage Mutant Ninja Turtles* and had sword fights in the garage. Our youngest sister, Emma, could tell you the velocity of

NASA rockets leaving the atmosphere or what a person's body weight was on the moon. She stargazed and dreamed and had the kindest heart I've ever known. She was too good for this world, and that's why she was no longer in it.

I glanced down the hallway to my old bedroom and sighed. Someday not too far off, I'd be sleeping in there again, door open so I'd be able to hear Dad get up in the middle of the night when he rose, thinking he was late for work. Back where I started life. Caught in a loop on the Loop.

When we were both done eating, I collected our plates and started doing the dishes, eyes mostly on Rachel's place up the street. After a bit I began glancing at the landline attached to the wall beside the stove, willing it to ring. Maybe she'd seen me walk over here, just like the time a few days after the kiss when suddenly the phone had jangled and Dad answered, then handed it to me.

Can you meet me? To talk? The tone of her voice had sounded like she was asking for the moon.

It was raining when I stepped into the little café in the neighboring town of West Forge. I hadn't asked why she wanted to meet twenty minutes away. You don't have to when your neighbor kisses you in her kitchen, then calls you at your father's a few minutes after you walk in the door.

Rachel was sitting in a far corner booth, hair wet the same as mine, coffee steaming in front of her. The café was mostly empty; we had half the place completely to ourselves. When I sat down across from her, she didn't say anything at first, just watched me until my own coffee was sitting before me.

She asked me if I was married, which took me by surprise. No, not anymore. Sharon and I had been together for about six years before she'd decided her cycle instructor would be a better fit. *You're always lost inside your own head,* Sharon had said as she packed the last of her things. *I'm tired of living with someone who's not here half the time.* It was ironic since she traveled a lot for work and wasn't home for long stretches. But she wasn't wrong. I did get lost in my stories, in scenes playing out that only I could see. Despite my books paying the bills, she needed more than I could give. I didn't blame her; it's hard to blame someone you still love. So Sharon went her way, and I stayed in our little apartment in the city until Dad called with some news after a doctor's visit.

I gave Rachel the shorthand version; my mother would've been proud. She seemed to digest it, staring at my left hand, I suppose looking at where my ring had been. Then she started talking.

First about the weather, then about the boys and what activities they were involved in. How Joey had a gluten intolerance so she packed his lunch every day before he went off to kindergarten at the school attached to the church on the hill. How he'd been anxious about going to school for the last couple of months and she didn't know exactly how to help him. She talked about her book club and how they'd read one of my novels years ago. Laughed when she told me the leader of the group had panned it. I laughed too. She said David didn't read much other than financial reports. That and a few sports websites on Sundays.

She'd looked down, staring into her coffee. Then she'd really started talking.

She said when she was eight, her father had taken away her nightlight. It was in the shape of Minnie Mouse, and the day her dad declared she was old enough to sleep without it was the first day she felt the beginnings of anxiety. A seed, if you will. Seeds can grow anything; it's hard to know what will sprout when they're planted until they bloom.

At night she'd sneak a desk lamp into her room and put it back every morning before her parents woke up. When she was caught doing that, she started sleeping with the lights on until her father told her she needed to grow up and he shut off the breaker to her room each night. It took the better part of a year before she was able to sleep with only the door cracked to the hall. After that, she started to worry. About

17

everything, she said. It didn't matter if it was something important or trivial. She fretted, chewed her nails, developed slight tics. She didn't blame her father. She thought the anxiety had always been there, just a part of the fabric of who she was. She glanced out at the rain when she said it.

Different medications while she was a teenager. A few helped, most didn't.

A teacher suggested a therapist. Her parents brought her to see Father Mathew at the church.

Confession was cleansing. It would wash away the worry. She actually smiled at that. By then she was dating David, her mother already planning their wedding. When she got pregnant with Asher, the planning kicked into high gear.

I love music, love to sing. Always wondered if I was good enough to record an album. Rachel paused, then went on. *I had one conversation with my mother,* she said, so quiet I had to lean forward in my seat to hear her. *I asked her if she ever wanted anything different for herself, her life. She told me if I didn't marry David, she and my father would never forgive me. The baby and I would be on our own.* She laughed sadly. *I already felt like I was on my own.*

When Joey was two, she tried a new medication. It was supposed to be a step up from the last one her doctor had prescribed, and the recommended dosage was slightly too high. It was a nice day, and she'd taken the boys into the front yard to play. She sat down in a lawn chair, and the next moment, she was waking up to the shriek of brakes. Asher was still playing cars on the lawn, but Joey was standing in the middle of the street a few feet from the bumper of an idling Chevy truck.

Rachel had paused there, swallowing hard for a second. Joey was okay, but the Loop had come alive at that point. The bird lady was suddenly outside, as were a half dozen others. All of them exclaiming and running over to see what the commotion was about. She'd rushed to pick Joey up, clutching him to her as if she could erase the past few minutes if she held him tight enough. The driver of the truck yelled at her, and Mrs. Pell from the other side of the street crossed her arms and shook her head.

It didn't help I'd had too much to drink at the last church social, she said, turning her cup around on the table. *Everyone thought I was a drunk and I'd neglected my son.*

I reached out and took her hand then. It was cool and soft in my own.

She sat looking at our hands. She took a deep breath.

David's business wasn't doing well. Hadn't been for a while. He'd gotten a loan from his parents for a start-up, taken on his best friend as a business partner against their wishes. On certain days he'd come home in dark moods, unspeaking for hours, silence filling up their house until she said something that would set him off. He'd never hit her, she asserted. She wanted to make that clear. The abuse was verbal, emotional, only bruising on the inside. So much better, I thought.

I wanted to ask you here to say I'm sorry for the other day in the kitchen. Everything had been piling up, and I don't know why the dam broke then and there during the party, but I'm sorry I did what I did. She didn't look at me when she said it, but I was still holding her hand. Everyone had a breaking point—I knew that. But I wasn't sure if that's what this was. For a moment my response balanced on an edge, then tipped over with the heavy beating of my pulse.

I'm not sorry, I said. And she looked at me.

The summer storm was in her eyes again. Could've swept me away. I would've let it.

Instead she slowly drew her hand back.

We sat for a while more, not talking, just finishing our coffees. I paid when we rose from our seats and stepped out under the café's awning. We were alone in the rain, and I felt I should say something more, some sentiment to put her at ease, let her know she could talk to me whenever she needed. Before I could say anything, she told me she'd rented a room at the motel just down the street. Her eyes met mine and slipped away. She was trembling.

We drove in my car.

The room was dark and warm when we went inside. She was another shadow, stepping close, wet clothes under my fingertips. She kissed me for the second time, much longer than in the kitchen. Over the pounding of my heart, I asked her if she was sure.

She was.

———

"Penny for your thoughts." Dad nudged my side, and I quit looking at the phone hanging on the wall. Came back from six months ago and started scrubbing egg yolk off a plate.

"I'd be ripping you off," I said, completing our ancient back-and-forth. He dried the dishes as I washed them. The sun shone over the mountains and hit the church's steeple.

When the dishes were done, we went grocery shopping. Kel and the girls were coming over later for a cookout, and we needed steak and beer. While I pushed the cart and Dad loaded it, I thought of ways to reach out to Rachel. All of them were risky. Who knew if or when our observer was watching? If I spoke to her, it would have to be 100 percent private or completely out in the open, just two neighbors chatting for a few seconds. Nothing to see here, move along.

There was a bulletin board at the exit of the grocery store. I grabbed a few job opening flyers. In the car, Dad said, "You thinking of quitting writing?"

"No. Just might need a little supplemental income. Last book hasn't earned out yet."

He frowned. "You're still working on the new one, though, right?"

"Yep."

"Then things might still be okay."

I gave him a smile. Dad was a romantic too. "They might."

As we were putting the groceries away, my phone pinged, and my blood pressure spiked. Rachel had never called my cell or texted, always ringing Dad's if she wanted to get ahold of me, but I knew it would be her. She would be distraught, furious, filled with regret. Or maybe it was our observer, stepping into the light just enough to make another demand.

It was Kel.

Did you hear about Mary Shelby?

No. What happened?

She died two days ago.

I sat down and waited until I could speak again to tell Dad.

4

You guide your car around the curves, up over hills, through a majesty of trees and sunlit spring grass in a daze.

You pass over a bridge, torrents of white water and rocks beneath, past an elementary school, past an overgrown cemetery, past a monument you've seen a hundred times and never stopped to actually see what it was a monument to.

You drive on automatic because a woman you wanted so badly to call *Mother* is no longer in the world.

I watched the scenery pass by and thought about second chances, about missed opportunities and clarity that only came with memory and looking back. Disbelief was a cloud around me. Since Kel's text, I hadn't felt like anything was real. The note and now Mary's death were contrived. Something none of my editors would accept in a manuscript.

Go back. Rewrite. Smooth it out. Too much tragedy all at once. Fix it.

The one time I'd be happy to edit.

Mary Shelby, who I only started calling *Mary* after I turned twenty-five, had always been in my life. Literally. There were pictures of her holding me hours after my birth—her grinning, me squalling my head off. She'd been the parish administrator, a wife, a mother, someone who never failed to send you a birthday card that arrived exactly on the day of, a woman who loved horses and riding them. And now she was dead.

I slowed the car as I came up around a steep curve, Mary's driveway being a blind approach directly on the other side. It was almost noon, the sky a cerulean bowl, and I had the window down, letting the air course over me. A blue jay called in the woods, and the gravel of Mary's drive crackled under my tires. No matter how much sensory input I registered, nothing felt real.

Two bends and the little ranch came into view. That's what she always called it: her little ranch. A few chickens, a cow, two dogs, a cat. And of course, her horses. I couldn't accept that they had been the cause of her demise.

The house stood to the left, tucked into the small clearing overlooking a meadow. On the right was the barn and stable, both a matching faded red. There was a light-gray sedan parked beside Mary's SUV in front of the house, no doubt belonging to her only son, Robert.

I pulled in beside the SUV and climbed out at the same time the door was opening on the house. Robert Shelby was a tall, willowy man who had started losing his hair in tenth grade, the last of it disappearing sometime in college. He wore a sport coat over a sweater, perfect attire for an accountant.

He tried to say something when we were a few steps apart and failed. I hugged my friend.

Inside Mary's house, he made us a pot of coffee, even though I was sure if I had one more sip, I'd lift off like a rocket. Robert fumbled around in the kitchen with the gaucherie of someone cooking in a stranger's house. He wiped away a few tears when he couldn't find the coffee filters. We looked for them together.

"I'm so sorry, Robert," I said for the second time. "I wouldn't have come right over except Kel told me you were here."

"No, no, I appreciate it. I got in late last night, and the quiet is . . . eating me up."

We discovered the filters behind a set of mixing bowls, and when the brew was finished, we took our cups into the living room. There was a hot coal perched on the back of my tongue, searing my throat shut. Every time I thought of something to say, the coal would flare and my eyes would begin to water. It didn't help that the living room was decorated with dozens of pictures. Mary at church. Mary with Robert, his wife, Lisa, and their two kids. Mary on vacation in Hawaii. Mary with her arms around my sister and me when we were teenagers. Mary with her horses.

I stared at the last picture for longer than I should have, and Robert noticed. "Yeah, I know. I told her she should've started boarding them somewhere else," he said quietly. "Then none of this would've happened."

"I still don't understand . . ."

He sighed and set his untouched coffee down. "It was Hocus. He was loose inside the stable when they found her. I guess Father Mathew sent Jill Abernathy over to check on her when she didn't show up for work and there was no answer on her phone." Robert struggled for a moment, then went on. "It looks like she was getting ready for a ride sometime Thursday evening. She let Hocus out into the main area, and he must've spooked. He kicked her." Robert gestured to his face. "One time. That was it. Pocus was still penned up."

I could see what had happened. Mary letting the big black stallion out of his pen, maybe feeding him a handful of oats as I'd seen her do hundreds of times over the years. Then grabbing the saddle and walking up behind him, and wham.

That's not what happened.

"I know. Freak accident," Robert said, noticing my expression. There was a tremor in his voice as he gazed around the room full of pictures. "I couldn't believe it when they told me. Still can't."

"Has either of the horses ever kicked her? Or each other?"

"No. Not that she ever told me." He laughed. "Not that she would. You know how she was."

"Tough as nails."

"Tougher. All I can think is she was distracted. She'd been a little scatterbrained on the phone the last few times we talked. Made a mistake the one time, and the one time was all it took. That's why mistakes are bastards; you only have to make one of them." He shook his head. "I haven't been home to see her since Christmas. Isn't that terrible?"

"It's not terrible. You had no idea this would happen. Your mom was in great shape. No reason to think—"

"I should've come home more." There were tears in his voice now.

I leaned forward and grabbed one of his hands. "Hey, how long we been friends?"

"Forever."

"Right. So if you can trust anyone to tell you whether you're a good son, it's me. Robert, you're a good son."

"Was. Was a good son," he said, and broke down completely. I sat next to him while he cried. Put an arm around him. I cried too. Mary had been more than the kind face at every Sunday-morning and Wednesday-night Mass. She'd been my mom's best friend. My dad's too. She'd been my godmother, the person who had defended me when my own mother wouldn't after I'd broken the church's stained glass window. She'd been a woman with something more than insight and empathy. She'd had grace.

We talked for a bit longer about her. Good memories this time: her infallible faith, how she'd been in great health and spirits right up to the last minute. Robert told me what the plans were for her service. I said I was there for him, whatever he needed.

On the way out of the drive, I couldn't help looking at the stable. Mary had trained all of us kids to ride. Kel still rode every so often out here and had told me several times she couldn't wait to get her girls on the horses when they were old enough.

I still recalled that first lesson when I was only six. The sharp scents of manure and oats. How the horse's eyes had been dark and knowing as I walked up to pet him. The soft mane under my fingers.

And prior to letting the animal out of its stall, Mary turning to me and bending down so her face was only inches from mine, saying, *The very most important thing about riding is safety, and safety comes from being aware, Andrew. Always be aware of where you are and where the horse is.*

And don't ever, ever walk up to a horse from behind.

———

"Don't turn this into one of your plots, Andy," Kel said.

We were sitting in the shade of Dad's backyard. Sweet smoke rolled from beneath the grill's lid, and the beer in my hand was so cold, it stung. Kel's girls, Alicia and Emmy, were trying to tackle Dad by holding on to his legs. He was dragging them along in slow Frankenstein steps.

"It's sad enough as it is," she said, taking a long sip from her beer. Kel had cut her hair the week before and was trying new blonde highlights that made her look younger than her thirty-one years, even though she didn't need it. I used to tease her about having a baby face; now I was starting to envy her.

"Gee, thanks."

"You know what I mean. Don't exploit this by making it into something it isn't."

"You ever see her walk up to a horse from behind? Ever?"

"No. But I didn't live with her either. Everyone gets careless and makes mistakes."

I looked up two houses into Rachel's backyard. It was quiet. Empty. My eyes shifted to Mr. Allen Crane's residence. I missed what Kel said next.

"What?"

"I said it's a tragedy—don't make it worse."

"I'm just sitting here with a beer in the shade talking with my sister. That's all."

"Then let's talk about something else or I'll start crying again."

"You know much about that Crane guy down the street?"

"The one who moved in last summer? No. Why?"

"Just curious."

"Haven't seen him since . . . the get-together over at the Barrens' last year."

My stomach clenched at that. I wasn't sure I'd seen him since then either. Wasn't sure if I'd seen him that day disappearing around the corner of the house after Rachel kissed me. Wasn't sure at all about Mr. Allen Crane from down the street.

"Steaks are burning," Kel said.

I leaped up from the chair and tended them. They weren't burning; Kel didn't know the first thing about grilling. I informed her of that by pouring a dollop of cold beer down the back of her shirt. She called me something that would've made our mother's head spin around in a circle and tried hitting me in the crotch. Sibling love.

The girls came bounding up and stood rocking from foot to foot, both asking the same thing but out of sync with one another. "Can we go inside and watch TV till dinner?"

"What did Grampa say?" Kel asked.

"That he's tired," Alicia said. We laughed as Dad dropped into a chair beside us with a groan.

"Okay then. Just until dinner, though." They were gone before Kel could finish the sentence. I was thoroughly convinced kids under ten years old had two speeds: zero and Mach 1.

"Those girls wear me out," Dad grunted, his voice saying he wouldn't have it any other way. He popped a beer and drank deeply. We couldn't let him have more than two drinks—otherwise it might interfere with his medications—but sometimes he managed to sneak a third.

Spring continued to be sprung around us. The birds were back, and the very last of the snow was finally melting in the deepest patches of shade.

"Can't believe she's gone," Dad said finally. We nodded. Mary had just been by to visit him the week before. She'd taken to stopping in regularly after our mother's life-ending stroke. By then, Mary's husband, Daniel, had been gone a few years as well. A part of me had wondered if she and my dad would get together in their twilight years. Some boyish part that always wanted to call Mary Shelby *Mom*. I never asked Kel if she had the same thought, but I wouldn't have been surprised if she did.

"Here's to her," Dad said, holding his bottle out.

We clinked ours with his and drank. I flipped the steaks.

"Makes you think," Dad said quietly, looking down at the deepening green of the lawn between his feet. "Life's so precarious. Easy to slip off the mountain. Doesn't take anything at all. That's why you have to drink moments in." He looked at us, none of the confusion there that sometimes clouded his eyes. "I'm thankful for this. For the grass and the breeze and the sun and the shade to sit in. I'm thankful for this cold beer and the way those girls inside giggle, and for sitting here with my kids. Things are gonna change, but nothing will change this. Nothing will change the way I feel now."

Kel's eyes were shining, and the coal was back in my throat. We hugged Dad. He hugged us back. The steaks were done.

After dinner, I walked Kel to her car and helped get the girls buckled in. "As shitty as today was, tonight was pretty nice," she said after I'd shut the back door on the girls' laughter.

"Yes, it was. Same next weekend?"

"Sure." She surprised me by hugging me hard. My little sister was normally as levelheaded as they came. She sat behind the counter at the local DMV for forty hours a week and listened to countless people piss and moan about paperwork and wait times and blah blah blah and didn't bat an eye. She'd taken Mark's cheating and their subsequent divorce in stride, only breaking down when Alicia had asked if she was divorcing her too. She'd been the rock of our family after Emma's and our mother's deaths, but now I could hear a strain in her voice as she spoke in my ear. "Thank you for taking care of him. I didn't know how I'd manage it with the girls and work. Thank you for coming home."

"It was easy to leave an empty apartment and the plants I kept killing," I said. She laughed and let me go. "I'm happy I can be here."

"We'll get through this, right? We'll take care of him?"

"Absolutely."

"Okay. Next weekend, then."

"Next weekend."

She was half in the driver's seat when she paused. "And leave the thing with Mary alone, okay? You're only going to torture yourself."

I told her I would. And I did.

For a while.

5

I dream of your wedding sometimes when I'm feeling especially strong.

It's a cool March day, because you loved early spring more than any other time of year. You said the air was clearer then, for better atmospheric observation. I believed you because you were always smarter than me.

You're twenty-three or twenty-four, just graduated from the college of your choice, and that's where you met her. She was in your second-year chem class. All alone at a big table, so you went and sat by her. Her name was Amy or Charli. You knew she was special from the start.

You brought her home for Christmas, and of course our mother was stoic and cold to both of you, but the rest of us made up for it. We sang carols and got drunk in front of the fireplace and opened gifts. We told her she was one of us. You proposed that night.

When you come down the aisle holding Dad's arm, you couldn't be more beautiful. You're both trying not to cry, but I see a tear leak from Dad's eye as he kisses your cheek and hands you off to Amy or Charli. Kel's up there as a bridesmaid, and Emmy is the ring bearer, Alicia the flower girl.

You give me that look before you turn around to say your vows. That look of questioning when you're afraid and not sure of yourself, that look I'm so proud to receive as a big brother, and I nod. You're ready. You got this. You're going to be so happy.

You grin, and it's radiant.

I dream about that day sometimes when I'm missing you, and it's so vivid, I catch myself thinking it might be true. That you and Amy or Charli live just on the other side of the mountains and we've made plans for a get-together at Dad's for the weekend. That I'm going to see you soon.

Then I remember.

———

It rained the day of Mary's funeral.

That big, dolloping, slow rain that soaks you through in seconds or spatters your pant legs even if you're holding an umbrella.

The church on the top of the hill was full. People milled in the atrium past a poster board checkered with pictures of Mary. The sanctuary was alive with muffled conversation. When I glanced inside, my eyes landed on the long mahogany coffin, and I looked away just as quickly. Dad shuffled beside me, and Kel held on to my arm. We were all dressed in black.

Robert and Lisa stood beside the poster board shaking hands with every person who filed past. Kleenex clutched between fingers, dabbing at eyes, the smell of pastry drifting out of the church kitchen. I didn't want to be here.

Elliot Wyman, one of the ushers at the church, came up and verbally accosted us with kindness and questions as we were crossing the atrium. Imagine Elliot as a fortyish boy with large, staring eyes and a mouth that won't quit moving about the Lord. He'd been at the church as long as I could recall, always volunteering and always wanting to chat whenever he wasn't glued to Father Mathew's hip. You didn't want to get cornered by him or a half hour of your life would be gone before you could say *Holy Spirit*.

We answered his questions as quickly as we could: yes, we were devastated by what had happened; no, we hadn't gone to the wake the day before; yes, we were aware Mary was in a better place.

When we'd extricated ourselves from Elliot, we greeted Robert and Lisa, asked about their kids, how they were doing. Fine, fine, as good as can be expected. I shot an unavoidable look toward the stairwell and the basement door that sent goose bumps up my arms. Then we were at the threshold of the sanctuary, and across it.

The first time in fifteen years I'd stepped inside the heart of the church. Christ hung from the cross, the ceiling soared, the lights were on full. The air was close and hot.

We sat near the back in the only free pew. It took me five minutes to spot Rachel and her family. They were in the front, of course, the boys dressed in miniature versions of their father's dark suit. Rachel wore a black dress, tasteful pearls draped around her neck. In the days since the letter, she hadn't reached out. This more than anything else told me she'd received a warning of her own. I could understand not wanting to risk it—she had so much more to lose than I did, specifically the two young boys sitting beside her.

I waited and watched, but she didn't look around, didn't look back at me.

Father Mathew entered shortly after. He loomed over the rest of the procession to the altar. He had been a big man when I'd first met him sixteen years ago on the first Sunday he took the pulpit, and he had only gotten larger. Athletic and tall, with a booming voice whenever he needed it, but most times he spoke in slow, quiet tones. He held his head up, scalp shining through a thinning crew cut, smiling an anguished smile of loss, which I'm guessing he felt was comforting.

God, I hated him.

As the service began, I focused on the last time I'd seen Mary. She'd dropped over to Dad's with a loaf of homemade bread and had watched a game show with him. Had she been distracted that day? I couldn't recall. Partially because it had been an ordinary visit, one of the many times she'd stopped by just to say hello, to bring a gift, to brighten the room with her presence. More so because I'd spent part of the afternoon with Rachel. So many things paled and lost their depth whenever I was with her. She distorted my space and time.

The ceremony proceeded. Father Mathew proselytized. People wept. I stared at the intact stained glass window and recalled Mary holding my hand in the police station. *It's just glass, for God's sake*, she'd said. *It's not like they quit making it.*

I was really going to miss her.

When the service was over, we didn't stop for pastries on the way out. Instead Kel and I drove Dad over to the cemetery on Lake Avenue and beat the funeral procession by a good half hour. We walked through the grass and dead leaves from last fall, stopping at the top of a little rise where the graves seemed to flow out in every direction. We stood in front of two headstones side by side.

RIANNE FLORENCE DRAKE

WIFE, MOTHER, CHILD OF GOD

1951–2014

EMMA LAUREL DRAKE

DAUGHTER, SISTER, GONE TOO SOON

1991–2006

We cleared away the detritus and made the graves look as nice as you can make graves look, then stood there, thinking our own thoughts.

I'd known Emma was gay before she'd come out to our parents. She hadn't told me, I'd just known. She knew I knew and that Kel knew, and it was a secret between us that I always thought helped give her strength. It wasn't my place or anyone's besides Emma's to reveal something like that. I figured when she was ready, she would let everyone else know.

Our mother saw her kissing a girl in a car one cold, gray afternoon in October. They were parked at the far end of the high school's lot. Em was fifteen; the other girl was a senior. Kel said later she thought it might've been her first kiss.

A nuclear explosion would've made a smaller dent in our mother's life. Or so it would seem. Her daughter was gay and the world was ending. Dad said later he'd been a little surprised, but not really. I think he always suspected, too, but never said anything since it would've caused an uproar Mom couldn't have shorthanded. But in the end it turned out to be an abbreviation anyway. A three-day saga punctuated by tragedy.

Like Rachel's parents, our mother brought Emma to church. Trust in the Lord and you'll never want for anything. I wonder now if Mom's faith was shaken then. She'd trusted fully in the Lord and he'd delivered her a gay daughter. It wasn't what she'd wanted.

Father Mathew counseled. He quoted scripture. He spoke in his loud voice, hammering home point after point about why homosexuality was a sin. It was a choice. One Emma could turn away from. I learned this all later from Kel, who had gone with them for emotional support but was made to wait outside Father Mathew's office. Dad had been against the whole thing from the beginning, but as in many instances before, he'd been overruled.

Emma called me on Sunday night, two days after all this.

She was serene. She explained everything to me calmly. What she left out was the content of the sermon earlier that day. Father Mathew had taken it upon himself to fashion a fire-and-brimstone oration decrying the depravity of homosexual sin.

Our mother had made Emma sit through it.

I asked her if she was all right. She said she was. I told her I'd be home in a few days and we'd sort this all out, that she wasn't alone. I told her not to worry. She said she wouldn't.

After she hung up with me, she went into our parents' bathroom and found the mostly full bottle of oxycodone from my mother's ankle surgery the prior year and took all the pills inside. Then she'd gone and lain down in her bed and drifted away forever.

We learned later she'd been bullied at school. On top of that was our mother's reaction, which was worse. But honestly, I think she would have made it through if it hadn't been for that sermon, the final blow while she'd been down. Because like all of us kids, she'd been raised to believe she had a soul and that there was something beyond this life. I think her stargazing and interest in the universe hadn't detracted from that belief; I think it had strengthened it. Added to the mystique and mystery of a higher power.

In the end Em could've handled the name-calling from peers. She could've withstood our mother's cold silence and short, cutting remarks. I think what she stumbled on was the thought that God wouldn't love her anymore because of who she was. And if he didn't, who else could?

I came back to myself as Dad knelt and pressed a hand against Emma's headstone, his head lowered. I guessed this was the one thing he wouldn't mind forgetting.

The funeral procession arrived. We made our way across the plots to where fresh earth had been turned and hidden beneath gaudy green cloth, as if the offense were the dirt.

Mary's coffin was brought to the grave. We gathered, and Father Mathew said the final words. Robert placed a lone white rose on the casket top, and it descended smoothly into the earth, one of the cable cranks on the lowering mechanism squeaking slightly.

Rachel looked at me from across the congregation, her eyes like our first kiss, there and gone.

When it was over, I ushered Dad and Keli away as Father Mathew started heading in our direction. I'm a romantic, but I can only take so much in one day.

At home I got Dad in and settled for the afternoon, promising to cook something better than our usual fare of sandwiches or burgers for dinner that night.

A car I didn't recognize was parked at the closest corner of the Loop, just down from the bird lady's house. I hadn't noticed it when we came home, but now it looked suspicious. There was someone sitting behind the wheel, a large shape that caused any inclination to walk over and get a closer look to evaporate like steam.

At home I showered to warm up from being out in the rain. As I was drying my hair, I meandered to the big windows to get a better look at whoever was in the car, but they were gone.

6

David Barren's business partner was dead.

Dad read it to me out of the paper nine days after Mary's funeral. We were sitting on the front porch, enjoying the first rays of sun prying over the mountains and sipping coffee strong enough to peel paint.

"Says Ryan Vallance was thirty-four years old, no spouse, no children. Found deceased in his home day before yesterday. Foul play hasn't been ruled out." Dad looked over at me. "Didn't you guys go to school with him?"

Yes. Ryan Vallance. Captain of the swim team. He'd enjoyed holding freshmen underwater until they nearly passed out. A real prince. Rachel had told me one afternoon while lying side by side in a motel room bed that Ryan was part of the reason David's business was lagging. Ryan seemed to think he was still twenty-three and stayed out late too much. More than once he'd missed client meetings and just the week before had been incommunicado for almost three days. Rachel said David had finally gotten a text from him and paid for an Uber back to Sandford from a bar in New York. Ryan seemed to have gotten in some kind of fight—she wasn't sure, only that he looked terrible the next time she saw him. Black eye, split lip. He made a quip about how she should've seen the other guy.

None of this had done anything to improve David's mood at home. I asked her again if he'd ever laid a finger on her or the boys, but she said no. Never. Just the yelling. The ranting. The insults. She always looked embarrassed when she opened up about it, like she was somehow to blame.

I wondered what would happen now that Ryan was out of the picture. Would things get worse or better for her?

"What a shame," Dad said, folding up the paper. "Anyone that young passes away, I always think of the parents." His voice thickened. "No one should have to bury a child."

Rancor for Ryan drained. I squeezed Dad's shoulder and asked if he wanted more coffee. He said sure.

As I was topping off our cups, I noticed a scatter of mail across the kitchen counter. Bills. Medical, mostly, with utilities and the mortgage thrown in for flavor. You'd think the medical bills were for Dad's checkups and prescriptions that were supposed to slow the process of his disease to a crawl, but many were holdovers from my mom's stroke. It was incredibly difficult to understand how three days in intensive care that ended in death could haunt the living for years to come, yet here we were.

In my mother's infinite wisdom, she had abstained from life insurance. I can't recall the reason why now but had overheard her say the word *waste* one evening when I was younger and the subject came up between my parents. *Waste*, however, didn't apply to the fact she'd willed half of her Roth IRA to the church.

I flipped the bill I was holding back on the counter and made a mental note to visit Father Mathew in the coming days. We needed to talk.

Dad wasn't on the porch when I came outside. His voice echoed from the open attached garage. "Where the hell's my shovel? Does Martin still have it?"

He was looking around at the tools aligned neatly on pegs studding the garage walls. His round-nose shovel, which I'd borrowed a few days ago to plant some shrubs at the corners of my walk, was missing.

"Martin" was a friend who'd owned my house prior and moved out several years back. The associations his mind made at times always made sense in a roundabout way. I'd taken the shovel, and I lived in the house across the street. Martin used to live there, thus Martin had his shovel.

"Martin took it to dig his potatoes," Dad said.

"I have it, Dad."

"You do? I coulda swore Martin took it."

"Martin moved quite a while ago."

The pause. The realization. It wasn't then, it was now. "Oh right. You took it for the shrubs."

"Yep."

His hands balled into fists, and he lowered his head. "This goddamned disease."

We stood there that way for a minute, the son in the doorway holding two steaming cups of coffee, the father near the back of the garage, impotent rage rolling off him like heat.

He followed me to the porch, and we finished our coffee. When I got up to leave, he asked how the new book was coming. Great, wonderful, flowing like a river.

At least it had been until the note.

The new story involved a man who suffered from a rare psychological disorder called Capgras syndrome. He was under the delusion his family members and friends had been replaced by identical impostors who wished him harm. And the rub was he might be right.

It was an idea from years ago I'd never done anything with, hadn't been able to find my way into the narrative at the time. After Rachel and I got together, the story started clicking, partially because I had someone to talk about it with. She listened, was curious and asked questions, seemed genuinely interested in my work in a way Sharon never had been. I was cautious, wanting the story to be as clean as I could get it since this might be my last chance at a good advance, which meant money to keep watching over Dad, but it was really humming along. I'd been at the 80 percent mark when I'd gotten the note.

Cue the screeching brakes sound, the record scratch. Since then, no words. No matter how long I sat in front of the computer, nothing came.

Well, not entirely nothing. I'd made a list. Of suspects, I suppose you could say. The note leaver. The bearer of bad news. The one who crept in the night. I had all kinds of names for the person who had stepped between us, many of which were highly offensive. My less derogatory list went like this:

- Mrs. Tross (a.k.a. the bird lady)
- Mr. Allen Crane down the street (a.k.a. Mr. Mystery)
- Mrs. Pell, who lived across from the Barrens (a.k.a. disapproving look giver who also sat on the church board with Rachel's husband, David)
- David himself (a.k.a. pissed-off husband)

But I still felt the last one didn't really fit. Although part of me wondered if David's angry bluster was just that—a front set up to protect a fragile ego. Had he learned of our affair somehow and it had crushed him internally to the point of writing an anonymous warning?

I couldn't discount it.

I couldn't write.

Couldn't sleep.

I knew what was wrong. I needed to speak to Rachel. At least to see where she stood. In the days since Mary's funeral, I'd seen her a few times from a distance, always with her boys or riding with David in his oversize SUV.

But this morning was different, and I had a plan.

The weekly farmers market convened in the church's parking lot. Shortly after the snow retreated, vendors began showing up with different wares, mostly early veggies and fruit with some homemade crafts thrown in. It was the weekly event for the Loop, and Rachel never missed it.

At least seventy people were milling around flatbed trucks and trailers arranged in the parking lot when I wandered up the hill, but I spotted Rachel at once.

She was wearing shorts and a light blouse, her hair pulled up in a bun, sunglasses on. I lost my breath for a moment and had to stop and pretend to examine a bin of freshly picked mint leaves.

I knew the difference between lust and love. I knew.

That was the problem. I cursed myself. I'd had no road map when this started, no guide to participating in adultery. I had my heart and longing and that was it. Yes, there was lust, but what attracted me to her was something so much more elemental. She listened, she was insightful, she was so funny when she let herself be. She was fragile, and much stronger than she knew.

Goddamn it. I was in love.

First mistake.

Deep breath. In. Out.

Mint.

I moved on.

Rachel was talking with Sadie Gardner, a woman in her early fifties, stout and muscular, gray hair tied in a no-nonsense pony. Sadie lived in the foothills, completely off the grid, if you could believe what people said. She'd been abused by her husband for almost ten years before she took away the fireplace shovel he was hitting her with one night and broke four of his ribs, two vertebrae, his nose, and one arm. Her husband got an extended hospital stay, and Sadie got a restraining order and a divorce. She mostly sold hydroponic lettuce.

As I approached casually from the side, I could see the two women were in deep conversation. Sadie said something, and Rachel nodded once before glancing around, eyes landing on me.

I wanted to hold her. I wanted to sink into the cracks of the pavement.

Rachel moved away from Sadie's table on to the next display of morel mushrooms. I sidled up a few feet to her right and began inspecting a container of fungi.

"I'm sorry," I said without looking at her. The entire parking lot was behind us. To anyone watching, it would look like we were just shopping in the general vicinity of one another. The table's vendor was chatting with Sadie. "Are you okay?"

She was quiet for a long time, and I thought she was going to walk away without replying. Then, "Andy, I can't."

Three words and it was over. I felt it. All the passion of the last six months, the long conversations, the laughter.

Done.

The question as to whether she'd gotten a note as well was answered. "Okay," I said. "This is what you want?" There was another option, one I'd laid out before, one that would blow up her world and mine. One I'd gladly choose.

She looked at me then, and I wished she hadn't been wearing sunglasses. I wanted to see her eyes. "It's what we need to do."

Then she was gone.

I swallowed hard twice, waiting to the count of five before turning to watch her go. She left the market with a final glance at Sadie, who returned the look before focusing on me. I looked away and saw Mrs. Tross's narrowed gaze pinning me down from where she sat on a bench across the lot.

I scratched my forehead with my middle finger. Her scandalized expression gave me the steam to get home. When I walked in the door, I realized I hadn't put the package of mushrooms back.

I hated mushrooms.

———

You won, blackmailer. Ender of good things. Cowardly, self-righteous note writer.

I milled about the house for the rest of the day, shooting poisonous looks out the window and at my open manuscript on the computer screen in equal measure.

In the cabinet there was half a bottle of good bourbon my agent had sent me after my last book was published. I took it out and sipped straight from the bottle, feeling like the epitome of a tortured writer, a lovestruck fool. I despised self-pity, so I put the bottle back and sat down in the chair before the computer and typed.

And typed.

And typed.

Until my back hurt and I had to piss. I wrote bad words, I wrote really good words.

It didn't matter. I lanced the story like a wound and let the infection ooze onto the page. Fuck perfection. I wanted completion. I wanted closure.

Finally it was done.

Around nine that night, I called Dad, asked if he'd eaten. He said yes. I told him I wasn't feeling well and was heading to bed.

I fell asleep roughly sixty seconds after lying down. Comatose.

But I dreamed. Great, vibrant Technicolor dreams. People on acid don't see things like this.

I was out in my front yard. The sun leaving the sky. Not setting, drawing farther away, like a thrown ball across a darkening field. The Adirondacks grew in height until they towered over everything, became an endless craggy wall. The grass was made of green glass shards, and even though I tried not to move, I started to walk. Then run. My gritted teeth cracked. A mouthful of gravel and blood. Then a sharp bang, like a thunderclap directly over my head, and I sat up in bed, reaching for my bleeding feet before I knew I was awake.

Two in the morning. Heart pumping hard. I waited, unsure if that last sound had been in my dream or not.

A car started up somewhere and drove away. A dog barked. Quiet.

I lay back down, staring up at the black ceiling, letting the sweat on my body cool.

I woke without recalling drifting off again and dragged myself to the kitchen. The last time I drank anything more than a couple of beers had been months ago, and my body let me know it wasn't a fan of bourbon no matter how expensive it was.

As the coffee brewed, the sound of a siren emerged somewhere in town and came closer, and closer, until it was on the Loop and I was moving to the window for a better look.

A cop car zoomed into view and slid to a stop in front of the Barrens'. An officer climbed out and started speaking to someone on the sidewalk. Mr. Allen Crane.

Another squad rolled up. And another. Then an ambulance.

I ran out the door.

7

You pace around the house you grew up in. You do this because you have no other place to go.

Not anywhere that's better. Nowhere the air won't seem thick and cloistering with your guilt.

Because you did this. Your selfishness brought you here, the starting line so distant in hindsight it's nonexistent. There is only now. Only the worry of what you've caused and its acid heat in your belly.

When I sprinted out of my house and up the street, I didn't think about it. I just ran, wearing only the athletic shorts and T-shirt I'd slept in. Hair askew, eyes wild, I looked like a madman.

It's no wonder one of the officers cordoning off the crime scene stopped me short. He was a big man, strong and powerful, and when he grabbed me, I had to stop.

Go back home, sir. You can't be here.

I took everything in. The early gray light of morning. The strobing flash of red-and-blue lights. Mr. Allen Crane standing off to one side holding the leash of his little dog, who was pissing in the grass between the sidewalk and street.

Go home. We'll be by to interview you shortly.

What had I done?

I kept moving once I got to Dad's. My nerves wouldn't let me sit down. I knew nothing.

Joe Hart

I knew everything.

Rachel and the boys were dead. Killed by David because he found the note. No, no. Rachel would've destroyed it. But what if whoever wrote the notes had seen us talking the day before at the farmers market? They'd tipped David off, expecting righteous retribution. And they'd gotten worse than that. So much worse.

Dad watched out the window. I couldn't look. He told me what was happening.

Two more cop cars were there, lights off, no siren.

Now an unmarked van. Men and women with paper gowns and booties carrying black cases.

Now the—

Now the what? I asked.

He looked at me gravely. Now the medical examiner was there.

An hour later a gurney was wheeled out, the flat black of the body bag darker than midnight even in the midmorning sun.

God. I'd done this.

We watched the officers canvass the neighborhood, the cop who'd stopped me earlier finally arriving at Dad's door. He came in and stood by the kitchen counter and asked us questions. Did we know the Barrens? How well? When was the last time we'd spoken to them? Had we seen or heard anything in the middle of the night? Anything out of the ordinary?

Dad had a strange look on his face when he shook his head to the last question. I bookmarked it and told the officer, yes, I'd heard a bang and wasn't sure if it had been part of a dream or not. He noted this and talked quietly into the radio on his shoulder. I asked him what had happened. He said someone would be by shortly to speak with us further. He thanked us and left.

We waited, the minutes elongating into hours. No more body bags were taken out of the house. Gradually the vehicles began leaving. The yellow crime scene tape stayed.

A knock on the door came later. Dad and I had just finished picking at our lunches, neither of us talking about the elephant up the street. In that time lapse after the officer left and before the knock at the door came, I so wanted to tell Dad everything. He would've understood. I could've let it all out just like I'd released the last of my book onto the page the day before. I felt sick, and telling him the truth would've been a relief.

But I didn't.

When I opened the door, a squat, dark-haired man stood there. I noticed his eyebrows first. They were thorny brambles across the lower part of his forehead, something I recalled being transfixed by fifteen years ago.

"Officer Spanner," I said, the name leaping from the nether of memory to my lips.

"Detective, actually," he said. "How are you, Andy? It's been a while."

Yes. Yes, it had.

The last time I'd seen Vince Spanner had been at the local precinct the night after Emma's death. I'd been drunk on a pint of cheap whiskey and wandered up to the church in the early-morning hours. Crying and shouting, I'd taken a stone the size of my fist and hurled it through the window of the sanctuary.

Officer Spanner had been first on the scene. He'd hauled me roughly off the curb where I'd been sitting and slammed me up against the side of his squad car so hard one of my ribs cracked. I couldn't breathe deeply without pain for several weeks. He was an Irish cop who had watched too many Irish cop movies.

He was also a certified asshole.

I invited him in.

He sat at the kitchen table, not touching the cup of coffee Dad poured him, and looked everywhere around the room except at either of us.

"So when did you roll back into town?" he asked finally.

"About a year ago."

"And your residence is across the street?"

"Yes."

"What's the address?" I gave it to him. "Phone number?" Rattled it off. "Place of employment?"

"Self-employed."

"What do you do?"

"I'm an author."

"Oh yeah? Have I read anything you've written?"

"How should I know?"

His expression hardened like curing cement. "In regards to the incident—"

"What happened?" I asked.

"I'd like to know what time you heard the sound you mentioned to Officer Reynolds."

I watched him. "What happened?"

"I can't divulge any details in an ongoing case."

"We'll be able to read it in tomorrow's paper."

"Then read it. I'm not here for scuttlebutt. I'm here to gather statements and evidence. Got me?"

"Detective." Dad had risen from where he sat and stepped in front of me. "I don't know what transpired up the street. I don't know what law enforcement protocol is. I only know Rachel Barren typically visits me once a week just to check in and say hi. Ask if I need anything. Her boys play with my grandchildren. She and her family are our neighbors. You live in the same community. We're concerned for the people we care about. Can you blame us?"

Spanner watched us like he was waiting for something more, then said, "David Barren is deceased. Rachel Barren, Asher Barren, and Joseph Barren's whereabouts are unknown."

I didn't know what I was expecting, but this wasn't it.

David was dead, and Rachel and the boys were missing.

I came back to the last half of Spanner's question and asked him to repeat it. "This noise you heard, a bang—what time was it?"

"Around two a.m., I think."

"Hear anything else?"

"No. A car, maybe, but that was all."

"Mm-hmm. And what is your relationship to Rachel Barren?"

I was a top losing its centrifugal force. Wobbling. "What do you mean?"

"I mean, are you a friend or just a neighbor? Something more?"

"We're neighbors. She's a friend. She stops in to check on Dad, like he said."

"So what were the two of you discussing yesterday at the farmers market?"

"We . . . she was asking about Dad. How he was doing."

"I thought you said she checked in on him herself."

"She does, but she hasn't been here in a while." That at least was the truth. She hadn't dared come over to Dad's since the night of the note.

"Uh-huh. And how did she seem to you? What was her state of mind?"

"Fine. I don't know. She was fine."

"Notice anything out of the ordinary? She say anything that seemed odd?"

"No, nothing. We literally talked for a minute."

Those beady eyes. Probing. Waiting.

Instead of asking any more questions, he stood and moved toward the door. "If either of you recall any other details, call the station. We'll be in touch if we have anything further. Thank you for your time." He stopped at the door and threw a half grin over one shoulder. "Oh, and Andy? Don't leave town."

8

When the snow had finally melted and stayed away for good a few weeks ago, Rachel and I met at a mountain lookout several hours from Sandford.

David was at a conference out of state, the boys on an overnight trip with her parents. She told me she was worried about Joey. He'd been distant and more anxious than usual. Hadn't wanted to go to school or anywhere else at all. She hoped the trip with her parents would do him some good. I asked if she wanted me to talk with him, see if I could help. I was thinking of Emma, how sometimes the quietest and most reserved people were hurting the worst. There was a long pause before she shook her head. So much in that small dismissal, a boundary between us I wanted to tear down.

During our marriage, Sharon and I had discussed kids. She'd been ambivalent, but I'd definitely wanted them. Just another set of lines in our relationship that had never intersected. In my secret heart I saw myself stepping into a role for Asher and Joey, someone more than the fun neighbor who played Frisbee or soccer with them from time to time or told them silly jokes—trying to make them laugh along with their mother. Someone they could really confide in and trust.

In other words, a father.

But it was something unsayable. At least then it was.

We left her car at the lookout and drove up farther into the hills, finally stopping at a pull-off I knew from childhood, one of Dad's many secret places where he took us camping when we were kids. Ours was the only vehicle in sight when we left it parked on the scant piece of blacktop.

We hiked for a few hours, the cool morning air slowly warming until we had to strip off our sweatshirts. The trail we were on switch-backed a dozen times before emptying out on a rocky spine overlooking a lake so crystal clear, it was tempting to drink from. At the end of the spine, an abandoned fire tower stood lonesome but sturdy. The day before, I'd deposited a picnic lunch in the tower: blankets, pillows, a bottle of wine.

We stayed there all day, swimming for a few freezingly brief minutes in the lake, drying off and lounging on the rocks in the sun before spending the afternoon in the tower. The scattered clouds were so low, they felt like ceiling tiles, and we could see into the distant horizon until it became a white-gray haze the color of infinity.

She sang a song she'd written, said it was her first time singing it in front of someone else, which made me a little sad. Her voice was breathy and light and sent a tingle across my skin when she hit certain notes. She blushed when I clapped at the end.

An hour or so before I knew we had to leave, I asked her what she wanted. Before she would have to go back to her regular life and me to mine and we'd have to pretend we didn't know each other beyond being neighbors.

She'd smiled and said she wanted to be asked what she wanted.

A life without corners.

Just a choice.

I told her she had it.

She smiled and pulled me close, and we stayed that way until it was time to go.

Yellow crime scene tape flapped obscenely up the street. I shook my head and looked down at my phone, reading the text I'd written. Deleted it. Rewrote it. Hesitated.

It was the first text I'd ever thought of sending to Rachel. We never called one another on our phones, always communicating through Dad's landline. She hadn't wanted to risk anything more than that. Nothing David could find and become suspicious of.

I deleted the text and set my phone down, hand shaking. Someone must've tried calling her by now. Many someones, I guessed. If they weren't getting through to her, I wouldn't, either, and in the process might make things worse for both of us. Especially if the cops were tracing activity on her account.

Instead I changed recipients and wrote another text, hit send. Regretted it immediately. All this technology in the world and you still couldn't unsend a text. Pathetic.

Dad was sitting in his recliner. I settled onto the couch and looked at him. "What?" he asked.

"Did you see something last night?"

A pause. "No. I don't think so."

"You had a funny look on your face when the officer asked you."

He mulled something over for a second. "I went to bed early since you weren't here for supper. Woke up after only a few hours. Couldn't sleep. I came out here and mixed a drink, thinking it might help. Didn't turn on the TV or anything, just sat in the dark." He hesitated. "I might have drowsed off for a minute, but then I heard a bang. Not too loud, like a car backfiring on the next street. I got up and looked out the window. Didn't see anything."

He stopped there. "And?" I prompted.

"A car started up way down the street near the cul-de-sac and drove by."

I leaned in. "Did you recognize it?"

"I . . . I don't know. It was dark colored when it passed under the streetlight."

"Did you see who was driving?"

"I did, but then I fell back asleep. When I woke up, I didn't think about it. Not until the officer came over and asked if we'd seen anything."

"Who was driving, Dad?"

"See, that's the problem. I keep thinking it was George Nell." He looked at me with an apology in his eyes. "But George is dead, isn't he?"

I settled back into the couch. "Yeah. Yeah, he is."

My phone rang in response to my text.

"Are you kidding me? What the hell is going on?" Kel's voice was shrill and loud. I pulled the cell away from my ear. "What happened?" I told her what I knew, which wasn't much. Again the urge to spill my guts came and went, a fleeting draft of cold air. "So we don't even know if he was killed, right?"

"No, I guess not. But if it was an accident, I don't think Rachel and the boys would be missing."

Kel sighed. "Okay. I guess that makes sense. Jesus."

"So since we don't know a lot, I was hoping you could get a little more info. Could you talk to Seth?" I asked with a wince.

Seth Goddard was the leading investigative journalist for the *Sandford Review*. He and Kel had dated on and off since she and Mark split, and I had the suspicion they still had a tangential relationship.

"I mean, I can ask him, but there's no guarantee he'll tell me anything. Especially if he hasn't printed the story yet."

"I know. I was just hoping you could check with him."

Long pause on Kel's end. "Is there something you're not telling me?"

"No, I just . . . want to know, that's all. They're our neighbors."

Longer pause. "Okay. I'll call him. No guarantees."

"None expected. Thanks, sis."

We hung up, and I stared out the window at Rachel's place, willing her into reality. Willing the boys to be there playing in the yard. Even willing David to be alive again because the fact that I loved his wife didn't mean I wanted him dead.

But it sure would look different to the cops. Or anyone else for that matter. The jealous lover would be suspect numero uno, the narrative easy to follow. Someone had caught on to our affair and delivered the notes. David had found out, and I'd intervened to get him out of the way.

Case = open and shut.

That was why I'd considered giving my note to the authorities to potentially aid in finding Rachel and the boys, and just as quickly dismissed the idea. I'd only be pointing the finger at myself while besmirching Rachel's reputation at the same time.

The note.

It was a splinter in my mind. I couldn't kid myself its arrival a short time before David's death was a coincidence. And there was Ryan's demise to consider as well. Two business partners dead within days. It all felt connected. I just had to figure out how.

On top of that, Dad might've seen the killer driving away from the crime scene, but the disease in his mind had replaced his identity with a man fifteen years dead. Or Dad might not have seen anything important. Who knew.

Movement caught my eye across the street. The twitch of a curtain in Mr. Allen Crane's house.

9

I'd only caught a glimpse of the person rounding the side of Rachel's house the day she kissed me, but if a gun were to my head (which is what it felt like now), I'd say that man had been Mr. Allen Crane.

Our quiet neighbor who no one knew other than from polite exchanges if you ran into him on the sidewalk or in the grocery store. The tall, dapper fellow perhaps in his early fifties who didn't seem to work and doted on his terrier mix, whom he never left home without.

He also appeared to have been the first person on the scene at the Barrens' home that morning.

I left Dad dozing in his chair midafternoon and crossed the street to home. The day was heating up, summer fully on its way. I needed to think, so I made coffee and took it into the living room before pacing in front of the big windows.

The twitch of the curtains in Crane's home was all I'd seen of him since that morning outside the Barrens'. I assumed he was the one who had made the call bringing the police to the Loop. Kel might be able to confirm or deny that he was the caller later this evening. For now I'd operate under that assumption. I'd also assume Crane was the one who had left the note or notes.

The note.

I needed to get rid of it. It was evidence, but mainly evidence incriminating me. I'd hidden it in the bottom drawer of my dresser beneath a pair of work jeans. I took it out and read it again before bringing it into the bathroom, gathering myself to tear it up and flush it.

But was that the smartest thing to do? There was a chance it would come into play later; how, I didn't know.

I did a weird dance half in, half out of the bathroom. Normally bathroom decisions weren't this hard. I opted to keep the note, folding it up tightly and burying it in a big jar of white rice in the pantry.

Back in the living room, sipping coffee before the windows. Thinking.

I needed to be careful. As worried and guilt stricken as I was about Rachel and the boys, I had to keep my thoughts collected. I wouldn't do them any good locked up on suspicion of their disappearances or David's death.

The Loop looked like an alien landscape. I'd grown up here. I knew every nook and cranny.

This was my first time seeing it.

I couldn't trust anything now. There were land mines outside my door, inside my head, and I had to be careful where I stepped.

———

Kel. Wonderful Kel had come through. I knew it the second she walked into Dad's house that evening with the girls. The glint in her eye. She had something, and she'd give it for something in return. We were twelve and ten again. Her holding my favorite squirt gun hostage while I stood with my hand out.

"What aren't you telling me, Andy?" she asked when the girls had gone out back with Dad to play and I'd placed a sweating beer on the coaster beside her.

"Nothing."

"No, that's *what* you're telling me. We grew up too close for my bullshit meter not to go off, so spill it."

56

I sat forward, calmly looking into her eyes. "Kel, there's nothing going on."

"I have my suspicions. You want me to lay them out?"

"Absolutely not."

She sipped her beer. "Will you tell me eventually?"

Little sisters. They never give up. "Yes."

"Okay, I'll take it. I spoke to Seth, and this is all strictly confidential. He didn't want to tell me, so I had to beg. He said if his source at the station gets wind of any leaks, he's done."

Here's what Seth knew:

The call that morning came in from one Allen Perry Crane, who was out walking his dog and happened to see a broken pane of glass in the Barrens' front door. When he went up to check on it, he could see someone lying in the hallway, only one bare foot visible. They didn't respond when he called out to them. Officers arrived on the scene and discovered David Barren deceased from a single gunshot wound to the chest.

"Point-blank through the heart," Kel said, finishing her beer. I got her another.

Rewind the tape. The prior day's timeline leading up to David's death went something like this:

Rachel was seen at the farmers market midmorning, as well as at the local grocery store in the early afternoon. Her car was spotted pulling into the church parking lot by another mom later, assumedly picking up the boys after school. If she returned home at any point after that, no one saw her or the kids.

David worked late that evening, arriving home at approximately seven thirty, according to a different neighbor who'd witnessed him pull into the driveway. He didn't leave the house again, from what the authorities could tell.

A break-in occurred sometime after midnight, the perpetrator gaining access by smashing the pane of glass in the front door and opening the lock. David had failed to arm the security system, so there was no alarm. Seth's source told him it appeared like a burglary gone wrong. David's office was in disarray, and so far it looked like some cash and jewelry were missing.

I could see it happening like one of the scenes I'd written about. David waking to a noise and climbing out of the bed to investigate, maybe grabbing some kind of weapon along the way. He surprises the intruder or vice versa, and the gun goes off. David falls to the floor, the life draining from him as the murderer flees the scene.

Kel said time of death was around two in the morning.

So I'd heard the gunshot. Dad probably had too. Which meant whoever Dad had seen driving away had most likely been the killer, and he couldn't remember who it was.

I don't know why I ever thought mysteries were satisfying, to write or read. They were pure frustration.

"So Seth didn't say there was any sign Rachel and the boys were taken?"

"No. Again, no one's sure they even came home at all." Kel stood and moved to the kitchen, and I followed.

"But they haven't heard from her."

"Nope. The police are set up at her parents' place in case it's some sort of ransom situation, though." She gathered the ingredients for stir-fry while I sipped my beer and watched Dad toss a Frisbee to Emmy and Alicia.

A ransom. Demands. *Do as I say or else.*

Deep breath. In. Out.

"You okay?" Kel had paused chopping up carrots to stare at me.

"Yeah."

"All this isn't research for a book, is it?"

"No."

"And you'll tell me at some point?"

"Yes." She went back to chopping. "Did Seth say anything about David's business partner?" I asked.

"Oh shit, almost forgot. Yeah, that's another really weird thing. So there hasn't been a final word on it yet, but it looks like someone tried making Ryan's death look like a suicide."

"You're kidding."

"Nope. Seth's source said everything looked like he'd killed himself—lots of alcohol in his system, gunshot to the head and whatnot, but the angle was a little off and there wasn't as much gunpowder residue on his hand as there should've been. Seth said he thinks it's going to eventually be ruled a homicide. He's writing the story tonight. Be in tomorrow's paper."

My head was filled with links of a chain, and it seemed to stretch back to the moment I'd made Rachel laugh. That end was in sunlight, topside, while the other stretched off into the darkness of an ocean trench.

I'd have to dive down to find where it led.

10

We ate stir-fry. The girls laughed. Dad told a few stories. Kel and I drank beer.

Nice night. Nice, normal night on the Loop.

I couldn't keep from glancing out the windows as the sunlight drained from the day. When it was dark, I walked Kel and the girls out on the way to my house. Kel asked about Dad's birthday. It was only a few days away. I told her we'd do something small, a get-together like tonight—he enjoyed that. Maybe a Yankees game later in the month.

"How's he been lately?" she asked.

"Fairly good." And other than the shovel incident and potentially misidentifying a murderer, it was the truth. I knew rougher seas were coming, but for now we should enjoy the calm days. Soak them up. She agreed.

"Good night, Andy. Don't do anything stupid." Before driving away, she gave me a look saying she knew a lot more than I was telling her. I waved and nodded.

Of course I wouldn't do anything stupid.

———

I was going to do something very stupid.

My stomach became a tempest the moment I walked through my door and decided I was going ahead with the idea I'd formed earlier in the evening.

Was I going to make Kel's nice dinner suddenly reappear? No. Nope. No way. Waste of food, waste of time, of energy. I was okay.

Instead of hurling, I spent a little time cleaning up the first draft of my novel. Really I focused on the last 20 percent. It was rough, but good. Maybe the best I'd written in a long time. When I was done, I emailed the manuscript to my agent. She'd be thrilled to see something new from me. I hoped. I did everything in a kind of semi-removed fugue. Because my mind wasn't on my characters or creating a list of comp books my agent could utilize while she read my words.

It was replaying a conversation I'd had with a New York City detective years ago. I'd been researching my second novel, a follow-up to my first using some of the same characters, and needed more insight into the daily life of a real detective. Sergeant Michael O'Rourke had allowed me to follow him around for the better part of a week, accompanying him on certain assignments, all the while talking out the side of his mouth in a Brooklyn accent.

Two things, he'd said, holding up his fingers to enunciate. *Two things to always keep in mind when trying to solve a crime. One, ain't no straight line in a case. You get a toehold and go from there, and the path always winds around, and if you're lucky, you stay on the trail long enough to put a close on it. Two, details. Some shit people pass by without noticing can be the most important part of the case. Blow it wide open.* Pointer finger—*No straight line.* Middle finger—*Details.*

What advantage did I have over the police? I knew things they didn't. I might recognize a detail they wouldn't. That's why I was going to break into Rachel's house.

I hiccupped into the back of my hand, willing the food to stay put.

Earlier I'd scanned the neighborhood for cops or any type of surveillance, but of course, there was the rub. Surveillance wasn't supposed to be obvious. If someone was watching Rachel's house, I probably wouldn't be able to make them. Then I thought of Detective Spanner and his sneer. His overconfidence. And I wondered if he'd even bother to have someone posted at the house. Maybe in his head, the deal was done. Burglary gone wrong. Dead man in the morgue. Wife and kids missing. Nothing to see here, folks. Everyone go home.

I paced by the windows with the lights off. Streetlamps showered the Loop in yellow pools. No one was out walking their dogs or jogging. It was quiet. I needed to get ready.

Black pants that didn't fit right since I'd bought them years ago and didn't wear black pants anymore. Black sweatshirt I yanked off a few seconds after putting it on since it had reflective stripes on the back. Instead I donned a black T-shirt and found a dark baseball hat in the closet. I caught my reflection in the hall mirror and paused.

Was I really doing this?

Was this going to help me find Rachel and the boys?

Was I going to get caught?

Yes.

Maybe.

Probably.

At a quarter after one in the morning, I quit drinking coffee and pocketed the tiny penlight I'd removed from my key chain. Out the back door and into the woods behind my house. I wasn't taking any chances by going out the front.

Circling around two other residences, I finally came out partway up the hill to the church, where there weren't any streetlights. The Loop was noiseless at this time of night, and every single breath and footstep I took sounded like a hurricane and falling trees. A dozen times I froze and knelt in the dewed grass, waiting and listening. No floodlights splashed over me, no dogs barked, nothing moved.

At the back of Rachel's yard, I waited, looking at the blackened windows and shadowed walls. A sharp-eared shape of a fox sat on the back porch next to the door. Not a real fox—a ceramic one with beady eyes and a badly painted tail. A kid's project, probably Asher's. This was what I was looking for.

Latex gloves out and on? Check. Neighborhood still quiet and serene? Check. Heart climbing the hell out of my chest like it's on a shuddering ladder? Check.

Go.

Across the backyard and up the stairs, sliding to a stop near the door. Still quiet, still good. When I tipped the ceramic fox to the side, I was devastated and relieved all in the same half second. The spare key wasn't there. Rachel had told me offhandedly one day they kept the spare under the fox in case the boys came home early or she wasn't able to pick them up. It wasn't there now, so they'd either moved it or an officer had followed their intuition and found it, taking it with them in case someone like me came along and—

A tinkling sounded: the key falling to the deck. It had stuck to the bottom of the fox.

Shit.

I picked up the key and slid it into the lock. Twisted. One. Two. Three.

Pushing the door inward, I readied myself to run the moment the alarm system started blaring.

But there was nothing. No one had armed it.

I pocketed the key and went inside.

For an agonizing second, I thought the adrenaline rush was going to make me sick. I planted my hands on my knees and breathed. When I was sure I wasn't going to pass out or throw up, I shut the door and listened to the house.

I'd always thought a house sounded different when everyone who lived there was gone. But what about when someone died there? What did that emptiness sound like? I was hearing it, and it made my skin crawl.

The penlight's little button clicked, and a tiny beam of blue light splashed the floor. I took a step into the back foyer and approached the stairs leading up to the kitchen. There was a gravity here I wasn't imagining. Everything weighed more. Each movement I made was a potential mistake. I had to be careful. So careful.

In the kitchen I took stock of the clean counters, the lack of dishes in the sink, the strange smell in the air. It was tangy and unpleasant, a sour scent of ammonia and something else. In the next room I realized what it was.

A dark blotch covered the hallway floor. Dried blood. David's blood. The man who I'd gone to school with, lived alongside, spoken to dozens of times—his blood coated the floor. The ammonia smell was probably from when his bladder let go after he died.

I gagged. No. You will not spray your last cup of coffee all over the crime scene, because if you do, you might as well drive yourself to the police station and confess you were here. It would expedite things.

The pungency of the smell eased, and my stomach returned to where it normally sat. Stepping carefully over the splotches of blood, I made my way down the hall, cupping the penlight with my hand whenever passing by a window.

A door to the left, one of the boys' rooms, bed made, toys on the floor. A door to the right, bathroom.

In the next room on the left, someone stood against the far wall.

A strangled shout of surprise died in my throat as I shone the light inside. A life-size cardboard cutout of the Patriots' star running back stared back at me. I cursed under my breath and saw the room belonged to Asher. Movie posters covered the walls, and there were some dirty clothes on the floor.

At the end of the hall, the last two rooms branched in opposite directions. One was the main bedroom. Inside, the two matching dressers jutted drawers and vomited clothing. More clothes were pulled out of the closet and strewn around the floor. The lamp on the right nightstand sat at an angle. I stared at the messy bed and wondered which side Rachel slept on. She always preferred the right when we were together.

Stop it.

I needed to focus. But on what? What the hell was I looking for?

Something out of sync. Something only I would pick up on.

I moved around the room, taking care not to disturb anything. Someone had gone through here like a whirlwind. They were looking for something. Kel had said cash and jewelry were missing. This seemed on point as I shone the light across a small necklace stand toppled over on a dresser. Earrings glinted in the carpet, and a wristwatch Rachel sometimes wore lay unclasped near the en suite bath. I looked at that for a long time before moving on to poke through the open dresser drawers, under the bed, and in the medicine cabinet.

Nothing. Nothing. Nothing.

The room across the hall was the office. A long desk, office chair tipped over, darkened computer, broken glass from a capsized lamp near the far wall.

Gathering what was left of my nerve, I began opening the desk drawers.

Folders with financial statements all bearing the name of David's lending agency, pens, printer ink cartridges. A leather-bound ledger caught my eye, but when I flipped through it, all the pages were blank.

I turned the computer on in the hopes it wasn't password protected, but it was. Turned it back off.

In the lowest drawer, under a fan of printer paper, was a scatter of business cards. Most of the names were local businesses in town. A few were out-of-state lending agencies and accountant services.

Just as I was sliding the paper back into place, words on one of the cards caught my eye.

New York, New York.
I picked the card up, exposing it fully.

HerringBone

Bar & Grill

5123 Prince Ave.

New York, New York

Something clicked and whirred in my mind, a processor chip coming to life. Nothing on the card stirred anything besides the city name. Then it hit me.

Rachel's story about Ryan's disappearance for three days. How David had ordered a car to take him home from a bar in the city. How he'd looked like he'd been on the receiving end of a beating.

I turned the card over. Written on the back in black ink was one word.

Speranza.

A phone number was jotted below it.

My heart moonlighted a funny shimmy, then went back to its day job. Okay, this was something. What, I had no idea. But it was the only business card I could see from the city, and definitely the only one with writing on it.

Okay.

I resettled the rest of the cards and paper back the way it was. Shut the drawer. Clicked off my light. Time to go.

Out in the hallway the smell of death hit me again. It wasn't as bad this time. Maybe I was getting used to it. I once heard that people are so adaptable, they can get used to anything, so chances were, if I hung out in this house long enough, I wouldn't even smell the last of David's bodily functions.

Yeah. Sure. Think the crazy thoughts and leave them behind.

Doing the macabre game of Twister for a second time, I stepped around the pools of blood and entered the kitchen. Over there near the counter, Rachel had kissed me. Over here in the hall, her husband had died. I wondered again if there was an invisible chain tying the two together. Maybe someone at the other end of the number on the back of the business card could tell me.

At the top of the stairs, I paused, listening intently, thinking I'd heard something.

There it was again. A quiet click. A clock ticking? There was a grandfather clock in the game room on the lower level.

No. The clicks were too far apart.

Again. Louder this time. It was coming from the rear entry.

A brief creak. Another click.

Then a deeper shadow filled the bottom of the stairway.

Someone was in the house.

11

That feeling you get when the traffic light switches to yellow and you're entering the intersection.

Too late to hit the brakes. Touch the gas and you're running a red light.

Indecision locked me in place. The shadow shifted, then came closer to the stairs.

I ducked down, crab walking sideways toward the front foyer. The front door—it was my only hope. I could let myself out and hopefully get down the steps and onto the street before whoever was inside saw me.

Light glittered across broken glass in the entryway.

They hadn't cleaned up the busted window yet. No surprise since there was still blood and piss on the floor in the hall. I couldn't go out this way; the intruder would hear the glass breaking under my shoes. A stair creaked.

Where could I hide?

Where?

Where?

The entry closet door was beside me, and without thinking, I pulled it silently open and stepped inside.

Darkness. Complete and total. The quiet was suffocating, all the coats and sweatshirts hanging around me dampening the sound to nothing. I wouldn't hear whoever it was approaching until they pulled the door open and blew my stupid brains out the back of my head.

I had to control my breathing. Sweat ran down my spine into the back of my pants.

Light suddenly shone beneath the door. Swept away. A flashlight.

The murderer. Obviously. They'd returned to the scene of the crime just like in every movie and book ever written. Why hadn't I thought of that? I was a fucking mystery/thriller writer. What a goddamned disappointment I was.

The light returned. Got brighter.

Brighter.

Glass crackled under a boot.

I bit the inside of my mouth. Tasted blood.

Psalm 23 came to me then, and I recited it in my head, not out of any sense of spirituality but because it took me away from the panic, from the knowledge that if there was anything after this world, I'd be seeing it in a matter of seconds. And if there wasn't, the darkness of the closet would be my new eternity.

The Lord is my shepherd.

The light shone bright enough under the door for me to see my feet.

I shall not want.

More glass crackled.

He maketh me to lie down in green pastures: he
leadeth me beside the still waters.

Footsteps and the brush of fabric against the closet door.
The light receded. Gone.

My breath slithered out of my chest, and I leaned against the back wall. What now? Stay here? Wait until whoever it was left? What if they came back?

I found the doorknob and turned it. Opened the door a crack. No flashlight, no sounds.

Wait—there. A drawer opening and closing down the hall. I could make it. I could get out without them ever knowing I was here.

Deep breath. Move.

My eyes had grown even more accustomed to the dark, so the house was more visible as I maneuvered around the glass on the floor.

Two steps to the hallway. Stop. Wait.

Light edged into view. They were coming back.

I glued myself to the wall, no time to do anything else.

They passed by the foyer into the kitchen.

I held my breath and sidled across the hall a half dozen steps behind them. It was a man, tall with rounded shoulders, wearing a similar outfit to mine. Black on black. He swept his beam of light around the kitchen and clicked it off.

Then I was to the stairs and going down.

Staying close to the wall so they wouldn't squeak.

Pulse pounding in my ears, head filled with helium and floating away.

Last step. Over to the door. Finally letting myself inhale. I grabbed the knob, eased the door open, shot one last look behind me up the stairs.

He was there, three steps down from the top. A deeper shade of black in the stairwell except for the glint of steel in one hand in the distinct shape of a gun.

We stayed that way for a second, an amber moment of time, each of us settling into our designated next moves.

I bolted out the door.

He followed.

Across the yard and I cut a hard right, angling into the next property. In between each heartbeat, I waited to hear the shot. The bullet would be white hot and drive me onto my knees and face, and I'd die tasting someone else's perfect lawn.

No shot came, and I launched myself over a kid's toy car that appeared out of the gloom, throwing a glance over one shoulder.

He was right there, running hard. Gaining.

No more looking back. Not if I wanted to live, not if I wanted to see the sun rise tomorrow. Not if I ever wanted to see Rachel and the boys again.

Head down, I ran.

Up around the side of the house, onto the sidewalk, then jagging left before I could sprint into a streetlight's glow. Because we hadn't seen each other's faces yet. That was the one and only thing I had going for me. He didn't know who I was, and I didn't know him. If I saw him and he ran off, okay. Maybe I could ID him, maybe not. If he saw me or chased me to my house, he could let me go and come back at a later date of his choosing and shoot me in my sleep.

Or shoot my dad.

I couldn't go home.

Across the darkest part of the street and up the hill toward the church. Hard right again, gaining speed and momentum until I was flying, feet there just as a formality to keep me in the air.

The hard line of shadowed trees and brush loomed, and I hurtled toward it. My salvation. I could lose myself in there. Lose my pursuer.

Branches and newly green leaves raked my face. Brush scratched and tried to tangle my legs. I didn't slow down. Ducking around trees and changing directions, first angling left, then right.

Up an incline, feet thrashing through fallen leaves and snapping sticks. I sounded like a bull moose plowing through the undergrowth, easy to track, but that was okay. As long as I kept moving, kept going deeper into the woods, there was a better chance the murderer would decide to turn around and leave me be.

At least I hoped.

The shape of a deadfall sprang out of the dark and caught me midthigh. I somersaulted over it and tucked my shoulder enough to roll back to my feet on the other side. Hot hammers of pain pounded my legs where I'd hit the tree. I ignored them and slid down a steep embankment.

I knew where I was.

We'd played here as kids. Cory had shown us the little hollow nestled between two larger hills the first time, but after that, Emma, Kel, and I came here on our own frequently. We'd try to leave Cory behind, but most times it didn't work. He was the oldest and fastest, and he'd shown us this place. The little stream winding down through the trees with its dark pebbles. The soft banks of sand you could lean against and let the sun's heat, collected there from the day, seep into your back. The massive hollow tree at the top valley we'd made into our clubhouse.

The clubhouse.

I hit the stream much sooner than I thought I would. Stumbling through it, wetting my pants all the way up to my crotch. Then I was on the other side, climbing the bank, fingers clawing at loose soil and rock, pulling myself up onto level ground.

I risked stopping and leaned against a tree. Each breath snagged in my lungs like a series of fishhooks. Over my ragged breathing, I listened.

Nothing.

Quiet.

Nothing.

Burble of the stream.

Branches snapping, feet crunching gravel and stones on the far side of the water.

Go.

I hurried across the spine of a ridge and thanked whatever power spun the universe on its axis the way was mostly clear. My footfalls went from thunder to the padding of a cat.

A few more yards and the clubhouse would appear. A few more yards. A few more.

Had I missed it? Had it rotted and fallen down in the intervening eighteen years or so since I'd been out here? Was I mistaken about where I was? If so, I was dead. The end.

No—there. There it was in all its leaning, hollow glory. The clubhouse tree. From this vantage point, it looked whole, and only when you went around to the northern side would you see a jagged split large enough to admit one person if they turned sideways and crouched. In the dark, the entrance would be almost invisible.

I careened around the side of the tree, hands fluttering against flaking bark until I felt open air. Turn, crouch, shimmy your adult body—that fits so much worse than your thirteen-year-old self—inside.

I was in.

The ability to keep my heart beating and my neurons firing for the foreseeable future depended on one thing now: if I could be quiet.

So many games we'd played here as kids. Tag, kick the can, hide-and-seek. This was the same except with much higher stakes. Hide out until you're the last one—you get the remaining grape Popsicle at home. Stay hidden now—you get to keep your blood and organs inside you.

My breathing slowed, and I cupped a hand over my mouth and nose to muffle the sound even more. A twig snapped under my heel, quiet, but I winced. Any sound now would be a giveaway. There were no do-overs. No restart of the game.

The hollow of the tree was still damp from the spring thaw. Moisture seeped through my T-shirt, and something with too many legs skittered quickly across my neck and was gone. A limited swath of night sky was visible through the gap in the trunk. Stars skimmed the treetops. Somewhere in town, a car horn honked. Other than that, it was silent.

Minutes ticked by. Sweat cooled on my body.

Maybe the killer had given up or taken a wrong turn at the stream. Maybe the sound of the water had hidden my passage and he'd gone back toward the neighborhood. That seemed likely if he thought he'd lost me, since he'd want to vacate the area as quickly as possible in case I called the cops. And I could do just that when I got home. No reason I couldn't let the police know I'd seen a flashlight sweeping around in the Barrens' house when I'd gotten up to get a drink of water. Maybe they'd send someone right over and bump into whoever it was—

The stars outside the tree went away.

For a second I didn't know what had happened. Then my guts shriveled.

He was standing directly in front of the tree, blocking my view. He was right there, close enough to touch. Facing toward or away, I couldn't tell.

Again time slowed. Drizzling out like chilled honey. It was beyond dark in the tree. My breathing came in shallow hitches, and part of me wanted to spring forward, try tackling him. If his back was to me, I might be able to do it.

But he also had a gun.

Another dozen seconds, my legs cramping from crouching for so long.

The stars came back.

The sound of his passage drifted away. Crackling leaves, a snapping branch, then nothing.

I sagged sideways and uncoiled my legs from beneath me. The cold air soaked through my saturated jeans. I shivered.

And woke up to my teeth chattering.

The sky was beginning to gray to the east, and the stars were fading. I'd fallen asleep somehow leaning against the inside of the tree. Once the killer had moved on, my adrenaline must've dropped and my ability to stay awake with it. I shuddered with cold.

Outside the tree, the little valley was still. A gentle breeze nudged the treetops, stirring new leaves. I picked my way down toward the stream and followed it as quietly as I could before climbing a gentle rise through a span of old-growth trees. Maybe the guy was still waiting for me, gun cocked and pointed at my head even now as I walked. I was too cold and tired to care.

The trees thinned, then vanished completely, and suburbia took hold. My backyard. I'd come out perfectly behind my house.

Inside I stripped off my damp clothes and snagged the bourbon out of the cupboard on the way to the shower. Underneath the scalding spray, I shivered and drank from the bottle until I was warm inside and out.

After toweling off, another kind of shakes hit me. I had to sit down at the kitchen table with my elbows on my knees, head down for several minutes, before I was steady enough to make a call.

The police dispatcher asked a series of questions in a calm, nearly bored voice. Had I actually seen a person prowling near the residence? Was I sure the light was coming from inside the house? Would I be willing to make a statement if necessary? Twenty minutes later a squad car rolled up and began combing the Barrens' yard with a spotlight. By then I'd hidden my sodden clothes in the laundry underneath a pile of blankets. An officer stepped out of the car after turning off the spotlight and disappeared around the side of the house. A few minutes later he returned and climbed back inside, then cruised slowly away, not even pausing before my place.

What the hell?

If the back door wasn't locked, it should've caused more concern. Definitely enough to stop and ask me a few questions. That told me that either (a) the cop hadn't checked the door at all (unlikely), or (b) the door had been locked. Which meant the killer had returned and locked it after losing me in the woods.

What the hell?

My mind was a mire of receding fear and overwhelming exhaustion. I couldn't reason or find a thread to follow that made sense.

In bed, covers up to my chin, a last conscious thought floated through my head. When I woke up, I'd have to make a casserole.

12

Condolence food was tricky.

A pie was too lighthearted to say you were sorry for someone's loss. Bake a cake and you'd probably get thrown out of the bereaved's home. But a casserole? That said, "Here, take comfort in meats and cheeses. I was thinking of you when I boiled the noodles and browned the hamburger. Sink into the savory goodness, and let it ease your heartache."

When I picked Dad up around noon that day, he didn't ask too many questions. I'd told him earlier that morning what I was thinking and to be ready by lunch. We drove out of the Loop with the smell of baked cheese and onions permeating the car.

The Worths lived on Upper Highland Road, which was a lot like the Loop except it ran around Sentinel Lake and the properties situated on it were typically twice the value. This was the main affluent neighborhood Sandford boasted. The place where BMWs sat beside Jaguars in three-stall temperature-controlled garages. The place where the only thing more important than your square footage and curb appeal was where your summer home was located.

We pulled up before the Worths' sprawling white brick three story, and I parked behind a squad car and an unmarked SUV reeking of law enforcement.

"Never been here before," Dad said, looking out the window. "You?"

"Been by but never inside."

"Neighborly support the only reason we're here?"

"Yep."

"Uh-huh."

"Let's go in."

The door opened to a plainclothes officer, who looked us up and down before asking who we were. I told her our names, that we were neighbors of the Barrens' and wanted to offer our condolences. She glanced at the Crock-Pot in my hands, and I held it out. "Cheeseburger casserole."

After disappearing for a few seconds, the officer reappeared and led us through a spacious entry and across a kitchen spanning about an acre. Every surface shone. The Worths sat in the lounge off the kitchen through a rounded archway. Glass lined the room from floor to ceiling, giving impressive views of the lake, which had a mild chop and mirrored the gray overcast above it.

William and Valorie Worth. Platinum hair—his short, hers long. He wore a button-up shirt and slacks still filled out with the remainder of his college football days, she a casual skirt and blouse revealing a figure so thin the only word that came to mind was *emaciated*. Both of them held glasses of wine.

"You can put it over there," William said, motioning to a table beside the doorway filled with Crock-Pots. All of them looked cold. I set mine in the middle.

"Hello, William," Dad said, shaking with the other man, then taking Valorie's hand. "I'm so sorry for everything."

"Appreciate that, my friend," William said, and I realized he'd already forgotten Dad's name. I followed Dad's lead in greeting, and Valorie gave me a polite half smile, her eyes chardonnay glazed.

"Please sit down," Valorie said. "Anything to drink?" We both shook our heads, settling onto a love seat. In the next room over, a folding table had been set up. The officer who let us in sat before a laptop and a jumble of electronic equipment. Headphones cupped her ears. Three cell phones sat on the table to her right, and a uniformed cop entered the room from a long hallway, the echo of a toilet flushing following him.

"It's an indignity," Valorie said, nodding at the police. "First you have a tragedy, then your home's invaded, so you can't even mourn in peace."

"Valorie, they're only here to help. We have to be ready in case . . . we get a call or something," William said. He sounded ambivalent and considerably less drunk than his wife.

"There's been no word, then?" I said.

"You mean a ransom demand?" William asked, eyeing me. "No, nothing yet. They seem to be expecting one, though."

"It's the best-case scenario," Valorie said. "That's what they told us. As terrible as it sounds, it is. I mean, if they wanted something else, then Rachel and the boys would've been there. They would've been just like David." She punctuated this with a half sob and a long sip from her glass. William placed a hand on her shoulder.

"How are the Barrens doing?" Dad asked.

"Not good. They were here until this morning, but they had to go home to . . . make arrangements," William said. "And on that note, not to rush you out, but we need to get back to a few things if you don't mind."

Dad and I stood, shaking hands with them again. William guided us out to the front door. As we left, I shot a glance into the next room where the police had set up their command center.

Rachel's phone sat among two others I didn't recognize.

Even at a distance I would've known hers anywhere, the rose-colored case with the sparkly jewels down its sides. She used to spin it idly on whatever surface was nearby, and it would flash and shine as it rotated.

My heart sunk. Seeing the phone was a hammerblow I wasn't ready for. I'd been operating under the notion Rachel and the boys had been taken, but her phone sitting there without her anywhere nearby was a confirmation that made me feel weak.

The drive home was silent, both of us lost in our thoughts. When we pulled up to Dad's, I went inside with him, half wishing I'd set part of the hot dish aside since it looked like it was going to go to waste anyway.

While I fixed us a salad, Dad came and leaned against the counter. He stared at me until I was forced to look back. "What's going on?"

"What do you mean?" I asked, cutting the last few cherry tomatoes into quarters.

"Son, I have regrets. Everyone does. You don't go through life without them clinging to you. I would regret not pushing you to tell me what's happening, because I think it's important, and I'd be disappointed if you wouldn't tell me."

Is there a master class parents take to learn guilt-tripping?

I held strong for maybe thirty seconds, half shaking my head. Almost like the denial you have before you vomit after being nauseated for hours. I wasn't going to tell him; I was going to keep him in the dark, safely in the dark and out of reach of whatever was happening. Because in all truth I didn't really know. So that's what I told him. I didn't know.

He sighed, unmoving. "I worked for umpteen years at that paper mill as night watchman. Unlike some of the other guys, I took my job seriously. I was observant, and don't think for a second all that's gone just because I came down with this shit. You got scratches on your arms that weren't there yesterday, you've had a stricken look on your face for weeks, and you've been seeing Rachel on the side for the last six months."

The feeling when you think there's another step at the top of the stairway and there isn't. Yeah, that.

"You knew?"

"I have dementia, Andy. I'm not stupid."

I withered. We sat at the table. I told him. Everything.

Until then, speaking the words my dad was hearing was one of my worst fears. Telling the secret. Because then it would be gone. It wouldn't be safe any longer. I learned that years ago when Emma's secret got out. I saw what could happen.

When I was finished, I watched Dad's face for the telltale signs I'd expected. Anger. Disappointment. Disgust. But they weren't there.

Instead he said, "Huh."

"Huh? That's it? That's what you're going with?"

"For now."

"Christ," I said, standing to pace the kitchen. When I finally stilled, he was looking at me. "Please say something. Anything."

He thought for a while. "I'm sure you've thought about telling the cops? About you and Rachel, the note?"

I nodded. It had been on a near-constant loop in my mind since yesterday morning. I could hand Detective Spanner the note. Come clean about the affair, about being in the house last night and the encounter with the killer. And where would that get me?

"They'd probably lock you up," Dad said, finishing my thought. "And with you in the crosshairs, they'd be less likely to find who actually did it."

Some of the angst I'd been feeling about keeping the note to myself eased. For now it would do more good to let the cops work the case without me as a suspect. And I could keep working from the inside.

"Do you care about her?" Dad asked.

"What? Of course."

"Do you love her?"

"I . . ." My hands fidgeted, feet shifted, eyes everywhere around the room. "Yeah. Yes. I do."

"Good. I'd be upset if you didn't. How about the boys? You care about them too?"

"Yes."

"Good. I won't say this isn't a mess you're in—it is—but sometimes wrong things come from the right decisions." He scowled for a moment, thinking. "There's one thing this disease has taught me, and that's life is like dementia. Anything can slip away at any time. You gotta hold on to the things that matter as long as you can."

I sunk into my seat. "So what do we do now?"

"We eat."

We ate.

An hour later when I crossed the street to home, I felt like I was backpacking in Nepal. Winding my way closer and closer to base camp with a hundred pounds on my back. I carried what Dad said and the fact Rachel's phone had been left behind. I carried the glint of gunmetal in the dark and the smell of piss and blood. Most of all I carried guilt— the majority of my provisions. The heaviest.

In the laundry room, I fished out my clothes from the night before, retrieving the business card along with the spare key. One was potentially helpful, the other damning. What explanation could I give to the cops about having the key? None that didn't land me in a cell for at least a short period of time, perhaps much longer if whoever had killed David and taken Rachel and the boys weren't caught. In my head I sat in lockdown, out for a few hours a day, meals on plastic trays eaten with plastic cutlery. A walk around the exercise yard and maybe a shiv in between my ribs if I looked at someone wrong.

The key I put in a jar of dried black beans in the pantry beside the rice with the note in it. My pantry of secrets. Jesus Christ.

The business card I took to the kitchen table. Moisture from my pants had seeped into the paper and made the word and number run. They were still legible but had a weird, ghostly look to them I didn't like.

Speranza. It meant hope, I learned from a quick internet search. Hope in Italian. For some reason knowing this didn't give me any.

The guy in Rachel's house had been looking for something. No other reason to be there, this coming from one breaker and enterer to another. I had maybe found something useful, but had he? Had he been looking for the business card and now realized it was missing?

All at once the card took on a new weight. If this somehow tied the murderer to David's and Ryan's deaths, it would be very valuable indeed.

Dad was right and so was Kel. I was in a mess, and this wasn't one of my books. I couldn't write the hero out of a tight corner; there was no deus ex machina to save me. All I had were choices.

I chose to go to the store.

13

The burner phone lay on my table, black and innocuous outside its packaging.

Of course, the manufacturers didn't call it a burner phone. The label didn't say BURNER in bold letters. There was no catchy ad copy on the package encouraging you to use this phone for any nefarious purpose since it couldn't be traced back to you without some sort of court order or sophisticated triangulation system.

In any case it was a burner phone. I'd gotten it uptown, and now it sat ready and willing on the table.

I picked it up and set it down. Paced. Went to the windows. Came back. Sat out on the porch. Talked to myself. Paced some more. Picked the phone up again and dialed the number on the back of the business card.

It rang. Once. Twice. The line clicked.

"HerringBone," a rough voice said. My throat closed to a pinhole. It was a struggle to swallow. "Hello?" the voice said.

"I'm looking for Speranza?" I finally managed, not able to disguise my voice like I'd planned. Nothing, it seemed, over the last few weeks was going like I thought it would.

"What?"

"Speranza," I repeated, my gamble either paying off or crashing and burning in real time.

There was some static from the other end, like maybe the guy was covering the phone with his hand for a second, then he was back. "Hold on," he said.

My heart went mustang. What the hell was I doing? My expertise in dealing with underworld types and mysterious figures in the dark with guns started and stopped in my manuscripts. I guess I was doing what Dad said, not letting go.

A minute later another voice came on. "Who is this?"

Imagine a smoke-filled room above a bar and grill in the middle of New York. The smoke is from good cigars, and there's a big safe in one corner of the room. A desk fills up most of the space, and a guy overfills the chair behind it. He's big, with heavy jowls, and he talks with a cigar clenched in his teeth. That's what I saw from those three words spoken in my ear.

"Someone concerned about Rachel Barren and her boys," I heard a reasonably steady voice say, then realized it was me speaking.

Long pause. "Don't know who you're talking about, friend."

"Whatever Ryan Vallance and David Barren had going with you, it doesn't involve Rachel or her kids. Just let them go. Her parents are waiting for your call. They'll pay."

Longer pause. Much longer. "You a cop?"

"No. Just a friend."

"Listen, I don't know anything about this. Best not call back, understand? Forget this number."

Then the line was dead.

I looked at the burner phone and shut it off.

Since I'd found the business card in David's desk, a seed of an idea had sprouted in my head. Rachel had told me David and Ryan's business had been hurting for quite a while now. This, combined with Ryan's three-day absence and meat loaf face when he returned, screamed he owed some serious folks money. Maybe he'd been skimming cash off the books and David had found out. Maybe a payment had been late and whoever owned the bill of sale to Ryan's ass had held him until David came through with some money. Maybe it hadn't been enough and someone had come to collect in full the other night and David had been able to pay only with his life.

Then they'd taken Rachel and the boys.

Whoever Dad saw driving away that night could've had them stashed in the back seat or in the trunk. That explained why Rachel's phone had been left behind—no way to track her. But that scenario left another large hole in the picture. If she and the boys had been taken, why hadn't a ransom been demanded yet?

Perhaps it was too soon. They'd only been missing for around thirty hours, give or take. Maybe a call would come in today or tomorrow. Maybe the kidnappers were biding their time for some other reason. Or maybe the call I'd just made would nudge them over the edge and they'd execute Rachel and the boys to cut their losses.

I was going to be sick.

Breathing heavily through my nose, I paced through the house and out onto the back porch. The fresh air did some good, but a solid piece of granite had settled in my center. Was I doing more harm than good? Should I just sit on my hands and let the police do their work? Could I do that? And how did the note tie into everything? It had come prior to all this. Had the same people who killed David sent it to cut me off from Rachel before everything happened?

It didn't really make sense.

"Here, Tosca!" Allen Crane stood in his backyard a few houses away. The terrier came flouncing out of the woods and stopped at his owner's feet. Crane bent and petted the dog, handing him a treat, speaking in a low voice. I watched as he straightened, taking in his height, the set of his shoulders, imagined him holding a gun in the dark and chasing me through the woods. Physically he fit the bill. If only I'd gotten a better look at the guy's face, heard his voice, something. Then I'd know for sure. At the very least he had been the one to discover David's body and call in the crime. Sometimes criminals would alert the authorities to their own misdeeds, thinking it removed them from suspicion.

Crane caught me looking at him. He didn't wave. Instead he clicked his tongue at Tosca, and they went back to the house, the dog oblivious, the master very aware.

Right. Time to call Kel.

———

"No. Absolutely not, Andy! I can't believe you're even asking me." Kel's voice was hushed but loud enough to reflect her anger at my requisition. "If I got caught doing an unregistered inquiry, that's my job. Done. *Finito.* Then what? Are you gonna support me too? Are the books selling that well?"

I sighed. "No. Not really."

She breathed out and swore quietly. "I'm sorry. I didn't mean that. It's just . . ."

"Don't worry about it. I get it."

"Why are you so interested in Crane anyway?"

"It's a long story. I just thought you could see where he moved here from or if there was anything fishy on his record."

"You think he killed David? And what, he's hiding Rachel and the boys somewhere?"

"I don't know, but . . ." But it was the only thread I had other than the HerringBone number. If Crane was the one who'd sent us the notes, he could be more deeply involved, tangentially or otherwise. Or maybe it was nothing. Maybe he was just a guy rounding the corner of a house after Rachel kissed me. Wrong place, wrong time. I was desperate and grasping at straws and I knew it. Nothing made sense. My compass spun.

"But what?" Kel asked.

"I don't know," I repeated. "No, you're right. Don't do a search on him. It's probably nothing. I'm just going a little stir-crazy over here, that's all. Haven't been sleeping well."

"I hear you. Hey, Dad's birthday—what do you want me to bring over?"

"The girls and your appetite."

"What, we're going to eat my kids?"

That pulled a chuckle from me. Kel could always make me laugh. "Make a salad or something. I'll take care of everything else."

"Sounds great. Sorry I couldn't help."

"No worries. I don't want you to get in trouble."

"No offense, but you were the only reason I was ever in trouble."

"What I'm here for."

"Big brother, good example, so responsible, blah blah blah."

"Goodbye, sis."

I hung up on her retort.

———

My agent loved the new book. *Fantastic. Inspired. Creepy. So readable. And the ending, nailed it!* The praise would've sent me over the moon a few weeks back. Now it barely made a blip on the radar. My career belonged to another life. Something before all this when the world made sense and people didn't die or disappear in the night.

Before I fell in love.

This stupid caring. This idiotic feeling. This self-absorbed yearning making you do foolish things, making you go on wild-goose chases and nearly get yourself killed in the middle of the woods.

All for those quiet moments of looking into the eyes of someone who understands you. Who you share secrets with. Who you trust.

I sighed and knew, given the chance, I'd do it all over again.

I wrote back to my agent saying great, wonderful, glad she liked it. What was she thinking for time frame on revisions? What publishing houses might be interested? All immaterial motions to maintain the semblance of normality. Mission control, everything is go for launch.

The rest of the afternoon whittled away an hour at a time. Check the news here, do some dishes there, prep a little dinner for Dad and me. Try not to think of where she is. Where the boys are or if they're afraid. Try not to worry you won't be smart enough to find them, to save them. Don't think about that.

Then the sun was settling into the horizon and the whole sky was on fire.

Dad and I sat in his backyard watching the light fade, talking a little but mostly just being quiet. I didn't know if anything had changed now that the affair was out in the open. I knew he didn't actually suspect me of murder or anything like that, but I wondered if there was a part of him that was disappointed. Maybe he'd felt the same way hearing Sharon and I were divorcing or that the last couple of books hadn't sold as well as my earlier titles.

Or maybe he was just worried about his son and the mess he was in.

After he was settled in for the night, I went home. The very last of the light caressed the church's steeple, making it glow. Glory on high and all that.

Around nine, as I was trying to consider heading to bed, a knock came at the door. When I opened it, Kel stood there bathed in the porch light, holding a bottle of wine in one hand.

"You're lucky I love you," she said.

14

"There's this one lady at work who runs the history of every cute guy who comes through the door," Kel said, kicking off her shoes in the entry. "Where are your wineglasses?"

"What? Corner cabinet, top shelf."

"I'm too short. You get those, I'll open this," she said, digging through my silverware drawer until she found a corkscrew. As I retrieved the glasses, she kept talking. "I started thinking about that after you called. Yvonne, she's divorced and always on the hunt for Mr. Right, or Mr. Right Now, as she puts it. I don't know how many guys she's looked up to make sure they aren't creepers or have any outstanding warrants and whatnot. So I thought if she does it constantly for selfish reasons and never gets caught, I can do it this once. What's the big deal?" Kel smiled and handed me a glass. "Cheers."

We clinked and went into the living room to sit next to the big windows. The street was empty outside, lampposts exhaling yellow breath into fog clouding the neighborhood. It could've been the end of the world out there, lifeless and quiet and gray.

"You didn't have to do it," I said.

"I know. The best things aren't done out of need."

"I'm stealing that."

"Go ahead."

"So what did you find about our friend down the street?"

Kel shook her head as she swallowed a large sip of merlot. "Nope. No more cloak-and-dagger. Yesterday I'm gophering after info from Seth, and today I'm risking my career for you—"

"I thought you just said it wasn't a big deal."

"—all so you can be clandestine and closed off?" Kel continued without pausing. "Uh-uh. No way. Spill it, Andrew Michael Drake."

I spilled it.

"I fucking knew it!" Kel said, leaping to her feet and pointing at me. "You were too happy the last six months. I mean, you're always happy, but you were really happy, and I totally knew it." She went from triumphant to indignant in a half second. "I can't believe you didn't tell me. This is such a mess."

"Dad said the same thing, but he took it so much better."

Kel spit wine onto my floor. "Dad knows?"

"He knew before I told him," I said, grabbing a napkin to wipe the floor.

She looked out the window at the house we grew up in. "Huh," she said. Like father, like daughter.

"I don't need a lecture. I know what we were doing was wrong." What I didn't know was what to say next. Kel's marriage had imploded because her husband cheated on her with a much older woman, no doubt adding insult to injury. My particular situation was different, but I wasn't sure how she would react. I didn't expect a hug.

"I'm glad you're okay. And I'm glad you two got together," she said after releasing me. "David was always an asshole. Not that he deserves to be dead. But wow, now I know why you were so edgy the last few weeks."

"So now that you're all filled in on the carnival ride that's my life, what did you find out about Crane?"

"First off, that's not his real name."

It was his *legal* name but not the one he was born with. All this became apparent in the few-minutes search Kel had conducted at the

DMV. Mr. Allen Crane had filed for a change of name with the state of New York two years ago, shortly before moving to the Loop. He had no outstanding warrants or speeding tickets, was not a registered sex offender, and his given name was Jimmy DeMarco Jr., but that's where Kel's research stopped.

"My supervisor came back from break, and I chickened out," she said, refilling her wineglass. "Otherwise I could've gotten more."

"No, this is great," I said, retrieving my laptop. "This gives us something to go on."

His original name was more than enough for Google. A half dozen hits came up, the first one sporting a photo of a slightly younger but unmistakable version of my neighbor.

Jimmy DeMarco Jr. had been indicted a little over three years ago regarding several faulty insurance claims on properties he owned in New Jersey. When it appeared he'd be spending a considerable amount of time behind bars, DeMarco flipped on a few other "business partners" who he testified were the investors and orchestrators behind the schemes. The business partners were fined, and two were sentenced to three years in prison, sentences suspended. DeMarco earned himself a plea deal and moved out of the state and into our neighborhood as Mr. Allen Crane.

"Holy shit," Kel said. "He's connected."

I let out a long breath. "We don't know that, but it's suspicious. Obviously he was worried enough to move and change his name."

"Something else I just remembered—at the Barrens' party last year, I overheard him talking to David. Just polite conversation, but I gathered Crane had his mortgage through David's company."

"You sure?"

"Yeah."

Interesting. I took a swallow of wine.

Had it been Crane/DeMarco who saw us in Rachel's kitchen that day? I thought so. Had he sent us notes about our affair? I couldn't be sure. Had he chased me from the Barrens' into the woods the night before? Maybe. If the guy was connected, could he have been some sort of liaison between Ryan and HerringBone? Maybe given David the business card with the number on it at some point?

It was a stretch, and I wondered, not for the first time, if we were dealing with one thing or perhaps with two or three all happening in tandem. There was no way to tell. Not yet.

Something struck me then—the fact I could say *we* now instead of *I*. Family—maddening, strange, tumultuous, and a blessing when you were hurting or in trouble. The people with their arms out when you jumped from the burning building you were in. No guarantee you wouldn't still hit the ground, but they'd try to catch you.

"Can you check with Seth to see if Crane's been questioned?" I said.

"Sure. I can ask."

"You two . . . uh . . ."

"None of your business."

"But Rachel and I are yours?"

"Different. This is dangerous." She reached out and squeezed my hand. "You realize you could've died the other night, right? That Dad and I would be the ones sitting here wondering what the hell happened. Why your body was found in the woods."

"I'm really, really trying not to think about that, but thanks for reminding me."

"Then maybe you should stop. If you don't push anymore, maybe everything will work out okay."

My little sister. Looking at me with the same eyes as when we'd sneak back into the house in the middle of the night after drinking with my friends and Mom was suddenly awake and coming down the hallway. The same concern, the same panic. That, coupled with the fact we weren't kids anymore—hell, Kel had her own little ones—sunk it home more than anything else.

This wasn't a game. It wasn't a story. It was exactly like she and Dad said: a mess.

One I might've helped create and had to clean up if I could.

Just like I saw the concern in her eyes, she saw the determination in mine. "Okay," she said, squeezing my hand one last time. "Okay."

A little later I watched her walk down my drive to her car, made sure she got in and pulled away before I shut the door. Then I went to my office and wrote the following words in a blank document:

> Ryan Vallance, and possibly David Barren, owed money to an individual or individuals at a bar and grill called HerringBone in New York. *Speranza* is either a password or a name. The individuals may be holding Rachel Barren and her sons hostage. Please notify the police.

A wild impulse to add *Do as I say* at the end came and went. I highlighted the paragraph and let my finger hover over the "Delete" key. Then I printed it instead. Using a pair of latex gloves, I plucked the printed sheet from the tray and folded it in half, then wrote Seth Goddard's name on one side.

Fifteen minutes later I walked down a fog-choked street parallel to the *Sandford Review*. I'd parked in an abandoned corner lot a half mile up from the paper and decided going on foot was the better choice. In the back parking area, I approached the employee entrance, making sure there was no one burning the midnight oil, and scanned quickly for security cameras. I didn't see any but pulled up the hood on my sweatshirt just in case as I made my way to the door.

Note out of my pocket. Press one corner tightly into the doorjamb. Turn and walk away.

Three seconds. Maybe less. Then I was out of the parking lot and on another side street, winding my way back to my car. The idea of leaving the note had come to me midway through our research on Crane/ DeMarco. I couldn't call the cops directly—way too many questions. Couldn't use the burner phone either—they'd track down where the phone was sold from and get the security footage of me purchasing it, and Bingo was his name-o. Leaving a note at the police station was super risky as well, so I opted for involving the press to get the word to Detective Spanner. Seth was a smart guy. He'd bring the note to the cops, and they could follow up on the claim.

Head down, walking up a dark, foggy street. A coward in the night.

Let the professionals do the work. Stand to the side. Get out of the way. Rachel and the boys' absence was eating me alive, and if this was the best way to get them back, then so be it. I just hoped I wasn't making another wrong decision in a long line of wrong decisions.

Back at home the tension eased a little. I finished off the last of the wine and stood looking out at the Loop. Dad was awake, but I could see he was just making himself a snack in the kitchen. Part of me wanted to go over there, but mostly I wanted to be alone. I was hollow from the last few weeks, nothing left to give.

The wine helped usher sleep in on burgundy waves that drew me out into deeper water. I nodded off in the chair, head drooped to one side, feet propped on the windowsill.

Dreams of the church basement door. Stuttering images like looking through the air over a fire. Stairs leading down endlessly into darkness.

I woke to a sound, soft but something my brain labeled as intentional. The dreams unwove, a tapestry coming apart. Blinking, I straightened in the chair, drew my legs down from the sill, and let the blood rushing back into them finish its buzzing work.

What the sound had been I couldn't say. A soft bump, like clothes flopping in a dryer. But I didn't have any laundry going. The house was dappled with orange sodium light from the street and oblong shadows. My eyes were gritty, and I rubbed them, making my way to the kitchen. An internal compass told me the sound had come from this direction.

I'd double-check the back door, then go to bed for some better-quality sleep.

Two things registered as I stepped into the kitchen. One, I identified the sound not as the flump of laundry going around in the dryer but of my back door's weather seal locking into place. And two, someone was sitting in a chair at the table.

Their shadowed face turned slowly toward me, and there was the click of a hammer cocking.

"Have a seat, Andy."

15

One Sunday when I was in fourth grade, Mom brought us all to church. It was like every other Sunday since she always brought us to church, but this particular time I decided to bring my Game Boy too.

Surreptitious. That's the word I would use now about how I thought I was being then. I sat to the far end of the pew, as far away from Mom as I could get, with Em and Kel in between me and Cory, since I knew he would squeal. I took out the Bible from the holder at the back of the pew in front of me, positioned it just so in my lap, and began to play my game.

It was perfect. The console was small enough to basically hide in my hands anyway, and with the Bible and the speaker system booming with the father's voice, I had all the cover I needed.

Until Mrs. Tross in the pew across the aisle spotted what I was doing. She didn't have her binoculars with her then, but I wouldn't have been surprised. She spoke to my mother after Mass, and I was summarily searched on the walk home, my contraband discovered.

One day, Mom said, in a measured tone that was more terrifying than if she'd been yelling, *one day you'll stand before the Almighty at the edge of your death, and what will you say when he asks if you've been attentive to his word? What will you do when you're at the end of this life and the beginning of the next?*

I knew the answer now, standing in the dark of my kitchen with an unknown man holding a gun on me.

I sat.

Closer, the gun was visible, some streetlight shine collecting on its barrel. I couldn't see the bore diameter but wondered if it really mattered how big the bullet would be that ended your life. The guy wore a dark coat of some kind and kept his hair short, the color indistinguishable. His eyes glinted just enough to make them look like they were lit from within.

We didn't say anything for a time, only sitting, contemplating one another. I wasn't sure how well he could see me, but I felt like I was on a dissection tray, slowly being taken apart.

"I'm a fan of your work," he finally said.

It was like he'd spoken in a foreign language. "My . . . what?"

"Your books. Are you not the Andy Drake who wrote the Laird Holmes series?"

"Yeah, I . . . I am." How ironic to not even be a bestselling author and be killed by a lunatic fan. Stephen King, eat your heart out.

"Good books. Read all of them. You got a knack for character. Especially the mob guys. They say art imitates life, and I'd say yours does."

"I'm sorry, can I ask what this is about?" My voice had quit shaking, but my hands hadn't, so when he slid something across the table, I didn't reach out to pick it up. I didn't need to. I knew what it was.

My note to Seth Goddard. The note I'd stuck in the doorjamb of the *Sandford Review*. Back on my table. Abracadabra.

The guy tapped it once with a gloved fingertip. "This, however," he said, before pulling the note back out of sight, "is not your best writing."

I didn't know what to say. This was the man who had chased me from Rachel's, who had pursued me through the woods. Somehow he must've figured out who I was.

"Are Rachel and the boys okay?" I asked when he offered nothing more.

He made a quiet scoffing sound. "See, I always thought writers were smart people. Worldly. Able to reason. But you, you, my friend, seem dumb as a bag of hammers."

"I just assumed since you brought the note back, you work for HerringBone."

"I do."

My mouth moved for a second before any sound came out. "So . . . I thought Ryan Vallance and David Barren owed money to HerringBone. To Mr. Hope."

There was a pause; then the guy burst out laughing. He had a good laugh, a deep chuckle that would make you look around if you heard it in a crowded bar. When he quieted, he said, "Mr. Hope—that's good. Yeah, Speranza isn't anyone's name, but I'm guessing you figured that much out on your own. As for Mr. Vallance, yes, he owed a considerable amount of money, and subsequently, so did Mr. Barren."

I watched him. Waited for the muzzle flash. This was all some kind of game ending in me bleeding out on the floor with my guts strung through the back of the chair I was sitting on. "I don't get it," I said when he didn't shoot.

"That's very apparent. What I'm here to make you get is you're barking up the wrong proverbial tree. The message is: do not bring my employers any deeper into this situation and you'll continue to cast a shadow."

"How do I know you don't have Rachel and her boys?"

"Because I'm telling you so." He shifted in his chair, getting more comfortable. "I been keeping an eye on things for a couple weeks, Andy. Been around steady ever since Mr. Vallance decided to check out early. Either that or someone checked him out, not sure yet. But I noticed you. You've been a busy boy. Nighttime exploits and visiting Mrs. Barren's parents. Now this." He patted his pocket where he'd placed the note. "I'd wonder what your angle is, but I think I know. Seen pictures of the missus. Pretty lady."

"I just want to make sure they're safe."

"And I want to make sure we understand one another."

I was quiet for a beat. "I'll give you the business card. That must've been what you were after the other night, right?"

"Sorry?"

"It was you in the Barrens' house. You chased me into the woods."

"Nah, friend. That wasn't me."

"Then—"

"But I will take this business card you're speaking of."

"It's in the black beans."

"What?"

"The pantry. I'll get it."

He panned the gun with me as I stood and crossed the room. I'd shoved the business card down in the beans with Rachel's spare key after making the call the day before. A quick scan of my surroundings told me there was no nearby weapon I could use before the guy at the table perforated my hide, so I went back to my seat and slid the card to him. He disappeared it like he had the note.

"If it wasn't you, then who was it?" I asked.

"Not sure. But I will tell you this: there's more players here than you think. We don't have the missing wife or her boys, but when they eventually do surface, we'd like to speak to her about potentially settling a debt. She should be well taken care of, what with life insurance and the like. When she shows up, you pass that message along."

"What if she's dead?"

"I don't get that feeling," he said, beginning to stand.

"What did Vallance owe you money for?" I blurted. What the hell was I doing? It looked like I might actually live through this little encounter with a mob enforcer, and here I was grilling him for info.

He must've been thinking the same thing, because his head tilted as he watched me through the dark. "Set of balls on you, don't ya?" He considered me another few seconds, then said, "Don't know what he was in deep for, but he said he had a foolproof plan to get paid up the last time he spoke to my employers. Then he was dead. Maybe that was his plan, maybe he was full of shit; who knows?"

The guy walked toward my back door and tucked the gun away beneath his coat. Before he let himself out, he said, "The reason your teeth are still in your head and not littering the floor is I like your books. But you do something dumb again like you did tonight? That's where my appreciation ends. I'll be around."

Then he was gone.

I stood from the table and crossed to the door. Locked it. The backyard was empty, and except for a faint trace of cologne, my visitor might've never been there.

My legs did a weird wobble, then unhinged. I sat down quickly.

With my back up against the nearest wall, my mind spun. When I thought I could stand, I got myself a glass and poured three or four fingers of bourbon into it, drank it down. Leaning on the counter in the dark, I tried processing what just happened the best I could.

So this guy, the Visitor, I'd call him (it had a nice ominous ring to it). HerringBone had sent him to check in on Ryan Vallance's death. Right after that, David is shot and Rachel and the boys disappear. But this guy says he has nothing to do with it, that he wasn't the one in the house with me the other night. I didn't know about the former, but the latter held some weight of truth. There's a distinct feeling in the air when someone wants you dead; I knew that now, and I'd never write another chase scene or gunfight the same way. When I fled from the Barrens', there was no doubt the man pursuing me wanted to kill me, yet if the Visitor was the same guy, he could've done it while I was asleep in the living room. Could've shot me when I walked in the kitchen or on his way out the door.

Comparing the build and general outline of the Visitor to whoever chased me brought something else to the surface. Dad had said he thought he saw an old neighbor, George Nell, driving down the street after hearing the shot. But George was dead. I conjured up how the man had appeared in life, and it gave me pause because he physically resembled both the Visitor and Crane/DeMarco. It wasn't a stretch to think Dad had seen one of the men and his memory had used George as a placeholder.

I doused the glass with another shot of bourbon and went into the living room, legs feeling more like they were attached to me with each step. Even if it had been the Visitor who'd chased me the night before, one fact remained unchanged: I definitely wasn't dead. So what did that mean?

"That he's a fan," I said to the empty room, and a wild laugh crept up out of my throat. I put one hand over my mouth because I didn't like the sound of it, but that only made me laugh harder. The guy had been a true-blue reader of my work, and my teeth were still in my head because of it. Goddamned hilarious. When the laughter finally faded to giggles, I swallowed the last of the bourbon and sat.

Really it came down to two things. One, did I believe the Visitor that HerringBone didn't have Rachel and the boys? And two, was I going to do what he said and quit looking for her?

Maybe.

And no.

Everyone has a breaking point—I knew that. I also knew I hadn't reached mine yet.

Not yet.

16

In the pale light coming around the curtains, I kissed the edge of her shoulder blade.

She slept on her stomach. I learned this after our third time together when she'd drifted off afterward. Bad habit, doctors would say. But how the valley of her spine looked in the light, the lines and shadows in the hollow of her lower back, I wouldn't have her sleep any other way.

Her face was turned to one side, a lank of hair draped there. I tucked it behind her ear, and she shifted, opening her eyes. A smile.

Those minutes, before we had to return to the world, were the worst and the sweetest all at once.

I thought of things to say, everything I wanted to tell her. How I knew her favorite color was an emerald green called Ireland. How one side of her mouth always quirked when she was watching her kids play. How she rubbed the same spot behind her right ear whenever she was nervous or worried about something, which was a lot. How I wanted to take that worry away as much as I could, as much as she'd let me.

All this I'd wanted to say and hadn't the last time we were together. Maybe if I had, things would be different. I didn't know. Words are funny things. They're warped mirrors of what we mean, and only once in a while do they reflect the truth. Maybe that's our fault, and maybe we can't help it. Maybe we do the best we can.

I thought about this as I sat at Dad's table, with the misted air clinging to the windows, obscuring the outside world. I hadn't slept. Hadn't even tried. My mind was a hamster, my head the wheel. Round and round.

How far would this go? What would my life look like in six months? If I kept pushing, would I even have a life in six months? What Kel said the night before kept rushing up and receding like an insistent tide. How I could've been shot and left dead in the woods and she and Dad would've been left with questions. I didn't want that, but what I wanted less was to find out Rachel and the boys were in some abandoned gravel pit or stuffed into a barrel somewhere. It happened. All the time. That the Loop was quiet and filled with retirees and young families didn't mean squat.

"Anything new?" Dad asked. He was finishing his second cup of coffee and watching me from across the table. I suppose I'd been too quiet during breakfast.

"No. Not really," I said, having decided the night before I wasn't going to mention the Visitor to Dad or Kel. They were worried enough as it was. "You been locking your back door?"

"Sometimes. Why?"

"You should make it a habit."

"We lived here forty years. Never had to worry about it before."

"Yeah, and people weren't getting killed up the street before." My thoughts were of the Visitor, but the lock on my door hadn't stopped him. Even so, some deterrence was better than none.

Dad grunted and folded the morning paper. "I didn't say it the other day because I know you are, but I want you to be careful, Andy. Whatever happened, it's still happening."

"I know, and I am." I started clearing the table and changed the subject. "Kel and the girls are coming over tomorrow for your birthday. Gonna grill ribs if that's okay."

"My favorite."

"Anything else you want?"

"Brain transplant."

"Already on the list."

"Good, good."

I told him I'd be back over around dinner and headed out the door. I sensed he was getting ready to approach what I was doing from another direction, and I didn't want to address it anymore. I wanted to act. To make progress. Wanted to make things right.

At my place I changed into a good pair of slacks and loose dress shirt. Checked myself in the mirror, then went to the bathroom and added some gel to my hair. I didn't look like me, which was good.

I needed to be someone else.

———

Layers.

Layers told a story. It's how books came to life. Characters are nothing but layers, emotions driving actions, actions having consequences, which fueled new emotions. Layer upon layer, a story is told. Truths learned. Secrets revealed.

I thought about how Rachel looked at her boys, how she looked at me in the low light of whatever room we were in.

I thought about this as I sat in the wireless carrier's parking lot watching the young clerk sell a phone to a middle-aged man.

Anything new learned had to be processed, evaluated, decided upon. I'd spent all night doing just that. The question I kept coming back to was if the Visitor was being honest. The impression he wanted to give was he was strictly here for business. Find the money owed and that's it. I'd replayed our conversation during the night when I should've been sleeping, and I still wasn't sure what his true intentions were.

Could you trust a man with a gun? It was a little like going to church. Putting your faith in the Lord. At any moment he could pull the trigger. Boom. You're dead.

Billions of people trusted God. I guess I could trust one guy with a gun.

That's why I was parked in front of the wireless store, waiting for the customer to finish up his purchase. I hadn't seen the Visitor or any suspicious vehicles on the Loop that morning when I left, but it meant nothing. The guy was good, had been keeping tabs on the neighborhood and me without being noticed. Yet another reason to believe he wasn't the man who'd pursued me through the dark—I got the distinct impression if the Visitor wanted you dead, you would be dead.

The middle-aged guy nodded and shook hands with the clerk before exiting the store. There weren't any other cars in the parking lot, and the clerk seemed to be the only one on duty. If I was going to do this, it would have to be now.

The prior night's fog had turned to a heavy mist sometime in the early hours, and it speckled my face as I crossed the lot and went in the store. Inside it was over-air-conditioned and smelled like new carpet. The clerk was maybe twenty-one and wore a button-up shirt with the company's logo on the breast. In the few seconds before he looked up from his tablet to greet me, I summoned the persona I'd been practicing all morning.

It was time to be a dick.

"Good morning, welcome to—" was as far as he got.

"Listen, bud, I need you to unfuck something for me real quick," I said, coming right up to the counter, talking fast. Hurried. I was in a hurry. Couldn't be bothered by pleasantries. "I just lost my wallet, my phone, and if you can't help me, about two hundred grand."

The kid's jaw opened and closed like a fish, and I immediately felt sorry for him. "Well, I . . . I'll definitely try."

"Here's the deal," I said, leaning my full weight on the desk between us, looking directly at him. "Late last night I'm at the gym, and some asshole breaks into my locker. Takes my bag with all my shit in it. Already canceled my credit cards, but what I really need is the last five phone numbers I called. If I don't make the calls I'm supposed to this morning, my ass is in a sling, you got me?"

"Uh, yeah, Mr. . . ."

"Vallance, Ryan Vallance." The kid looked relieved that he could focus on something other than me for a second as he started tapping at his tablet. "See, I'd just get a new phone and sync everything myself, but all my cards are canceled and I gotta close a deal this morning. I can't dick around that long. Ryan Vallance—it should be under Valiant Lending Agency." I rattled David and Ryan's business address off, which I'd memorized that morning.

All of this—a long shot. I wasn't sure Ryan Vallance had his account through this carrier, wasn't sure he ran his phone through the business, and definitely wasn't sure this kid would give me the last few numbers called on Vallance's account. But it was all I'd come up with since the Visitor had walked out my back door last night. If I could find out who Vallance had been in contact with before he died, then maybe I could figure out why he owed HerringBone money and what his "sure thing" for paying them off was. One layer leading to another I hoped would lead me to Rachel.

"Here we are, Mr. Vallance. Yes, I got your account pulled up. Um . . ." The kid shot a look around the empty store, maybe searching for help or to see if we really were alone. "The only problem is I'm not supposed to release any information without proper ID."

"So did you not hear me earlier? All my shit was stolen. I have no ID until I hit the goddamned DMV later, and let me tell you, I ain't looking forward to that."

"Yeah, still. I'm uh—"

"Are you serious? Do you know how much business I do in this town? How long have you worked here?"

"Two . . . little over two months."

"Two whole months? Okay, lemme talk to your manager."

"Um, well, she's not in today."

"Of course she isn't. What a fuckin' shit show this is. You know what? I'll come back when your manager's here and explain how your little policy lost me one of the biggest deals of the year. I'm sure that'll go over well."

All the cards on the table, I stalked away. He wasn't going to stop me before I hit the door. He was going to tell his manager, and she was going to realize Ryan Vallance was no longer among the living, and she'd file a complaint with the police. They'd come down, review the store's surveillance footage, and there I'd be on camera—big as life.

Four steps from the door.

Three.

Two.

Hand on the handle.

Pushing out into the mist.

"Hey, Mr. Vallance?"

I stopped, glad I was facing away so he wouldn't see the pure relief on my face. I turned around.

The kid was writing on a piece of paper. "Here you go." I went back to the desk, and he gave me the paper with five numbers scrawled in hasty but readable script. "Please don't mention anything to my manager. I'd get in trouble either way."

I tapped the paper once and then slapped him on the arm like I figured Vallance would. "Not a word, bud; you really helped me out. Thanks a million. Or two hundred thousand, I should say." I laughed loudly, and the kid joined in half-heartedly. He looked glad I was leaving.

That made two of us.

17

The sanctuary of home.

Or so I hoped. I spent the first ten minutes checking the entire house to make sure the Visitor hadn't come visiting again. Maybe spurred by my slicked appearance and trip to the local wireless carrier, no matter how innocuous I tried making it look. Maybe this time he'd shoot first and not ask questions later.

The house was empty, all the locks still locked.

Out of paranoia, I'd almost destroyed the burner phone and thrown it away after my call to HerringBone but decided to keep it at the last moment. I was glad now, given the task ahead. The kid at the wireless store had drawn arrows after the phone numbers, a couple pointing away and the rest pointing in. It took me a few seconds to realize he'd delineated which calls were outgoing and incoming. Nice attention to detail. If he didn't get fired for the little stunt I'd just pulled, he might have a future in telecommunications.

Not really wanting to call each number to find out who they belonged to, I tried a reverse lookup online first. No go for three out of the five since they were cells. The other two were a sporting goods store downtown and a Chinese takeout in a nearby strip mall that served the best pork fried rice I'd ever had.

Deep breath in. Out.

The first number rang three times, then a female voice came on saying, "Hello? Hello?"

I was prepared for this. I started to panic.

"Hey, hi there, hi," I sputtered. "I'm not sure I've got the right number."

"Who is this?"

"This is John, I'm a friend of Ryan's. Ryan Vallance?" I said his name like a question. I was terrible at this.

"Okay, what do you want?"

"Oh, sorry. Yeah, I was just going through some of his things, and he had a few numbers written down on his desk, and I was checking them. Seeing if anyone . . . needed anything."

Long pause, and I felt like there was a drain in my center and someone had just pulled the plug. I was about to end the call when she spoke again. "No, I got all of my stuff when I moved out like four months ago."

Okay. Girlfriend. Ex-girlfriend. "All right, that's good. I don't think we've ever met."

"Probably not. Ryan didn't have a lot of friends."

"Yeah, no, that's true. I'm sorry, your name was . . ."

"Marla."

"Right, he did mention you before. Thanks, Marla." I had no idea why I was thanking her. "You know, I wanted to ask—did Ryan ever seem strange or distant? Did you notice anything before . . . you know . . ."

She breathed out, long and slow. "When wasn't he distant? We'd only been living together for about three weeks when I realized it wasn't going to work. All he wanted to do was hit the bars and talk about money. How much cash he had, how much he was going to make. It was a nightmare, glad I left when I did. Gives me the creeps because he called me a day or two before he died. Probably wanted to hook up. Who knows? Maybe he would've offed me along with himself if I would've still been living there."

"Yeah, well, who knows? Uh, did he say anything to you specifically about money, because when we talked, he seemed especially stressed when that came up."

"Probably, I don't know. When we first got together, he was always flashing cash, and later we were splitting the bills. Guessing his get-rich-quick scheme didn't pay off. He said it was a long-term investment, but Ryan wasn't a long-term guy. In *any* respect, I can tell you that."

"Do you know what that was? The investment thing? Because he mentioned it once and never told me anything more."

Long pause. "Doesn't sound like you guys were very good friends."

I laughed nervously. "Like you said, he was always distant."

"Mm-hmm. Some biotech thing. I don't know. Then he quit talking about it. Listen, I gotta go. I don't have anything at his place, and if I do, throw it away—I don't need it."

"Okay, sounds good—" But she was already gone.

I looked at the phone, then set it down. Long-term investment. Biotech.

What the hell?

Scenarios and rickety conclusions formed in my head, and I shook it to clear them away. It was important not to assume anything. Just label the layer and move on.

The next number down the list rang four times, then went to voice mail.

"You have reached Collin Dressler with Westex Therapeutics. I can't come to the phone right now, but—"

I hung up and tapped out the company's name on my laptop and searched. Lots of hits.

Westex Therapeutics was a biotech start-up company out of Texas specializing in immune system therapy. It was started by one Collin Dressler, CEO, and his business partner, Steven Fairchild, CFO. The first article I read stated Westex had formed early last year with several private investors and a healthy portfolio of both technology innovations and cash depth.

The latest article, dated a month back, was only three paragraphs long, though they could've shortened it into one.

Westex was bankrupt and shutting down. Their offices and labs would be shuttered in the coming weeks, and plans of going public with stock options were obviously off the table.

I closed my laptop and looked out the window.

If I were writing this scene, it would go something like this:

Ryan Vallance, wannabe big shot—large fish, little pond kind of thing—hears about a neato start-up on the frontlines of medicine. Maybe he got a hot tip somewhere, maybe the "CEO" of the company took him for a ride while they both sat at a bar after meeting by chance—who knows. Ryan then goes to David for a loan, but David says no or won't give him the full amount. Ryan takes a trip to the big city and asks around, eventually ending up at HerringBone. Speranza. Hope. Loan goes through, and presto—he's an investor.

Then disaster strikes.

Westex has setbacks in funding. Setbacks in research. Employees start leaving in droves like rats from a sinking ship. The shades lower, and away goes Ryan's money, which he owes to serious individuals. Perhaps he starts skimming a little off the lending agency to make the payments on time. Maybe one month he doesn't come up with all the cash and he gets a visit from the Visitor, along with an all-expenses-paid ride down to New York for a weekend of bleeding, cowering, and pleading for his life. Then a phone call to David and the truth comes out. David bargains with HerringBone to get his business partner back in one piece. And then?

"Then they fall short on money again and they're both dead," I said to the empty room. Only problem there is the needle pointed back to HerringBone and the Visitor as the culprits. Why wouldn't they have asked for a ransom by now? Why would the Visitor still be hanging around the Loop?

The other option was the Visitor was telling the truth. They didn't kill Ryan or David, didn't have Rachel and the boys, and there was another party involved.

My cell rang, so loud and sudden I flinched. I muttered something, seeing Kel's picture on the screen.

"Hello?"

"Hey, how's it going?"

I sighed, looking at the list of phone numbers. "Okay. How about you? Didn't get fired for helping me yet, I hope."

Kel laughed. "No. I'm not too worried about that." She paused, and I could hear something in the quiet. Sometimes it was people's silence that said the most. If you loved someone, all kinds of conversations happened without words.

"What's wrong?" I asked.

"It's Dad. He called me this morning."

"Why? What's going on?" I was on my feet and over to the window, half expecting his house to be engulfed in flames.

"I guess he got a notice from the insurance company. The payment didn't go through."

"What? Can't be—I've got that on autopay."

"Then his account's overdrawn."

"No, that's—" I was going to say "not possible," but it was. Imagine a guy juggling bowling pins. He starts with two and slowly works up to more. Every so often one drops, and he has to keep the others in the air while picking up the dropped pin. Dad and my bills were the bowling pins, and the juggling act was finances versus timing. Somehow I'd miscalculated, and a bill must've come out before a payment went in.

"Shit, I'm sorry. Guessing I forgot something."

"Not like you don't have other things on your mind. I think that's why he called me instead. He didn't want to bother you with anything else."

I sighed. "Sorry. I'll take a look."

"It's okay, quit apologizing. Honestly, I knew this day would come. I've been putting a little aside for the last six months or so—"

"Kel, no. I've got this."

"You don't, though. You can't. Do you know how much his care is going to be? Insurance is only going to cover so much each month."

"I know, I've looked it up." Dad losing his health insurance was one of the things I feared the most. Only in America could you be crushed by the wheel of medical expense before the disease being treated actually killed you.

"I'm going to help with the cost, Andy."

"You need your money. The girls—"

"We'll be fine."

I moved through the house wanting to strike something. To break and shatter. It would feel good to pass some wreckage on. "I'll figure it out."

"What? Are you going to call Cory?"

I snorted. "Fuck no. Are you?"

"Not a thousand wild horses . . ."

Our older brother, Cory. Tall, dark haired, suave, never swore, went to church on a regular basis. Male version of our mother. Cory worked in finance in Chicago and came home once a year on Christmas. It was more than enough. By the end of his stay, I'd be sitting on my hands whenever he was in the room, and Kel would be drunk by ten in the morning. Even Dad would be more stressed than usual. Cory had that effect on people. He was a comb run through your hair the wrong way, a hangnail that tore. He was also loaded, but asking him for money was going to be my very last resort.

"I've been thinking," I said. "Mom's Roth IRA."

"Yeah? What of it?"

"I was going to talk to Father Mathew about getting the church to revert it to Dad."

Kel huffed a laugh. "The church give up money? Sure, sure. Please do let me know when you get blood out of that particular stone."

"I know, I know. But if I explain the situation, he can't turn us down, right? Even though it was in her will, there has to be some way to reroute it to Dad. Even if it's accepting the money each month and making a charitable donation back to him."

"I mean, that sounds good. But I don't know if—" She stopped, and I heard a lot more in her silence again.

"If what? If I should be the one to talk to him?"

"Well . . ."

"It was a window, for God's sake. I didn't set fire to the church."

"Still."

"It'll be fine. I'll go up there this afternoon before I make supper for Dad. He can't say no."

"Five bucks."

"You're on. Except I'll have to make payments if you win."

"Ha, ha, ha."

"Bye, sis, I'll call you later."

"Bye, Andybird."

That stopped me. I held the phone pressed to my ear even though she'd hung up, her adolescent nickname for me bouncing around in my head. Kel was worried. She joked around and reverted to nicknames when things were the worst. It was her defense mechanism, a time machine of sorts. Her way of going back to before when everything was better. The last time she'd called me that was during her divorce.

I sat down at the table. Put my head in my hands. What did Mom always say about life being the ultimate crucible? I didn't care. Her abbreviated wisdom had always fallen short for me. Right now I needed to keep my mind clear on every front, and that included the ghost of my mother's voice.

Instead I thought of what Winston Churchill had supposedly once said. If you're going through hell, keep going.

Yes. Right. No stopping now. No way to turn back anyhow.

I was about to get up and change out of my faux dress clothes and wash the gel from my hair when I realized I hadn't called the last number on the list I'd gotten from Ryan Vallance's carrier. After considering waiting until that evening, I punched it into the burner phone, readying my new cover story.

Five rings, then voice mail. A voice came on, and I froze.

Because I recognized it. I'd listened to it hundreds of times over the years, booming and echoing throughout cavernous spaces, speaking of damnation and redemption.

"You've reached Father Mathew Travers. I can't answer the phone right now, but please leave me a message and I'll return your call as soon as possible. God bless you."

18

I stared at Mary Shelby's empty desk.

The seating area outside the glass enclosure near the sanctuary was quiet, and I was alone, looking at the place where she used to work. On another timeline, I'd be sitting in front of her desk, kicked back and at ease in her company. Mary's eyes would be twinkling with whatever story she was telling about a parishioner, her horses, grandkids, it didn't matter. She'd always been so *alive.*

And now she wasn't. It was very hard for me to accept the fact.

Her desk appeared untouched, its neatness betrayed only by a few sticky notes stuck to the dark computer screen. I could almost see her fixing a cup of coffee across the room and bringing it over to where she'd sat for the better part of twenty-five years, day in, day out. Everything was a potential echo chamber for someone who'd moved on. It wasn't just houses that could be haunted. Hearts could be too.

Especially hearts.

Elliot Wyman pushed an electric lawn mower past the nearest window. Besides his being an usher, it now looked like Father Mathew had him doing groundskeeping as well. He saw me and waved enthusiastically. I waved back and was semi-horrified as he left the mower and stepped inside.

"Andy, how are you?" Elliot said, coming too close to shake my hand.

"Good, how're you, Elliot?"

"Blessed. Just blessed. What a beautiful day."

"It is."

He glanced at Mary's desk. "So strange not seeing Mary sitting there, isn't it?"

"Sure is," I said, not happy with him voicing my earlier thoughts.

"But strangeness is part of faith, isn't it?"

"I'll say."

"It's the mystery. We don't know when our time is up, and that's a blessing!" He laughed, leaning close again, and I nodded, resisting the urge to sidle away. "He works in mysterious ways, and we just have to trust in him, don't we?"

I was saved from answering by footsteps coming down the hallway. Father Mathew. All six feet one and two hundred pounds of him. He looked bigger in casual dress than he did in the ceremonial outfit, if that was possible. I knew he took care of himself, saw him jogging around the Loop from time to time. Maybe he CrossFitted.

"Andrew," he said, his voice carrying across the space, and I was hearing him on his voice mail again before I'd hung up an hour ago. Hearing his recorded words because he had called Ryan Vallance's cell phone shortly before Ryan died.

I took his offered hand, and he squeezed mine firmly before addressing Elliot. "How's the lawn looking?"

"Beautiful, just beautiful," Elliot said. We stood in an awkward silence for a beat before Father Mathew raised his eyebrows slightly. Elliot grinned and nodded. "I'll just get back to it." He gave me a final wave and exited.

When I returned my attention to Father Mathew, he was looking me over, a complacent smile on his face, like an uncle or grandfather examining a wayward son. "Thanks for meeting with me on short notice," I said.

"No problem at all. Let's go in my office, shall we?" He started across the lobby, talking over one shoulder. "Actually a great time to catch me. Most days around now, this place is pretty quiet."

Quiet was an understatement. The whole sprawling building felt like one large tomb. Somewhere, a printer was printing over the sound of our padded footsteps. Nothing else.

His office sat at the back of the building's long hallway, and I resisted looking down the stairwell toward the basement as we passed it. When we were inside, he closed the door and gestured toward the seat across the desk as if he thought I might stay standing.

"I just got back from our sister parish," he said, settling his bulk into a leather office chair. "Father Thomas is out with a nasty cold, so I was making a few rounds for him. Confessions for the elderly who can't travel, that sort of thing. Good to get out and about once in a while for sure." He steepled his fingers and watched me over their peaks. "So how're you holding up, Andrew?"

"Ah, good, good."

"And your father?"

"He's doing well. As well as can be."

"Such a terrible disease. I can't imagine. We're all thinking of him—can you pass that along? We haven't seen him as much lately on Sundays."

He let it hang out there, but I didn't take the bait. You mean he hasn't been coming to church as much since I came back to care for him, I thought. It wasn't true—Kel said years ago Dad had dropped his attendance to once a month. Church had been more our mother's thing, not his.

"I'll let him know," I said, clearing my throat. "That's kind of what I came to talk to you about, actually. I'm sure you're aware my mother set certain guidelines in her will regarding her Roth IRA."

He nodded. I waited, but that was it. A nod. I went on.

"So I'll be honest with you: financially, we're in a bit of need. Dad's pension only covers so much, and my sister and I are both pitching in, but we're stretched pretty thin. So I was wondering if there was a way to revert the funds back to Dad? Possibly a monthly donation from the church?"

Father Mathew watched me for another beat, just long enough to be uncomfortable, then pulled his hands apart. "Andrew, are you familiar with the story of the widow's offering?"

Sweat crept down the back of my hairline and into my collar. "No, I don't think so."

"One day when Jesus was at the temple, he saw the rich men donating their wealth to the treasury. Then an old widow came along and put just two coins in the coffer, and Jesus said, 'This poor widow has given more than anyone else.'" He blinked a few times. "You see, she had less than anyone else but still gave."

"Yes, I understand the parable," I said. My hands had curled in on themselves.

"Your mother was a woman of great faith and great generosity. Faith is a sacred thing. Who are we to question her ideals? Who are we to rescind her wishes?" I was speechless for a few seconds, unable to process what he was saying. He took it as a cue for him to continue. "Now, there's no reason we can't figure something out. We have a dedicated volunteer care staff and food delivery service. I can make a note for Jill to call you; she's been filling in here since Mary's passing." His expression darkened. "I'm still trying to accept she's gone. So strange to walk past her desk and see it empty. It's just wrong. But—"

"But God has a plan for everything—is that what you were going to say?" I asked. My hands weren't hands anymore. They were fists.

"I believe he does," Father Mathew continued, unfazed. Unaffected. "As painful as someone's passing can be, all is for a purpose in something greater we don't always grasp."

"My dad won't know who I am in the coming years. He'll die living minute to minute, not understanding why he's where he is, or potentially who he is. And he knows that now. He knows it's coming. Like seeing a train hurtling toward you without being able to step off the tracks. What purpose does that serve?"

"Andrew, listen—"

"I'm sorry if you're still upset about the stained glass. I'm still upset my sister's lying in the cemetery across town. Now, I came to ask for kindness, for mercy, for help. I thought this was supposed to be the building you went to for something like that." All my anger, my frustration, my helplessness from the last weeks came pouring out.

"I understand you don't believe, but your mother did, and you should at least respect that even if you don't respect a higher power."

"My mother was half the reason my sister killed herself. Forgive me, but my respect for her diminished some time ago."

"Andrew, please—"

"Look, I'm not here to debate belief or faith or religion or anything else. I want to know if the church can help my father. If it can't, I'll be on my way."

Father Mathew pursed his lips and sat back in his chair, which squeaked under his weight. "I understand your family's plight. Let me do this. The church board will be meeting on Wednesday evening after Mass. I'm sure you're aware we are now missing our chairperson."

David. I'd almost forgotten he'd chaired the church board. I nodded.

"I'll bring up the issue then, since it's partially out of my hands anyway. The board has to agree to any financial adjustments or donations, but let me assure you, I'll make it a priority. Now, if you'll excuse me, there's some paperwork I have to attend to."

Just like that, dismissed. He began moving a few folders around on his desk. I suppressed a reflex response to thank him. Instead I said, "A lot of tragedy lately in the community, isn't there?"

"Yes, there most certainly has been."

"First Mary's accident, then the Barrens, and Ryan Vallance before that." Father Mathew set down the folders and looked at me. There was no congeniality now. Only a coolness about him. The limb I was standing on was bending. I went out a little farther. "Someone told me you talked with Ryan before his death. Did he seem upset or disturbed? We were friends in high school," I quickly followed up. "It was quite a shock."

He glanced out the single narrow window beside his desk and became very still. "David told me he was worried about Ryan, asked me to talk to him. I did, briefly. He seemed okay then, but I wish now I would've pressed harder. If I would've known . . ." Father Mathew brought his gaze back to me. "You aren't the only one with regrets, Andrew. Please know that."

———

I went for a walk.

Besides drinking an inordinate amount of coffee, it's what I did when I needed to think. We used to walk the Loop as a family when we were younger. Normally Dad wasn't with us since he was either at work or sleeping, but sometimes he would come along, usually in the early dusk of evening when the light was leaving the air and everything looked smoky. The neighborhood houses would start to glow, and the Loop would reverse, all the exterior life and activity of the day receding inward, which we could see snippets of through golden squares of glass as we went by.

I walked past homes that had been on their foundations since I was born and others much more recent. Layers upon layers. Stories all behind closed doors. Secrets everywhere. I had a momentary sense of tipping, of disassociation. Nothing was what it looked like. I wasn't in my neighborhood anymore. Everything was a prop, false fronts to create a semblance of normal everyday life.

My breath tightened in my chest, and I stopped, leaning momentarily on a lamppost, vision swimming in the corners of my eyes. Was this what Rachel went through on a daily basis? Her worry like a drop-off in the ocean, a dark trench steps away waiting to swallow her up? Of course it was. As I started to imagine what she must be going through at that second, I pushed away from the post and hurried back the way I'd come, trying to leave the idea behind.

Back in the house, there were a few texts from Kel I hadn't noticed when she'd initially sent them.

Hey, talked to Seth about Crane/DeMarco.

He said the police interviewed him and he didn't have an alibi for the night of David's murder.

They already searched his house, guessing because of his history, and came up with nada.

Still no ransom demand . . .

Anything else you want me to ask him for?

I stood at the side window looking down the street at Crane's house for a while, then typed **thanks** and **no** back to Kel. I wouldn't involve her anymore if I could help it.

Going forward, I'd be on my own.

19

When Crane backed out of his garage around 9:00 p.m.—streetlights reflecting on the perfect black paint job of his Lexus—I was ready.

The evening had passed like most others. I went over to Dad's and cooked dinner; we ate, shot the shit, watched some TV, I came home. Only difference was where I'd sat in his living room and kitchen—a different angle to keep an eye on Crane's house. What would I tell Dad if I saw our mysterious neighbor leaving his place and I suddenly jumped up and ran out? I don't know. Probably wouldn't have had to tell him anything.

Now my legs hurt and I was chilled from standing in my garage, glancing out the window every so often to make sure Crane hadn't left. There was no assurance he was going anywhere tonight, but I was beginning to hear the pitter-patter of desperation's tiny feet. The dead end I'd been fearing was fast approaching, and when I got to it, I had no idea what I'd do.

As Crane drove slowly past my place, I left the window and hurried to my car. Door up, back out, accelerate up the Loop, and just like that I was tailing him.

Every movie, stupid TV show, and thriller I'd ever read where someone followed someone else surfaced and submerged. This was like fiction and different at the same time. Sure, tailing someone in crowded traffic was fairly easy. Changing the setting to late-evening suburbia was another story. Hard to hide behind traffic that wasn't there. Instead I stayed back as far as I could while still keeping Crane in sight.

The Lexus cruised, slow and purposeful, through the dark streets, a shark prowling a midnight reef bed for prey. And what was I? Maybe one of those little parasitic fish swimming under the shark's belly. I wondered if sharks knew those fish were there and just ignored them. I wondered if Crane was watching me in one of his mirrors.

I dropped farther back.

Downtown Sandford was dead. A few cars loafing along Main Street heading out toward the interstate. Businesses were closed or closing, traffic lights the only colors in the night. Crane took a left on Main and accelerated, leaving me farther behind. I wouldn't lose him even if he got a half-mile head start. It was that quiet.

Fog rose from the ground and draped itself across yards and sidewalks like ghost garlands. Crane's taillights flashed once, twice, then stayed on as he made a right down a side street. I took a chance and cruised past, turning at the next street and coasting down a long hill, flashes of the block over visible every so often between buildings. A right at the next intersection, then a left, and there he was again. I congratulated myself on being so sneaky.

As we wound our way through the east side of town, I told myself Crane could be going to get takeout, he could be going to a friend's house, to pick up dry cleaning. All possibilities. Did I believe any of them? Not really. It was just as likely he was on his way to check on Rachel and the boys—make sure their ropes were still knotted or the cage he had them in was still secure.

Nefarious.

The word suited Crane/DeMarco to a big old capital T. I'd felt it the first time laying eyes on him. The feeling hovered around him like flies around roadkill. Knowing now of his shiny new identity and corroded past only supported the notion.

At the next intersection, Crane went straight across into the industrial development. Lots of sharp rooflines and towering storage buildings cut dark against the rest of the night. Yellow security lights punched holes in shadows here and there, but for the most part that section of town was lonely and dim.

For the second time in my life, I wished I owned a gun. The first time had been years ago, shortly after Sharon and I were married and living in the apartment she would eventually leave me alone in except for a few straggling plants on their way out. We'd been asleep in the mid hours of the night when someone had thumped against our door. Not uncommon. I'd rolled over to drift off again, then Sharon had been clawing and shoving at my shoulder, telling me to wake up, that someone was trying to break in. I hadn't thought about it, had only climbed out of bed and listened for a second as someone attempted to force the door open in the next room. Then I'd whispered for Sharon to call nine-one-one and walked out into the hall.

A gun. My hand had flexed for one as I'd stepped into the kitchen with a clear view of the entry. Instead I grabbed a broom, all the inadequacy inside me summed up in its flimsy length. Someone would come through the door any second and they would attack me and I would die and Sharon would die. I would fail.

The fear of being unable to keep those you love safe is a fear unto itself. Its own genus and phylum.

In the end I'd called out for the person to go away, that the cops were coming. And they had. I don't know if Sharon ever guessed how afraid I'd been. I never told her. But I couldn't forget the crushing sense of helplessness. It tattooed itself on my soul, and every so often when the light was right, I'd catch a glimpse of it.

Like now. Right now.

Dad had a pistol locked in a little gun safe in his bedside table. He'd taken me targeting a few times when I was younger. I remembered how to shoot. I knew the pass code to the safe. Give me a time machine so I could go back and punch those numbers in.

Instead I pulled forward.

Chain-link fencing. Gateposts. Short paved drives. Everything passed by mirrored in long shadows at their bases. Crane had disappeared. His car was nowhere to be seen in the deserted parking lots or wedged up behind any of the buildings.

I'd lost him. I was so bad at this.

In a textile manufacturer's turnoff, I spun my car around and paused, waiting, thinking. Could this be where he was keeping them, in an abandoned building? Or maybe he'd seen me and only pulled into the complex to shake me loose. Maybe he'd doubled back somehow and I'd missed him. Who knew? After a few minutes of sulking, I pulled up to the street and caught a flash of taillights near the loading bay of a building across the way.

A light-colored truck had drawn to a stop, and a man climbed out, giving a half wave to someone I couldn't see. Then, in the low light of a distant security lamp, Crane appeared.

I doused my headlights.

Crane and the unknown man shook hands. They leaned against the guy's truck and looked down at whatever was in the back. A few minutes of talking, then mystery man pulled something from inside his coat. At the distance it was mostly undefinable, but with a gun against my head, I would've said it was an envelope. Crane put it in his pocket. Another handshake. They went back to their vehicles.

My hand found the shifter, and I threw the car in reverse, backing farther up the drive until the car was enshrouded in the shadow cast by the company's sign. On the street, first Crane appeared, then the truck following closely behind. When they were two blocks away, I rolled back onto the street and turned on my lights.

Deep breath. In and out.

Stay far enough back so they don't see you, don't suspect anything, because maybe, just maybe, you've stumbled onto something useful. If the stars align, maybe you've hit on something like salvation.

I trailed so far from them, their taillights nearly vanished at the next intersection. More fog lifted from the ground and encroached the road. Another car joined our little procession, and I relaxed a bit. When the street emptied out onto Main, my cover turned left while Crane and the truck went right. I waited at the stoplight, but no more vehicles presented themselves. Soon I'd lose them. No choice.

At the bottom of Main, we crossed a canal and entered a livelier part of town. More fast-food neon, a movie theater, bars. Just when I was thinking of turning off to try to rejoin them a few streets over, the truck swung hard into a burger joint. Crane kept going.

Decisions, decisions.

There was only one car in the burger place's lot. I'd stand out like a sore thumb. I kept going.

Crane guided his Lexus out of town, heading east again toward the mountains. Fewer and fewer streetlights sprouted from the roadsides until there were none. Vast emptiness broken only by the occasional home set back from the highway and the fog rolling up and across fields like something alive.

Ten miles from the city limits, Crane slowed and turned onto a county road. Dirt and a single sign marking its vein into the foothills. No pretenses of anything civilized beyond.

I never touched the brakes, flew past at sixty and kept going. When I'd rounded the next curve, I swung a U-turn and headed back, inching up to the road Crane had disappeared down until I could see.

At least a mile away, his taillights flared before fading around a bend.

I turned in.

Black, skeletal trees crowded the ditches, snuffing out any ambient light from the sky. Dirt pecked and snapped at the undercarriage like a hungry bird. I flipped the headlights off and turned the running lights on, staining everything a yellow orange.

Digging out my cell, I threw looks from the dirt road to the screen over and over. Call the cops? Kel? At least let someone know where I was so they have an idea of where to look for the body?

Not yet. I didn't know anything for sure. But I could see it unfolding in my head.

A few miles in and a single overgrown lane would appear, the last trailing lights from the Lexus disappearing. I'd park the car and head after Crane on foot. Deeper in the woods, the drive would open up to a clearing holding a ramshackle farmhouse with only candle glow from inside. I'd sidle up to the nearest window, and Crane would be there, standing over Rachel and the boys, who would be terrified but unharmed. I'd make the call and bring in the cavalry.

Game over. Day saved.

The other possibilities were too much to envision.

Around the curve Crane had disappeared behind—nothing, darkness. He was still ahead of me quite a bit. My foot pressed down; the trees fled past on either side. I watched for a break in them, some indication of a driveway leading off to the dilapidated shack, but there was only the forest and the indifferent stain of the mountains beyond.

One mile.

Two.

Three.

No mailboxes, no signs. Sweat beaded on my forehead.

Another turn. Still no taillights, no side roads. I was driving slower now, half expecting to suddenly come upon Crane's car pulled off on the side of the road. When I'd gone another mile and seen nothing, fear began worming its way through my stomach.

I thought of gazelles pulling their heads up from feeding as the amber eyes of a lioness watched from the long grass. Of an insect trundling its way closer and closer to a trapdoor and the eight-legged horror waiting beneath it. Of a seal outlined against the shimmering light of the water's surface and rows of white teeth emerging from fathoms below.

My headlights shone on something, and I braked, blinking without comprehending.

The road ended in a high bank and wall of trees.

No Lexus. Nothing.

Instinct took over, and I whipped the wheel to the right, then left, making a sweeping turn in the dead end, but even as I started accelerating back the way I'd come, lights appeared, center of the road, high beams speeding toward me.

The black paint of the Lexus wasn't visible behind the lights, but it didn't need to be. I knew who was behind the wheel even as I slid to a stop and the car rolled closer.

Back up? Get out and sprint into the trees? Try to skid past on the right or left?

In the end my panicked brain couldn't decide. I thought of Dad's safe and the combination to open it again.

A gun, a gun, my kingdom for a gun.

The headlights flickered as someone passed in front of them, then Crane was there, tall and dark, squinting down at me through the window, one hand inside the coat he wore. I rolled the window down.

"Hi," I said.

Crane's squint narrowed. "The fuck? Aren't you the guy down the street?" he said.

"Uh, yeah. Andy Drake."

"The hell are you following me for?" The hand under his coat twitched as if it wanted to draw whatever was concealed there.

"I—I'm not following you." It was all I could come up with. He just watched me. Mentally, I calculated how fast I could release the brake and hit the gas. Faster than he could draw a gun?

"I'm not gonna ask again," he said.

If I was going to die, I was going to die knowing the truth. "Did you take Rachel and the boys?"

"Rachel and the—what the fuck are you talking about?"

"The Barrens."

"Across the street. The guy who got plugged? You a cop or something?"

"No."

"Listen, whoever you think I am, I'm not. And I'm definitely not a person to follow at night, got me?"

"You sent me the note," I said.

Crane shook his head and finally withdrew his hand from his coat sans gun, to my eternal relief. "You on drugs or something?"

"The day at the party last summer."

He watched me for a beat. "Yeah, I saw you two. Don't know anything about a note, though." He leaned closer, placing his gloved hands on the window frame. "Lemme give you some advice, friend. Do not go sniffing around where you aren't wanted. These woods are deep, and no one lives out here. Someone could easily get lost and never found. Happens all the time."

Then he was striding back to his car. The Lexus made a quick three-point turn, and all I could see was the deep red of his fading taillights. A second later, they were gone.

I put the car in park and rested my head on the steering wheel.

The horn honked, and I let out a short scream.

20

Abject: adjective—sunk to or existing in a low state or condition.

Yeah, I could relate.

The drive home passed in a blur. Garage door up, pull in, door down. Engine off. I sat behind the wheel for a few minutes, absorbing what had happened. The fear had ebbed, and all that was left was a profound confusion. For the second time in as many days, the confusion's source was my continued existence.

There had been nothing keeping Crane from blowing me away on that back road. Nothing tying him to me or my demise other than living in the same neighborhood. If he was involved with Rachel and the boys' disappearance, if he'd chased me from their house the other night, snuffing me out would've been a reflex.

Yet I was still here.

I showered and lay in bed on top of the blankets, staring at the ceiling in the dark. If Crane's meeting with the guy in the truck hadn't been about Rachel or the boys, what was it about?

"Could've been anything," I said to the empty room. Knowing his history, it might've been a new fraud scheme or some type of correspondence with his past life. In any case one thing was for sure: he'd been genuinely puzzled when I'd mentioned the note. He had seen us in Rachel's kitchen, but I didn't get the impression he cared one iota.

I saw the dead end of the dirt road and felt as if I were still there.

This wasn't working. I wasn't smart enough. Didn't have the where-withal to figure out the next move. Every single lead I'd followed ended with disappointment or more questions, and I was no closer to finding Rachel and the boys than I had been the morning sirens invaded the Loop.

I tossed. Turned. Couldn't get comfortable. When I slept, I dreamed of roads tinted in red. Of hands scrabbling at the insides of steel doors. Of being alone in a sprawling field and feeling like there was someone else, unseen but watching.

Cold sweat and late slanting light. I'd slept until almost noon. As I dressed, something nagged me through my thoughts of the night before, and it took until the coffee was finished brewing before I realized what it was.

Dad's birthday. Today. Damn it.

Plans I'd had for his breakfast and morning movie, *The Fugitive* (he loved anything Harrison Ford), came apart as I hurried across the street. There was a car in his drive I didn't recognize and a voice I did in his kitchen when I went inside.

"—more than anything. His love is bigger than that. It was pro-found when I realized it, a real life-changing event, you know?"

Elliot Wyman.

When I entered the room, his moonish face and wide eyes found me, and they lit up with even more holy zest. "Hello, Andy! So good to see you!" He pumped my arm as if we hadn't crossed paths in years. "I was just telling your father about my awakening when I was thirteen. It happened after I fell through the ice while fishing."

"Yeah, I remember," I said. Everyone in the parish knew Elliot's story. How his father had taken them fishing on Sentinel Lake in late December after a warm spell, and when young Elliot had wandered while his father drilled them several fishing holes, a dark patch of thin ice had given way and he'd gone under.

"I knew in that second I was going to die. And you know what I saw?" Elliot asked. I knew, but I let him go on anyway. "Light. Pure, warm light. I wasn't cold anymore. And after that I was at peace. I felt love. His love. I was calm in the frozen water, and when my father pulled me free and I was rushed to the hospital, I didn't worry, because I knew even if I did die, I'd be taken care of." He grinned, swiveling his head from one of us toward the other.

"It's a great story," I said, trying to busy myself in the kitchen.

"Sure is. You ever thought of writing it down?" Dad said. He had more patience than I did.

Elliot nodded. "I have, many times. I think it would be inspirational for so many who are lost and struggling."

"You know, Andy's a writer," Dad said. I froze. "He's got about a half dozen books published."

"That's right!" Elliot exclaimed. "Sorry to say I haven't read them. If I recall, they're of the thriller and mystery genres, aren't they?"

"Yep," Dad said, and I turned to pin him to the wall with my gaze. His eyes twinkled back.

"Yes, I don't partake in any questionable media," Elliot said, looking at me.

"Well, even so," Dad went on. "Maybe he could give you a few tips on writing your story down and publishing it."

I'm shocked I didn't burst into flames.

"Could you really?" Elliot asked.

"Umm," I rasped, then cleared my throat. "I'm pretty tied up at the moment."

"Oh, I bet it wouldn't take that long," Dad chimed in. Elliot looked at me hopefully, eyebrows raised in anticipation.

"Yeah, sure," I finally said.

"Fantastic!" Elliot actually clapped his hands. "You never know what blessings the Lord will bring you. Let's set up a time for me to stop by and we can discuss it further. Tomorrow I'm busy with the church luncheon, but the next day—"

"Sure. By the way, to what do we owe your visit?" I said, cutting him off.

"Oh, I brought some foodstuffs down for Mr. Drake." When I just blinked at him, he continued. "Father Mathew said he and you spoke about food service for your father?"

The bastard.

"Yeah, great, thank you."

"So do you really think you could get my memoir published? I mean, that would be amazing, and I really think my story has such inspirational messages and themes. Do you have an editor, or could you put me directly in touch with your agent?"

"You know, it's Dad's birthday, so we were going to head uptown in a few," I said, ushering the usher toward the front door. "I really appreciate you stopping by and dropping off the food. I'll call Father Mathew and thank him personally."

"So what would be the best—"

"I'll catch up with you soon, just under some tight deadlines right now. Thanks so much," I said, and gently closed the door as Elliot started talking again.

I stood with one hand pressed to the wood until the sound of Elliot's footsteps faded and his car started. When I turned around, Dad was standing on the border of the living room and kitchen chewing back a smile.

"You dirty old bastard," I said, and Dad put his hands on his knees and bellowed laughter. "Threw me to the wolves."

He couldn't speak for a while. He leaned against the doorway to keep himself upright. Between gasps he said, "Teach you . . . to . . . over-sleep . . . on my . . . birthday." Then he couldn't talk again. Tears leaked from the corners of his eyes, and I couldn't help but chuckle as well.

"It's not funny," I said, which made him laugh harder. "He's gonna be stuck to me like a goddamned barnacle now."

"*Godblessed* barnacle," Dad said, and sunk down to the floor, waving his hand. No more, no more. I stepped over him on my way to the kitchen, giving his leg a half-hearted kick on the way by.

"Happy fucking birthday," I said, starting to gather sandwiches for lunch.

"Don't, I'm gonna piss my pants."

"Good. Serves you right. I'm going to tell him *you're* my agent."

By the time I had the sandwiches fixed, Dad had mostly regained control of himself, though every so often he would hiccup a laugh and shake his head.

As we sat down to eat, I said, "Glad to be a source of amusement. Anything else I can get for your birthday?"

"Nope, that's the gift that keeps on giving."

"And here I was feeling sorry I'd overslept."

"You're forgiven." We ate in silence for a bit. "Out late last night?"

I cleared my throat. "Were you up?"

"Couldn't sleep again."

I changed the subject. Maybe I didn't want to worry him with what had happened the night before. Maybe I didn't want to worry myself. I could hear a second hand ticking away, had begun hearing it sometime in the last forty-eight hours. It was for Rachel and Asher and little Joey, who had anxiety like his mother. It was for me, too, because I still felt responsible. I'd made myself responsible by starting down this road. The ticking clock was for me because if I wasn't able to find them, I'd never forgive myself.

I started laying out the afternoon and evening's plans. Dad was thrilled about Kel and the girls coming by and about the ribs I was planning for dinner. It was a beautiful day outside, warm but not hot. Sunny but not blinding. A real good day to get a year older, Dad said.

I couldn't argue that.

———

We went shopping, and even though I shouldn't have, I pulled out all the stops. Bought fresh ribs from the meat counter instead of the ones shrink-wrapped in plastic. Bought the fixings for potato salad and a package of cheese sticks rolled up in thin slices of prosciutto. We stopped at the liquor store, and I splurged for a bottle of Dad's favorite bourbon.

We got home midafternoon, and I prepared the ribs with apple cider and rub while Dad poured us a couple of splashes of the good stuff. He chopped potatoes and onions, and I thawed meat for the girls' burgers.

We talked about the time he and Mom took us across the country to see the redwoods. How Mom had gotten food poisoning along the way and we'd had to stay in a shitty motor court for an extra two days. The place's pool only had an inch of water in it, and the cable didn't come in clearly on the TV. We ended up playing with the owner's dog for hours, chasing this big greyhound around and around the empty parking lot while semis whistled by on the highway and Dad sat in the shade, sipping a beer and urging us on. It hadn't seemed like a ton of fun at the time, but I couldn't help smiling now.

It's funny the things you remember and what you forget. All of it's important, every last second.

Kel and the girls arrived an hour or so later just as I was laying the ribs on the grill. Alicia and Emmy had made cards for Dad as well as a photo album of their year at school. I wondered if Kel had nudged them regarding the type of present. Wondered if she was thinking about the coming months and years when he might have to consult some of the pictures to recall a certain day or year when something happened. Kel caught me out by the grill, and I told her it had smoked up a minute ago as I wiped my eyes.

We all drank a little too much before dinner. That was okay. There were no more tears. Lots of laughs, and the girls decided to run through the sprinkler. After a while so did Dad.

I locked that moment in. Dad soaking wet, arms raised over his head and growling as he chased Alicia and Emmy through the rainbow sheen of water, the girls hysterical. The warmth of the sun. All of us here, nothing different yet.

When the ribs were done, I pulled them off, and we all headed inside. Dad and the girls went to change, and Kel and I were alone in the kitchen.

"You look tired," she said, stirring the potato salad.

"See, if I said that to you, it would be offensive."

"Perks of being a chick."

"I guess."

"Make any more headway?"

"No. Not really."

"You thinking of staking Crane out? See if he goes anywhere suspicious?"

"No."

"Really? Why?"

"I get the impression he's not involved."

"Yeah? How?"

"I just do. Thanks for talking to Seth, though. I appreciate it."

Kel's eyes narrowed, but she nodded. "Sure, anytime." I could see she was about to say something else when I caught the sweep of a car's front end swinging into Dad's drive.

"Who the hell's this?" I said, moving toward the door. "Everyone I know is here." Visions of Elliot ambling up the front steps to ask further advice about his memoir loomed in my head, and I concocted an escape plan as I peered out the window.

A new-model sedan was parked in front of the garage, and a second later a guy climbed out and grabbed something from the back seat. There was a second of disorientation as he rounded the back of the car carrying two bulging bags with the emblem of Sandford's only Thai restaurant on their sides. Then I sighed and prepared to open the door.

Cory was home.

21

"Surprise!" Cory yelled as he stepped inside.

Yes. Surprise.

He was dressed in gray slacks and a dark polo. He sported a new hairstyle swept back and to one side, and the sunglasses he wore cost more than I made in a month.

"Little brother, how you be?" His hug was all toned gym muscle and expensive cologne. He brushed past me and embraced Kel, whose mouth hung slightly open. The bags from the Thai place sat near my feet, steaming.

"What are you doing here?" Kel asked when he released her.

"Gee, nice to see you, Cory. Glad you could make it for the old man's birthday. Thanks for bringing dinner." He laughed.

"No, you just didn't let us know you were coming," Kel said, visibly faltering. She looked how I felt. Cory's visits were always an assault on the system. Like a virus you had no choice but to suffer through until it burned itself out.

"Like I said, surprise! Had some PTO built up and thought I'd swing east for the big day. Where is the birthday boy?"

Dad came down the hall and stopped short, eyes going wide. "Cory? What're you doing here?"

"Geez, starting to feel like I'm not wanted. How are you, Pops? Happy birthday." He crossed the room and gave Dad a hug. Kel and I shared a look.

"Uncle Cory!" Alicia and Emmy called in unison, coming out of the bathroom. They rushed over and grasped either of his legs. Cory hoisted them up, one in each arm.

"Baby pies! How old are you now? Fifteen? Sixteen?" They giggled. "Go out in the back of Uncle Cory's car and get your presents."

The girls scrambled out of his arms and rushed through the front door. "You don't need to bring them presents every time you come," Kel said.

"Gotta spoil my nieces."

A hush fell over the house. I could have sworn I heard paint peeling somewhere. "So," Dad finally said, breaking the silence. "How was your trip?"

"Oh, you know, going through O'Hare is like running the gauntlet of hell, but I flew first class, which is always nice. I wouldn't have made it at all, but the deal I was closing went through quicker than I thought. Did you change the carpet?"

Dad looked around at the floor. "Nope. Same."

"Huh. Thought you said you were going to."

"Yeah, well, I was thinking about it but . . ."

The girls came bustling back in, concealed behind a stack of boxes and bags in their arms. As they started tearing the presents open like hyenas around a kill, Cory plucked a slender bag from the ruins of tissue paper and handed it to Dad. "Happy birthday."

"Oh, thanks, son. You didn't have to."

"It's no problem." Dad unwrapped a bottle of cheap whiskey and held it at arm's length. "It's your favorite brand," Cory said, grabbing one of the Thai bags from beside me. Dad's eyes flickered from the bottle to Cory to Kel and me. It wasn't his favorite.

"Andy, bring that other bag in here, and give me a hand setting up the buffet," Cory called from the kitchen. Kel and I locked eyes again, then I brought the food into the other room.

Cory had pinched the tinfoil covering the ribs and pulled up one edge. "Did a little BBQ, huh? Cool." He pushed everything we'd prepared down closer to the sink, clearing a spot to deposit the dishes from the bags.

"You didn't have to bring dinner," I said, opening up containers of tom kha kai and pad thai.

"It's fine. I'm seeing this girl, totally gorgeous, met her through a friend at church, and she introduced me to more traditional Thai. Not like this stuff—most places are perversions of the original recipes. That's what Tanya says anyways—her name is Tanya. There's this place on the lake called Delphi's, and it's amazing. She's totally opened up my tastes. I never realized there was more than General Tso's and whatnot."

"That's Chinese, but—"

"So how've you been? Publish any good books lately?" Cory laughed and dug a beer out of the fridge. "I read your last one and had a question—wouldn't Holmes have caught the guy sooner if he'd just followed up on the lead that prostitute had given him in the first act?"

I drained my glass of bourbon.

———

We sat around the kitchen table in a weird quasi scene that could've been our childhood, except two of the members were missing and had been replaced by two of the next generation. A casting change in the suburban drama of our lives.

Cory attacked a heaping plate of food, mostly Thai, but there was a considerable hunk of the ribs I'd cooked mixed in as well. Dad had a small portion of everything even though I knew he didn't care for some of the dishes—still trying to keep things even and fair among us kids.

Kel and I ate little and drank more. The girls chowed overfull plates of spring rolls and pineapple fried rice. The burgers I'd grilled for them sat on the counter untouched.

"So what's going on around here?" Cory said. "Anything new on the Loop?"

"It's been pretty quiet," Kel said before any of us could answer. She'd worked her way through her second beer and was on to a glass of bourbon. More than I'd seen her drink since the last time Cory was home.

"See, that's the nice thing. The city's so fast paced, it's great to come here and decompress," Cory said. "You get caught up in the bustle and don't stop. There's always someone calling or a cocktail party. My boss, he's the COO of one—no wait, now it's two—Fortune 500s, he threw this get-together at his place the other night, and wow. I mean he pulled out all the stops. Three hundred people there at least, and French champagne for everyone. He's got a two-tiered pool, and he dyed the water this turquoise that you only see in the Caribbean because that was the theme and—"

"Gramma Mary passed away," Alicia said quietly.

"Who?" Cory asked, scanning us.

"Mary Shelby," Kel said.

"Oh really? That's too bad. I guess she was getting up there."

"She had an accident with her horse," Alicia said.

"Horse?" Cory asked.

"Yeah, we can fill you in later," I said, panning my eyes to the side at the girls.

"Huh, well they are dangerous animals," Cory said, continuing to eat. "Kevin, one of the guys I work with, his kid got thrown during a riding lesson and broke his collarbone and a couple fingers."

"Can Asher and Joey come over to play?" Emmy asked.

Kel blanched and shook her head. "No, not tonight, honey. Tonight's for family."

"So what are you working on now?" Cory asked me. "Same series or something new?"

"Uh, something new. It's in the basic stages. Lots of editing to do."

"Mmm, yeah. Must be a lot like putting the final touches on a proposal. We have a few interns to do all the basic stuff, but then I fine-tune it. Make it sing." I just nodded. "So I was going to tell you, one of Tanya's friends is a screenwriter. She did that movie last year with Bruce Willis and Ryan Gosling, the sci-fi one where everyone's living in space? She's making bank. That something you ever considered? Try to get one of the books made into a movie?"

Deep breath. In. Out. "Yeah, it's a process."

"Grampa, is it okay with you if Asher and Joey come over to play?" Emmy said.

"Uh . . ." Dad glanced at Kel, who reached across the table to take Emmy's hand.

"Not tonight, honey. I already said no, okay?"

Emmy pouted and pushed her plate away.

"No, I get it," Cory continued. "But that's where the real money is, film. No offense, but books are sliding more and more out of social circles. No one's talking about what they've read—it's all movies and TV shows and video games. Man, if you could get a gig with a video game producer, that would be the big time."

I started clearing the table and piling dishes in the sink.

"How about you, Kel? How's government work?" Cory said, switching his aim.

"Oh, you know, same old."

"I heard about that new license thing they're coming up with. That's going to screw up the system royally in my opinion. Just another check on the average person. Like all these regulations on productions. You wouldn't believe how many hoops these corporations have to jump through to qualify for a loan. I mean, the government's got businesses totally pinned down with environmental restrictions and whatnot.

They're so worried about keeping some wetlands and a few species safe, they don't care they're killing the economy. Honestly, if they aren't careful, the cure's going to be worse than the disease."

Kel's fingers were white where she gripped her glass. Dad must've seen it, too, because a thought seemed to strike him, and he changed the subject.

"Hey, how's that pretty girlfriend of yours you brought home for Christmas? Was it Carri? I was telling someone the other day how funny it was with your names being almost the same."

Cory tilted his head, then shot a look at Kel and me before focusing on Dad again. "We broke up, Dad. Like four months ago. I called you after it happened. I've been talking about Tanya all evening. Don't you remember?"

The light went out of Dad's eyes. He blinked. "Right. Yeah, sure, I forgot. Sorry."

Cory sent a quizzical look at me, and I resisted the urge to leap across the table and strangle him.

"Grampa, I'm done. Can I go outside?" Emmy said, lower lip still stuck out.

"Sure, darlin'. I'll go with you," Dad said, standing up. Alicia followed them out the back door, and the house was quiet again.

"What the fuck is wrong with you?" Kel said.

Cory recoiled. "What do you mean?"

"Do you not understand what's happening to him?"

"Look, I know he's getting forgetful, but I don't think he was listening to me at all. I've been talking about Tanya and—"

"He's got dementia," I said. "It's not forgetfulness, it's a disease."

"Well, now that you bring it up, it would've been nice to go to one of his appointments and actually meet with the doctor. Or better yet, he could've come to Chicago and seen someone there like I suggested, but no one listens to me apparently."

"He got two opinions," Kel said. Her voice was starting to shake. "One of them was in the city. You could've come to either."

Cory ignored this. "I didn't think it was this bad. Neither of you said anything to me. Business as usual, I guess."

"We told you this was going to happen at Christmas," I said. "Maybe you were the one not listening. It's not our fault you only swing by when it's convenient."

"Right, penalize me for having a career and getting out of this Podunk town."

Kel made a sound of derision and shook her head. She grabbed her plate and moved to the sink. "No one's penalizing you for anything. You do that well enough on your own, Cory."

"No, I get it. It's the gruesome twosome all over again. Wait, no, it never stopped, did it? You always teamed up against me, always tried to undermine me as kids, and it's really sad you're still doing it. Grow up."

"Listen, I don't know if you're in denial about what's happening," I said, trying to keep my voice even. "But it's happening whether you're here or in Chicago. It's going to get worse. And the last thing Dad needs is someone asking him why he doesn't remember something."

"Sure, sure. It's funny, I take time off from work, bring gifts, bring supper, and this is the thanks I get. You know, Mom was right," Cory said, crossing his arms. "You guys never took anything seriously. Not church or school or any of the stuff she tried teaching us. You didn't listen, and I guess that's why you're where you are now."

"And where are we?" Kel asked.

"You tell me. You're divorced and stuck at a menial job with two kids to feed, and Andy moved back home when he couldn't cut it in the big city." He cocked his head. "You guys made fun of me the whole time we were at home, and now you're jealous."

"Christ, how do we all fit in here with your ego?" I asked.

"Don't use his name in vain," Cory said, pointing at me. "This is our mother's house."

"It's our father's house," Kel said. "Mom's dead."

"Yeah, so is Emma. She should've listened to Mom too."

It was like all the air was sucked out of the room.

"Take it back," Kel whispered.

He started to say something else. It might've been an apology or what passed for one for Cory, but we never found out because I launched myself across the room and tackled him out of the chair.

My feet clipped the table as we toppled over and dishes flew. Glass shattered. Kel screamed.

I barely registered any of it.

Imagine a trip wire attached to a claymore mine. Think of that wire slowly tightening, getting tauter and tauter as days and weeks go by and the weather does its work. There is a breaking point, when the tension on the wire will finally be too much and trip the blasting cap. Boom.

As we hit the floor, I could almost see the words *FRONT TOWARD ENEMY* hanging in the air.

Cory issued a surprised squawk, then a grunt of pain as I landed on him. He tried saying something, but by then I was pistoning my fist into his jaw. All at once we were teens again, except this time I was on top and he was taking the beating.

He rolled to the left to get away from me, and I responded with an elbow to the side of his head. He must've thrashed his legs around, because a second later the table tipped over and spewed the remaining dishes and food onto the floor.

"Jesus! Stop it!" Kel yelled, but all I could hear was an echo of Cory saying what he'd said about Emma. Gentle Emma, who only wanted to be a physicist or an astronomer. Who never hurt anyone but herself.

Cory flailed with one arm, and his fist caught me on the side of the head. Supernovas of black stars in the corners of my vision. He was strong from all his workouts in whatever swanky gym he belonged to, but he wasn't angry.

I was distilled rage.

I wound up a haymaker that connected with his mouth.

Blood flew.

I think it was the sight of so much blood that finally stopped me. Both his lips had split deeply on his teeth, and drops of crimson pattered and smeared on the tile. An abstract painting of our relationship there on the floor.

I climbed off him, heaving breaths, still angry but growing cooler as the adrenaline unstacked and I looked around at the mess.

Cory touched a palm to his lips and stared at the blood before looking at me with eyes so wide they seemed to fill up his face. "What the hell is wrong with you? Are you crazy?"

Suddenly I didn't have the energy to reply. Kel did it for me.

"I think you should leave," she said, gesturing toward the door.

Cory climbed to his feet and swayed there. He swiped at his mouth again, more blood smearing down his forearm. "I always knew you hated me. Both of you. But you've gone too far. I'll be talking to my lawyer. Neither of you are fit to take care of Dad."

"Cory . . . ," Kel said, sounding even more exhausted than I was. "Just go."

It looked like he was going to reply, then thought better of it. He turned from us and kicked a takeout container of shrimp and noodles. It flew across the room and spattered against the wall, bits of spice and peppers dripping down in the sauce.

The front door opened and slammed shut. An engine started. Tires squealed.

Cory was gone.

We stood there for a while in the dinner wreckage. Not saying anything, just being. Absorbing it all. Then we started to clean.

I picked up bowls and pieces of broken glass while Kel took a washrag to the beer and sauces on the cabinets and chairs.

We didn't get far. A noise came from outside, jerking both our heads up. The whoop of a police siren. Once and gone, but close.

We picked our way through the debris to the window and looked out.

Up the street, a patrol car had rolled to a stop before the Barrens' house, and a cop was rounding the front of the car, hand resting on the butt of his weapon.

He was beelining across the lawn toward Dad, who stood on the Barrens' porch, knocking on the front door.

22

Out the back door and across the lawn.

Kel said something to me as I rushed toward the Barrens' place, but I didn't catch it, barely registering Alicia and Emmy standing in Dad's backyard, a Frisbee on the ground between them.

By the time I made it within shouting distance, the cop had already grabbed Dad by the arm and was dragging him off the porch.

"Hey! Hey, stop! That's my dad," I said, jogging up to them.

The cop was young, maybe midtwenties, built like a bull. He could've picked Dad up and carried him over his head with ease, but there was plain uncertainty in his features. "What's going on here?" he asked.

Dad glanced from the cop to me to the Barrens'. "I just came up to ask the boys down to play," he said. "The girls wanted them to come over." A haze of confusion floated behind his eyes.

"I'm sorry, he has a condition," I said, trying to draw Dad away from the cop's grip, but he didn't let him go. "I think he got mixed up for a second."

"We got a call someone was prowling," the cop said. "You know this is a crime scene, right?"

"Yes, yes, we're aware. Like I said, he has a condition."

The cop finally released Dad's arm as another vehicle pulled up, and something inside me withered as Detective Spanner stepped out and headed toward us.

"I'll take it from here, Ronny," Spanner said.

"You sure, sir?"

"I'm good."

The cop nodded, giving us one last look before heading back to his cruiser.

Spanner stopped before us, took in the food stains on my shirt and pants, the drying crust of Cory's blood on my knuckles. I put my hands in my pockets. "What the fuck is going on here?"

"The girls—" Dad started, but I cut him off.

"Can he go home, please, while we talk about this?"

Spanner chewed on the side of his mouth, jerked his head once.

I pointed Dad in the direction of his house, where Kel was waiting on the edge of the yard, one hand held to her brow to block the late-evening sun. "Why don't you go sit with Kel and the girls, Dad." His face darkened, and more awareness seemed to come over him. He nodded and started off.

When Dad was halfway down the street, Spanner said, "Drake, I got about five minutes for this and patience for two. Speak."

I told him about the girls' request, how they weren't aware of what had happened at the Barrens'. Dad must have had a lapse, forgotten, and come up to the house to ask if the boys could come play. That was all.

Spanner pointed at the house. "Crime scene."

"I understand."

"Then seriously, do your dad a favor and find someone to watch him full time if this is going to be an issue."

"I'm taking care of him."

"Coulda fooled me." I gritted my teeth. Didn't speak. "And what the hell happened to you? Is that blood on your hands?"

"Cut myself on a broken dish."

Spanner studied me for another second, a man looking through a microscope at a petri dish, then scanned the neighborhood. "I don't need calls coming in for shit like this. We have enough on our plates as is. Keep your dad under wraps or there'll be consequences."

He turned and headed back to his car, giving me a dead stare as he swung the vehicle around and pulled out of the Loop.

I sagged, my body an old balloon losing air. The press of eyes followed me back to Dad's. Watching from doorways, peering from behind curtains. I wanted to flash the middle finger to all of them, tell the whole Loop what I thought of their rubbernecking.

In the backyard, Kel and the girls waited by the rear entry. Kel wrung her hands. "I tried to stop him from going inside," she said.

I glanced at the house. "It's okay. I'll clean up." Alicia and Emmy were motionless, not looking at either of us. Silent tears slid down Emmy's cheeks. I knelt before her. "Hey, you okay?" Barely a nod. "Everything's all right. You're not in trouble, right, Mom?"

"Right," Kel said.

I wiped Emmy's tears away with the cleanest part of my hand. "Grampa's gonna take a little rest. His birthday tired him out. Okay?" Both girls nodded, and I hugged them.

"Go get in the car," Kel said, and they circumvented the house for the front drive. When they were gone, she sighed and rubbed one side of her face. "What a nightmare."

"Wasn't exactly what I had in mind for his birthday."

"Yeah, me neither."

"Where do you think Cory went?"

"Who cares. Asshole," she hissed, and I wasn't 100 percent sure she was talking about him.

"I'm sorry about . . ." I gestured at the house.

She shook her head. "I'm going home. Text me later. Let me know how he is."

"I will."

She started off around the house and paused at the corner. "You still think everything's going to be okay?"

I wanted to assure her, to be who I usually was. I wanted to say yes, that everything would work out. In the end I didn't say anything. Kel gave me a last look and was gone.

The blood on my hands was darkening, appearing more like ink stains in the low light. I rubbed them against each other, and little flakes of my brother drifted off. I went inside.

Dad stood in the doorway to the kitchen, surveying the mess. It was even more impressive coming back to it with fresh eyes.

I watched him track the broken dishes and overturned table to the spilled beer and spilled blood.

"Hey, Dad. This—"

He raised an arm and pointed at the door.

"Listen . . . ," I tried to continue, but then he faced me.

There is something elemental passed down through generations that transcends species and gender. It is a river running through the lifeblood, an unspoken connection between parent and child, able to convey everything within a look. The undercurrent flowing in Dad's eyes said it all.

Too much. Go away.

I'd seen my father furious only a few times in my life. It was enough.

I swallowed and looked at the floor. Some spicy sauce had seeped over into Dad's sock and stained a portion of the fabric near his little toe. Without another word I left by the front door, closing it on the sounds of broken glass being stacked together.

The sun had dropped below the trees, and all the day's warmth was gone. The radio said earlier a front was moving in. Cooler weather and rain for the next few days. Crossing the street toward home, part of me hoped Cory would show up again. I wouldn't fight him; that was through. I'd tell him he was so very wrong. Wrong about Kel and me. Wrong about Dad. And so, so wrong about Emma.

My rage had curdled to sadness. Not ever a big leap.

The bird lady sat on her front porch in an ancient Adirondack chair. Her binoculars were on the left armrest within easy reach, but what gave me pause was the object on the opposite side.

A cordless phone.

She watched me slow. Then stop. I looked up the road to the Barrens', traced the unobstructed view back to her porch.

Her eyes widened.

I headed toward her.

She tried heaving herself up out of her chair, once, twice, the third time making it to her feet.

"Hey," I said, crossing her lawn. She shot a look at me and shuffled as fast as her spindly legs would take her toward her front door. She opened it, swung herself inside, and was trying to slam it shut when I put my foot in the way.

"Get off my porch!"

"Why'd you call the cops on my dad?"

"I never." She tried yanking the door shut again. "This is assault!"

"What the hell did he ever do to you? You know he's sick, right? You must be aware with your addiction to gossip and those fucking binoculars stuck to your face all day."

She blanched, and I wondered how long it had been since someone had spoken to her like this, if ever. "You . . . you have no right."

"Why are you like this? What do you get from someone else's misfortune? Huh? Entertainment? You get a high from calling the cops?"

"I—"

"Be thankful you aren't suffering like him. Keep sitting in your chair, keep spying, feed your little addiction. But leave my dad alone."

I yanked my foot free and turned away. When I was halfway down her steps, the door creaked, and the bird lady stepped back onto her porch. Intending to throw her the most scornful look I could muster, I glanced back.

And stopped.

Tears shone in her eyes, and her lower lip quivered. At first I didn't hear what she said, but then she cleared her throat and spoke louder.

"I'm sorry." She shrugged and held out her hands. "I didn't mean to cause trouble. I saw him up there and didn't recognize him at first. My eyes aren't the best anymore." She shook her head, and a tear fell free of one eye and hit the decking at her feet like a raindrop.

Without looking at me again, she turned and went into her house, shutting the door behind her.

I made my way back home. Tired. Beyond tired.

A shower sluiced through the Thai food and blood clinging to me. I stood there a long time in its stinging blast as if it could wash the entire evening away.

Finally clean, comfy sweats, a cup of tea I couldn't get myself to drink. The windows looking out toward Rachel's house were inside me, the view peering inward.

The dead ends.

The questions.

The secrets.

And now another failure. This one a birthday party for an old man who one day wouldn't remember he'd taught me how to ride a bike or that I was afraid of spiders. The life he'd lived would be new secrets, unknowable even if I told him.

Enough. That was enough for one day. Plenty.

A quick text to Kel letting her know Dad wanted to be alone, then bed.

As I drifted off to sleep, I wondered if Rachel was somewhere warm. If she was hurting. I hoped not. And if she was beyond all that, I hoped the end had been brief and painless.

We wish our loved ones long lives and quick deaths. It's what separates us from animals.

No dreams. Just falling asleep and waking. The morning was oppressively gray, like night had refused to relinquish its hold fully. Over coffee, my thoughts turned on an axis, rotating through the panorama of the day before.

Whenever I wrote a character, I always asked why they were the way they were. Kel and Dad were easy, Cory less so. For me he'd always been a source of anxiety. Childhood with him brought bruises and humiliations—adulthood, verbal barbs and jabs that stung on the inside. At least until last night. Cory had been our mother's favorite, hands down. But there was some truth in what he'd said, that Kel and I had banded together. Mostly because he'd tormented us and there was strength in numbers. Maybe part of the reason he'd picked on us was the feeling of exclusion, which had been because of his bullying. An ouroboros of behavior.

I didn't know. It was nearly impossible to say unless someone was totally open and self-reflective.

Like the bird lady.

Her vulnerability had caught me off guard. She didn't have a son or daughter to check on her. She had expensive binoculars, vicariously allowing the entire Loop to become her family. I let our confrontation do a rerun in my head and felt like a shit.

Leaving the dregs of my coffee, I started out the door, then jogged back to the refrigerator after a moment's thought and grabbed the remaining three doughnuts from the dozen I'd brought to Dad the other day.

Knocking on the bird lady's door, holding a half-eaten box of doughnuts, I didn't really expect an answer. I hadn't shaved, hadn't combed my hair, was still wearing my sweats.

Crazy person.

She'd be right to turn me away. So when the door cracked open and she peeked out at me, timid as a mouse, I lost the thread of what to say for a second.

"Mrs. Tross . . . here." I held out the doughnuts. Her eyes went down, back up, but she didn't open the door. "I apologize for what I said yesterday. It was . . . a stressful afternoon."

Slowly the door opened. She surveyed me, maybe wondering if it was a trick and I'd suddenly berate her again. When I didn't, she said, "Don't apologize. You were right."

We stood that way for a second, a standoff. I flipped the box open. "Doughnut?"

———

Her sitting room smelled like some kind of old potpourri—cinnamon and cloves. The furniture was all floral and sat in carpet longer than I kept my lawn. She brought us coffee, and we chewed on the doughnuts. They were a little stale.

"Been years since someone came by to visit," she said, finally giving up on her pastry. "Your mother might've been the last person to stop in." My reflex was to say I was sorry. More so because Mom had been her last company. I just nodded. "When Tom was still alive, he said a good neighbor is someone who'll help you change a flat tire, but you never have to learn their last name. Looking back, I don't think he was right." She glanced at a framed photo of her and her husband from perhaps twenty years ago. When I thought about it, I never actually recalled speaking with Tom. I'd always assumed he'd been the brow-beaten husband kept separate from the rest of the community by his sharp-tongued wife.

Layers. More layers.

Something occurred to me then, the beginnings of an idea that sent moth wings through my chest. "You . . . keep an eye on the neighborhood. Have you seen anything out of the ordinary in the last few weeks?" I motioned toward the Barrens', giving her a half smile. "Anyone else besides my dad snooping around?"

She blushed a little. "I already told the police everything I know. They stopped by that morning like they did with everyone else on the block." I nodded, knowing she'd told the cops all she'd gleaned during her hours of surveillance. But my hope was there'd be something that had flown under the radar, some detail that might mean something to me.

"Any strangers hanging around?"

"No, not that I noticed."

The Visitor was good if he'd eluded Mrs. Tross's watchful eye. Very good. "How about the day it all happened? Anything odd then?"

Her brow furrowed, and I pictured a server of gossip and reconnaissance being accessed. "The boys went up the hill to school that morning like always. David left for work. Rachel went to the farmers market." She faltered there, most likely recalling me flipping her off after catching her watching Rachel and me. I fought to keep a straight face. "I didn't see her come home, but that night I fell asleep early. New medication for my arthritis hit me hard." She searched her memory for another moment. "That's all I can recall. Is there a reason you're asking?"

A field of land mines stretched out before me.

"No, it's just I heard the shot that night. Thought it was a car backfiring or someone shooting off a firework. I was curious."

Her eyes narrowed a little, and I could see she was holding back questions. Pointed ones possibly concerning Rachel's and my schedules and how we sometimes left the neighborhood within ten or fifteen minutes of one another. Dangerous questions.

"How about beforehand?" I said, trying to train her focus elsewhere. "Anyone come by their house prior to that day?"

"Well, sure, lots of people, but just the usual, I suppose. The mailman, UPS, David's business partner a couple times." She shrugged a set of bony shoulders.

I withered internally. Another dead end. I'd really hoped she'd seen something or someone, but realistically the police would have already followed up on any potential leads. I was reaching past my skill set again. Trying to be smarter than I really was.

As I started to rise, an excuse to get going forming on my tongue, she tilted her head to one side, another data set being retrieved. "You know, there was one thing that struck me as odd. It was quite a few weeks back, now that I think about it. David came home in the middle of the afternoon one day while Rachel was out. Wasn't like him to be back before evening. He was a very hard worker, you know?" I settled back into the couch, a tingle of something in my nerve endings. "But that day he was home just after lunch. I remember because I was on the porch having tea. I always have tea at one thirty after the midday news. Another car pulled up to the house after a bit, and I only figured out who it was when I fetched my binoculars. My eyes aren't so good anymore, you know?"

I'd scooted to the edge of my seat. "Right, you mentioned that."

"I guess I should've known by her car—Lord knows I've seen it enough times over the years."

"Who was it?"

"Well, it was Mary Shelby. Come to think of it, that was the last time I saw her. She died a few days later."

23

Galaxies colliding. Stars aligning. Gravity settling things into place that only could have fit where they did.

Mrs. Tross was still speaking. "David let her in, and they talked in the living room. I could see them through the window. Mary seemed very . . ." She searched for the word. "Perturbed. I could see it on her face even at a distance, and after a while she was waving her hands around. David looked like he was trying to calm her down. He did this—" She surprised me by reaching across the little table between us and gripping me by the shoulders with surprisingly strong hands. She was in full chin-wagging mode now, finally with a (literal) captive audience. "I think he was comforting her. They talked for a little bit, then she nodded, and he gave her a hug." She released me and settled back in her seat. "That was it."

For a second I was lost. Pictures forming and dissolving in the darkroom of my mind. "Did David seem angry?" I finally managed to ask.

"No, not that I could tell. If you ask me, he was just trying to calm her down."

When I didn't say anything more, she changed the subject, turning to the latest political gaffe, the weather front coming in, small talk she didn't get to share with anyone else. I listened, agreeing with whatever she was saying. I might as well have been hearing static.

I was a thousand miles away.

At the earliest break in conversation, I told her I had a doctor's appointment. Nothing serious. A minor issue. I promised to stop by again, and I would. At the end of the day, she was an old lady living alone who only wanted someone to talk to, someone to listen to her. Once the layers were drawn back, it was strange how different everything looked.

Through Dad's window I could see his TV on, him moving past every so often. He was okay for now, probably still upset about the day before. Not in the mood for company yet. Later.

I called Robert, Mary's son, chatted a bit. Asked how he and the family were doing.

"Adjusting," he told me. "Still so strange to go to call her and remember all of a sudden." I thought of the thousand times I'd played Emma's life out differently, picturing every happiness for her. How each time the realization she'd never get to live it was still a cold punch to the stomach.

We talked a little about his kids. He asked about Dad and Kel, thanked us for the card and gift of money we'd sent. Sure, of course, no problem.

Near the end of the conversation, when it sounded like he was ready to get off, I said, "You mentioned your mom had been scatterbrained the last few times you talked. Any idea why she was preoccupied?"

Long sigh from his end. "No; I mean, not really. She'd been filling in for Jill Abernathy over at the sister parish. Jill was on maternity leave early in the spring. I think Mom was just stressed with the increased workload."

"She didn't say anything to you out of the ordinary? Anything strange?"

"No, why?"

What could I say? Nothing. I had nothing. No evidence except a circumstantial account from an old lady.

Nothing but a heaviness in my center that wouldn't go away.

Joe Hart

I asked him if I could swing by his mom's place and grab a couple photos from one of her albums. I wanted to make copies for Kel and Dad and me. Was that okay?

"Of course," he said. "You know where the key is."

———

All the color had been leached from the day. The burnished greens of foliage were dull, the mountains heaps of ash to the east. The air hung with a heaviness, and a light rain fell.

When I climbed out of the car at Mary's ranch, I pulled my shirt collar up over my head and went around the back of the house. No barking dogs announced my arrival, no sounds of chickens in their pen. The spare key was underneath a loose brick in a little raised flower bed where Mary used to grow perennials.

Inside I brushed away moisture from my arms and face and made my way through the house. Mary's ghost followed me. The smell of the place, the art on the walls, how some of the floorboards creaked.

A newish desktop computer sat at a compact workstation in her office. The surface of the desk was clear, a calendar beside the mouse listed appointments that would never be kept.

I went through the drawers first, avoiding eye contact with the painting of Jesus on the wall. Typical office supplies in the first one, a blank daily journal in the next along with some tax records. Pens, printer paper, nothing.

My fingers hovered over the keyboard. I punched the space bar. The screen lit up.

Only Mary's avatar appeared. No password sign-in. I clicked.

The computer's desktop appeared—the background a sunset picture Mary might've snapped herself at some point. Very few folders lined the digital fringes of the screen. One near the top was marked PARISH.

162

I clicked the mouse, and a warm breath brushed the back of my neck.

Even as my stomach curdled, I registered the quiet hum of the furnace in the basement, the heating vent directly behind me. Fun, fun.

Inside the folder were more folders, all arranged by date. Monthly amendments to the church schedule, expenditure reports, notes from board meetings, quarterly finance reports, Father Mathew's travel schedule, special guest speaker events, etc.

I pored over everything.

Did I know what I was looking for? Not really. Something strange. A red flag. Another ping on the radar. As I searched, my thoughts flitted back to Mrs. Tross's account of David and Mary's meeting.

Mary had obviously been upset about something. Upset enough to ask David to meet her. David had tried consoling her, tried calming her down. A few days later she was dead. A couple of weeks later so was he.

I had a tolerance for coincidence, but I was also a crime writer. It only went so far.

So what was the connection? Could only be one thing.

Mary Shelby was the parish administrator. David was the chair of the church board.

Files upon files. My vision blurred. Outside, the wind picked up, drifting rain across the meadow and spitting against the window. Soon all I saw was Mary's shorthand, her abbreviations. Spreadsheets, columns of numbers. Projections and schedules.

The last file was dated two weeks before her death. I scanned its contents. More of the same. I was about to click out of it and begin a search spanning the rest of the hard drive when a line of text at the very bottom of a finance report caught my eye. It was spaced so far from the last entry, you'd have to either know it was there or stumble on it.

Another spreadsheet. This one different from the others. It was simple, columns and rows delineated with months and numbers headed by dollar signs.

The figures themselves didn't mean anything to me. They seemed to be mostly random, but on closer inspection, they trended downward as time went on. If they'd been a graph, it would've looked like a gentle sledding hill. Not too fast, not too slow. Just right.

I looked at the spreadsheet awhile longer, then searched all the other files for something similar.

Nothing.

Just one spreadsheet buried at the bottom of a boring monthly finance report.

I closed everything out. Put the computer to sleep. Looked out the window.

Ryan Vallance had been in trouble. Which meant David was in trouble. Rachel had told me the business had been hurting for a while. How bad had it been hurting?

The photo album rested at the very bottom of a bookshelf in the living room. I took it to the couch and sat down, leafing through the plastic pages.

Here Mary was in her garden. Here she was on vacation in the Black Hills. Here was Robert naked in the bathtub, all of two years old. Here were Kel and me sitting astride horses in the meadow outside the house, waiting anxiously for Mary to quit taking our picture and bring us on the ride into the foothills a few miles away. I recalled how we'd been anticipating the ride for weeks.

The hot coal was back in my throat, and I pulled the pic of Kel and me free of its clear pouch. Held it for a second in the ashen light. Then I put the album back and went out into the rain.

Across the yard the stable stood grim and silent in the dampening weather. On instinct I bypassed the dryness of my car and jogged to the building, both glad and disappointed it wasn't locked.

Old hay, grain, faint smell of manure. The high ceilings and exposed beams were coated in shadow. Some of it dispelled as my hand found the light switch. The alley running in front of the stanchions was spick and span like always. Mary hadn't tolerated mess. She'd painted the exterior of the structure and had repairs done inside whenever an issue arose. She'd loved her horses, and they'd loved her.

What you love could kill you.

What else could?

In the center of the aisle, between the stanchion gates and the far wall where sacks of grain were stacked—this was where it had happened. Where they'd found her. If I wrote the scene, it would go something like this:

Mary comes home after work. She fixes herself a little dinner, maybe watches some TV, since there's no one else there. A ride, she thinks. A ride would be nice after eating. She puts on her riding clothes, and there's enough day left to get an hour, maybe hour and a half, in. That last light coming over and through the trees is special; it's clear while making everything look different, like it's all imagined. All a dream.

She goes to the stable, gets the tack and saddle situated, and tells Hocus he'll be the one carrying her tonight. He whinnies, stamps—he's ready. She goes to unlatch his gate and—

I turned toward the window, fully expecting to see someone standing there. It was empty. Just the rainswept yard, the wind.

Mary unlatches the gate and lets the big horse out, maybe brushes his mane a little before retrieving the saddle and then walks up behind him and—

I squeezed my eyes shut. No. The scene stops there because it doesn't hold water. It was a plot hole a mile wide.

Turning in a slow circle, I counted the angles and corners that could hide someone. Looked at the empty stanchions, at all the blunt objects near the walls, the tools to bludgeon. If the house was haunted with Mary's ghost—her presence, a lingering memory—this place was haunted by something else.

A shudder ran through me, and I rubbed the gooseflesh from my arms. It was time to go.

The rain had tapered slightly to a heavy mist. Halfway to my car I gradually slowed, then stopped, despite the blanketing moisture. The driveway was empty, and so was the meadow. When I brought my gaze up to the windows of the house, I braced myself to see the flit of movement, the twitch of drapes sliding back into place. Nothing.

And yet . . .

My scalp tightened, and the hair rose on the back of my neck.

In the car, three-point turn, out the driveway to the paved road, fifty, sixty, seventy miles per hour—the driveway growing smaller and smaller behind me, then it was gone.

24

The sister parish was in the next burb over. A place called Brighton.

Little town, much smaller than Sandford, if that were possible. A gas station, two bars, a bank, apartments, and the church.

The parking lot looked mostly empty, only a maintenance truck and a Subaru near the very back entrance. When the front door of the church remained firm, I went around the side and found the janitor smoking near a butt can. Yeah, Jill Abernathy was in, he said. Right through there and take a left.

Jill's office sat near the boiler room behind a stack of legal boxes and some cleaning supplies. It was a small space with a checkered linoleum floor, cracked but concealed by an old maroon area rug that looked wildly out of place.

When I knocked on the doorjamb, the sole occupant startled, her chair creaking as she pushed back from a narrow desk.

"Jesus, Andy! You scared me." As she realized what she'd said, Jill's eyes widened, and she put one hand over her mouth. I laughed.

Jill and I had dated very briefly in high school. Nothing more than a few burgers and a movie or two. She'd been sweet and funny, but ultimately we'd decided our relationship was most definitely a friendship after a botched attempt at a first kiss that left us both shaking our heads.

"Good thing Father Thomas isn't in today," she said, laughing now too. "He's not keen on blaspheming, especially here." She'd cut the long, dark hair she'd had in high school so now it framed her face, a pair of reading glasses perched on the bridge of her nose the only other new addition. "The famous author back in our midst. I saw you at Mary's funeral, but you and your dad skedaddled before I could talk to you."

"Yeah, sorry. That was a tough one. Just needed to get Dad home."

"Totally understand." Her expression fell.

"You were the one who found her, right?"

"Yeah. It was . . . horrible. She was just there on the floor of the stable. I . . . I knew right away she was gone." Jill shook her head, blinking. "Sorry. Still makes me queasy to think about it."

"I'm sure."

"So to what do I owe this honor?"

I glanced up and down the quiet corridor, making sure we were alone. "It's actually about Mary."

Jill scooted a little closer in her work chair. "Okay . . . ?"

I mentioned speaking to Robert, how his mom had seemed distant, a little frazzled in the weeks before her death.

"Probably my fault," she said. "She was filling in for me while I was out on maternity leave."

"Yeah, hey, congratulations by the way."

"Thanks."

"Boy, girl?"

"Boy. Justin Michael. Showed up in the wee hours of March tenth. He's a little joy."

"That's awesome. Congrats."

"Thanks." Jill frowned. "Yeah, so Mary was taking care of things here while I was out. We've got less workload since the parish is about a quarter of the size of Sandford's. It was still extra hours for her, though. Probably stressed her out a little. But you know Mary, never said no to anyone needing help. Still can't believe she's gone."

"Me neither." I shifted in the doorway. "So you didn't notice any-thing odd while she was filling in? Didn't say anything to you that was out of character?"

Jill cocked her head. "Mmm . . . no. No, don't think so. Why?"

"Robert mentioned she might've been concerned about the church finances. Didn't know if that could've been part of it." I felt bad telling her a lie, but if it came back to bite me, it was the least of my worries.

"She never said anything to me if she was. Father Thomas has been out sick more than usual lately, and Father Mathew's been filling in for him, so both he and Mary were pulling double duty. It could've been just the back-and-forth between parishes that wore her down. What's this all about, Andy?"

"Guess I've been having a tougher time accepting what happened. Trying to make sense of it."

"I know. I suppose it goes to show you there's no guarantees. Anything can happen."

Anything can happen, and according to Murphy's Law, will happen.

Jill and I small talked for a while longer, then I wished her and her new family well. Outside, the janitor was gone, only the smell of his last cigarette lingering in the cool air.

On the drive home my thoughts wheeled from one end of the spectrum to the other.

There was nothing going on. I was stupid and paranoid.

There was definitely something going on. I was smart and right.

My handle on the situation was so comforting.

At home. Coffee. Change of clothes. I absently checked my emails. There were a few from readers, one from my editor, another from my agent. I couldn't concentrate.

Closing the laptop, I sat before the big windows in the living room, looking at the Loop through the rain that wouldn't stop. Something Jill had said tolled a quiet bell in my mind, but after replaying our conver-sation a half dozen times, I couldn't for the life of me figure out what it was. For some reason I thought of my dreams over the past few days, of hands scrabbling at steel doors and long stairways leading down to darkness.

What was worse than not knowing? Wondering about anything serious wasn't fun. Schrödinger's cat was a great thought experiment, but I think he missed the crucial point—human beings weren't meant to live in a state of uncertainty. Never looking inside the box to see if the cat was alive or dead would drive us insane. A deer, a bear, a lion—they didn't worry about the unknown, about mystery. Hunger and thirst and the need to procreate. If one of their kind disappeared, so be it. Time to move on. Hunger. Thirst. Sex.

That's all, that's it.

But for people, mystery was horror.

I envisioned every parent or spouse of a person who had gone missing and how after years of wondering, of worrying, of the unknown, even bad news would be welcomed. Finality is better than nothing at all.

Dad's TV flicked on through the weather, and I got up and found the umbrella in the hall closet and went out.

He was sitting in his easy chair when I came in and shook off the rain. I sat on the sofa and didn't say anything. We watched an episode of some game show, then a half hour of news before Dad hit the remote and powered the TV off. He didn't look at me.

"I don't want to know what happened," Dad said. "I can pretty much picture it anyway. It's why I tried changing the subject at dinner, to avoid it all, but then . . ." He trailed off. "I want to say something, and I want you to really listen, Andy. Don't just humor me. You do a lot around here, and I appreciate it, but don't just humor me. Listen. Okay?"

I gave him a nod.

"Cory is a lot like your mother," he said, sitting forward in his chair.

Part of me leaped to interrupt, to insert an eye roll, an "Of course he is; do you think I didn't grow up with both of them?" But I kept all that to myself.

"Now I know your mother had her faults just like I have mine, like you do yours, and she seemed to pass many of them on to Cory. He's afraid, Andy. That's why he says and does the things he does. It isn't any excuse, I'm not giving him a pass, but he is my son just like you are, and I love him. I love all of you kids." His eyes grew distant. "We made a huge mistake with Emma. Your mother relied on her faith to understand what she was going through, and I didn't put my foot down hard enough. We fought, but she forged ahead anyhow. That's a regret I'll live with until . . . the end."

I heard Father Mathew's voice then. *You aren't the only one with regrets, Andrew. Please know that.*

"Dad, you—"

He held up a hand. "Let me finish. I should've stopped your mother from taking Emma to church, physically if I had to. It might've made a difference in the long run, and maybe it wouldn't have. I don't know. What I do know is your mother regretted her decision too. She realized her mistake much too late, and in my heart, I think that's what killed her. They called it a stroke, but guilt is dense. It's heavy, and it builds up over time." He sighed, and in the storm's light he looked very old. "What I'm trying to say is this: Cory is your brother. He can be insensitive and rude and pushy, but he's also very generous. When I'm gone, I don't want you three fighting. You're family, and if you can give me one thing, it's your word you'll be good to one another. As good as you can be."

I wasn't ready to forgive Cory, and I surely wasn't ready to forgive my mother. Maybe there was a part of me that wasn't ready to forgive Dad either. A part I kept locked away in a deeper place, a gag in its mouth to muffle its cries, because I loved the man sitting in the chair across from me. I loved him deeply.

You lie to the ones you love sometimes. You lie because you love them. You lie to yourself.

"Sure, Dad. We'll be good."

"Okay."

The rain came down and we listened to it. I made dinner, and things swung around almost back to normal.

As I was placing the last of the silverware in the dishwasher, Dad's landline rang.

It would be Rachel. She'd been found and the boys were okay. She was calling to tell me, to hear my voice and so I could hear hers. I'd go to wherever she was, and I'd hug her, kiss her. Note be damned.

I was so convinced of this when I picked up and heard a voice on the other end, I nearly said her name.

It was Jill.

"Andy, is that you?"

Gears freewheeling. Engaged. "Uh . . . yeah, yeah. Sorry."

"Hey, apologies to bother you at your dad's, but I don't have your cell number. Your dad's is still listed."

"Sure, no problem. What's up?"

"Well, it's funny. I got thinking after you left, what you said about Mary being concerned with finances and whatnot?"

My posture straightened, senses sharpening to points. "Sure, right."

"There was something, actually. When I came back from maternity leave, there was this spreadsheet in the printer. I think Mary must've printed it out and then forgot it. I filed it away in case it was something she needed, and then it slipped my mind. Then she was gone, and I didn't remember until you came by."

"What was it?"

"It looked like she was tracking some of our collection plate donations. We have a master data sheet for that, but she'd made her own, kind of."

"You still have it?"

"Yeah, like I said, I just set it aside and never got around to giving it back or asking her about it."

"Could I see it?"

"Oh, Andy, I don't know. That's parish information. I'd have to check with Father Thomas first. I mean, what does it matter now?"

I turned and looked out the window. My gauzy reflection stared back. "I'm not sure. But I'm trying to find out."

25

Dad fell asleep in his chair before the ten o'clock news. It was okay; I might as well have been on another planet for as much company as I was.

There's a deep place in the center of everyone where suspicion lives. It's a rabbit hole going down and down without an end. One passage leads to another, and after a time you realize you don't remember how you got there or what the sun looks like. You want to turn around, but the hole won't let you. It's go forward or stay there stuck in the dark of your own thoughts.

I'd gone down the hole after getting off the phone with Jill. Just dug right in and dove deep, and the tunnels led me to this:

David had been skimming money from the church.

He was the chair of the board not only for Sandford's parish but for Brighton's as well, since they shared a lot of resources. He had access to the money. I knew this because I'd asked Jill how the collection plate and monthly donations were handled. After being collected, cash and checks were counted, usually by someone like Jill or Mary with one of the fathers or another member of the board present, and then the cash went into a safe until a deposit could be made at the bank. She told me that a lot of donations were going digital, but the parishes still hadn't fully embraced the online options, and around 90 percent of their funds came through physically.

The chair of the board had access to the money.

So Ryan Vallance gets himself in over his head, and David starts bailing him out with the only resource he has available, because he can't go to Mommy and Daddy for another loan. Rachel had told me more than once how upset they'd been about David taking Ryan on as a business partner. If he went crawling back to them for money, he'd never live it down, and them denying him was a definite possibility as well.

So David skims from the collection cash—maybe before it's counted or prior to a bank deposit. A little here, a little there. At first maybe no one notices; months go by, then Mary starts to catch on. She sees cash donations gradually declining over a period of time and begins to suspect something. She maps it out, sees a pattern, and finally confronts David.

That's what Mrs. Tross saw the day of her spying—Mary finally having it out with David. What had he told her? A sob story? Something kind-hearted Mary would accept for the time being? Maybe even that he would pay everything back with interest if he could have a little time?

I thought of her holding my hand at the police station. How forgiving she was. How trusting.

And it had gotten her killed.

Her horse hadn't kicked her. She would've never made that mistake.

David felt himself being crushed between a rock and a hard place. Don't pay HerringBone for Ryan's debt—dead. Don't pay back the money taken from the parishes—jail.

So he'd murdered Mary. Made it look like an accident.

There it was. Could I see him doing it? Planning it out, then actually doing it?

I thought of Rachel telling me about his anger, his stoic silence and outbursts. Thought of how she'd looked ashamed. Not for the first time, I wondered if there was more she'd been holding back.

Yes. I could imagine it. It wasn't hard.

But there, as the Bard once said, lies the rub.

If David had killed Mary, then who killed him? Where were Rachel and the boys?

Screeching brakes. Trains coming off the rails. A hole that only went deeper.

I had no idea. Crane? The Visitor? Another unnamed party?

It was equivalent to drawing a circle and never quite being able to fully complete it. It was wondering if the cat is alive or dead and not being able to look.

And what could I do with this hunch, these bits of information I'd pieced together into a half-assed puzzle? Bring it to Spanner? He'd laugh in my face. Go to Seth at the paper? Better, but I guessed he'd tell me it was too thin to run with.

Where did that leave me?

"Square one," I murmured.

"What was that?" Dad asked from the bathroom. He'd woken and shuffled in there a few minutes before.

"Nothing."

He appeared in the hallway. "Okay. Going to bed."

"Sounds good. I might sit here awhile if that's okay."

"Me casa, you casa."

"Su casa."

"I know, smart-ass. Sleep good."

"You too, Dad."

His footsteps faded. The house settled. I didn't.

I paced for a bit. Spooned a little ice cream out of the carton in the kitchen and stood looking out at the street. The rain had tapered off again, and a cool vapor hung beneath the lampposts. In the living room the couch accepted me, molded around my shoulders and back just like it had when I was a kid. We still had the same appliances and furniture since the beginning of time. The couch was worn and uneven and a comfort, something reliable that didn't ask anything of me, didn't need me to be smarter than I was.

I slept.

When I woke, the room was filled with morning grayness, and lava oozed from my skull, slid down the back of my neck, burning.

I couldn't breathe.

A rotten egg smell permeated the air. What air? I couldn't get any, could barely roll myself off the couch.

A quiet hissing from the kitchen. My vision swam, thoughts treading water. I retched, coughed out last night's dinner onto the floor. I had to get to Dad. Something was wrong. Very wrong.

Crawling across the room was momentous, arms barely dragging me along, legs useless bags of watery muscle.

My chest brimmed with hot liquid and the smell, the rotten eggs. Brimstone. I was in hell.

Down the hall, air thick, clinging to my face. Reaching up, fingers brushing the partially open door.

Dad's bedroom, the air no better. I crawled across the floor and pulled on the comforter. Croaked Dad's name. Twice. Nothing.

The last of my strength, yanking myself up and onto the bed. Dad on his side, a shape beneath the blankets. I said his name again, rolling him over as my head sloshed like a fish tank. He didn't open his eyes, wouldn't wake up.

I stumbled to the window and fumbled with the latch, fingers huge and unwieldy. Finally got it open.

Cool. Blessed. Air.

I coughed and dry heaved, stumbled back to the bed and yanked Dad out of it. Dragged him across the floor. Got him to his feet.

Shoved him out the window.

He tipped bonelessly through, feet coming up like counterweights. I eased him to the ground outside as gently as I could, but then I was coughing again, tears flooding my eyes. By touch only I slid out after him. Crumpled into the grass and dirt. Lay there sucking wind.

Sweet, sweet oxygen.

When I could lift my head and my limbs started doing what my brain told them, I rolled over.

Dad lay next to me, like he had been in bed—on his side facing away. I said his name, pulled him over.

His eyes were closed, lips bluish. I leaned close to him, heart doing a strange stutter step in my chest, and pressed my ear to his lips and nose.

He wasn't breathing.

26

You can't remember how to do CPR.

There's a big white gap in your brain where that knowledge hung its hat before. It's something you learned years ago, never had to practice, but it's there just in case.

Like a gun.

Now there's only a hole filling up with panic because your father is dying or dead and you don't remember how to help him.

I came out of the two- or three-second fugue, and then the memory of chest compressions and assisted breathing was there. But first I felt for a heartbeat.

Fingers on his carotid. Waiting. Waiting.

Oh God.

There. Faint. Erratic. But there.

Thirty chest compressions. Two breaths.

Nothing.

Thirty more. Two breaths.

Still nothing.

No, no, no, no, no.

On the third round Dad took a big, sucking drag in through his nose and started gagging.

I rolled him over as he convulsed, sicking up his dinner. He coughed and coughed and coughed, but the color had come back to his lips. I checked his fingernails. They looked normal.

We needed help.

My phone wasn't in my pocket, and I had a half memory of setting it on the coffee table in the living room.

A short yapping came from the street, where none other than Mr. Allen Crane, a.k.a. Jimmy DeMarco Jr., stood with his dog. Tosca was straining at the end of his leash, barking and whining at us.

"Help!" I yelled. It came out as a shouted whisper. My voice wasn't my own. Someone had run a steel file across my vocal cords, shaved them flat. I mimed at my dad, who groaned something between clenched teeth before he started gagging again.

Crane/DeMarco hesitated a second, then pulled out his phone and started talking into it.

After that, everything softened around the edges.

Sirens came from the east and got louder until they filled up the world. Flashing lights. Paramedics and cops asking me questions. A fire truck bleating its low horn as it pulled up to the curb. Guys in gas masks going in through Dad's front door.

Then there was a mask over my face and all I could see was the roof of an ambulance.

Cue darkness.

Flashes of fluorescent light. A hallway. People in gowns. A sharp poke in the arm. Then Kel standing over me, hand in mine, telling me everything was going to be okay. I tried asking about Dad but couldn't seem to form the words.

Later I opened my eyes to a hospital room, a large window on the right pouring sunshine through half-closed blinds. A cooling chunk of iron sat at the back of my skull, its glow throbbing with the bellows of my pulse. The door across from the foot of my bed opened, and Kel stepped out of a little bathroom, drying her hands on a paper towel. She saw I was awake and hurried over.

"Can you hear me?"

"Yeah," I whisper said.

"Holy shit, Andy." She more fell than sat in a chair beside the bed. "Holy shit."

She held my hand for a little bit. We didn't say anything—Kel because she was crying, me because it hurt to talk.

When she'd dried her eyes on the paper towel she'd been wiping her hands on, she cleared her throat and said, "Dad's okay. You asked about him while you were out. You said a few other things too."

"Like what?"

"You said Rachel's name."

Oh.

"Anyone else . . ." I gestured at the surrounding walls.

"No, no one else heard."

"And Dad's really o . . . okay?"

"Yes. I talked to him twenty minutes ago. He was asking about you." She squeezed my hand. "Jesus Christ, Andy. What the hell happened?"

"Water," I whispered, and she got me some. It was cool and crystalline and basically the best thing I'd ever tasted. I kept drinking even after my stomach recoiled and tried to do a magic trick and make the liquid reappear. Kel took the glass from me when it was empty.

"Gas," I said, and this time my voice was a semblance of normal. "The gas was on when I woke up."

Kel nodded. "Yeah, that's what the fire chief said. All the burners were on and not lit."

I processed this. Lay there watching Kel watch me. "You think Dad did it?"

She took a minute answering, and I resented her a little for it. "I don't know. He's never done anything like that before."

"He didn't do it, Kel. He went to bed before I did."

"He gets up in the night."

"Right, but he's aware. He gets a little confused, but he knows what he's doing. He's not that far gone yet. He wouldn't start the stove and walk away. Besides, he'd have to blow all the flames out first."

"You know that stove's older than dirt. The back two burners don't always light when you turn them on."

I shook my head, and the iron inside it stoked, glowed molten. I was about to say something more when the door to the hall opened and a doctor appeared. "Hi there, I'm Dr. Johnson," he said, coming over and shaking my hand. "How are you feeling, Andy?"

I told him like shit. He said that would happen when you huff propane in for several hours instead of oxygen. He told me we'd been lucky, me more so than Dad. My oxygen levels were good, and so far the tests they'd run had all come back negative for any alarming damage.

Dad was a little different story.

He'd actually stopped breathing. The tests for his heart had come back inconclusive, and they were going to need to do more of them when he was in better shape. For the meantime, though, he was stable.

"You'll probably be able to go home this afternoon or evening," Dr. Johnson said. "But we'll need to keep your dad here for a few days under observation." Kel and I thanked him after a couple more questions, and on his way out he turned back and said, "There's a Detective Spanner outside waiting to speak with you. Are you feeling up to talking, or should I ask him to come back later?"

Kel and I shared a look. "Send him in," I said.

Spanner looked tired and was wearing too much cologne. I guessed he hadn't slept the night before, judging by the rumpled look of his clothes. A thirteen-o'clock shadow crept across his jawline, and he grunted when he sat down beside my bed.

"I just checked on your father. He couldn't tell me much, so you'll need to fill in the gaps." Spanner took his phone out of his pocket. "Mind if I record your statement?"

"No."

"Can you tell me what happened at your father's residence last night?"

I ran him through the evening. How Dad had gone to bed and I'd fallen asleep later on the couch. How I'd woken unable to breathe, with the sound of gas hissing in the kitchen.

"Then you managed to go down the hallway and get your father out of his bedroom through the window?"

"Yeah," I said, searching for the little button they sometimes give you to administer your own pain meds through the IV. I couldn't find one.

"So given your father's condition, I'm going to go out on a limb and say he got up to cook himself something in the middle of the night and forgot to shut the gas all the way off."

"No."

"No? Enlighten me."

My tongue felt lead lined, heavy from all the things I wanted to say. Tell Spanner everything? Spill my little conspiracy theory to the one person least likely to believe me, or keep it locked up? Spanner watched me, thick eyebrows raised almost to his hairline.

"I don't know."

"You don't know. Well, what's the alternative? Someone else broke in and did it?"

"I don't know. Did anyone dust for prints?"

Spanner turned his phone off and put it away. "Listen, I'm sure all this has been tough. My pop had that shit, too, before he passed. Wasn't pretty. But denying it ain't gonna make it go away."

"We're not in denial," Kel said. She'd crossed her arms over her chest and sat forward. I could hear the definitive edge in her voice normally reserved for her hours at the DMV. "We know what's happening to our father. All Andy's saying is we don't know for sure what happened last night."

Spanner glanced from her to me. "Okay. Fair enough. I'm writing it up as an accident. Feel free to stop by the precinct if you have anything further to add."

When the door shut behind him, Kel said, "I've got something further to add. You're an asshole."

She glanced at me, and we burst out laughing. Gradually my laughter became coughing. Kel got me more water, and a nurse came by to check my vitals. When we were alone again, Kel said, "Don't look at me like you did earlier."

"Like what?"

"Like when you asked if I thought Dad turned the gas on. I'm not saying he did, it's just the most likely."

"It's definitely a great cover story, that's for sure."

"What, you mean if someone were trying to kill both of you?"

"Not both of us, just me. Dad would've been collateral damage."

Kel looked around as if to make sure we were alone. "I thought you said the guy at Rachel and David's place didn't see who you were."

"I don't think he did, but . . ." I trailed off, stopped again at the wall I'd met talking to Spanner. I could tell Kel anything, but should I? I pictured her house late at night, the girls sound asleep, Kel watching TV or getting ready for bed. She hears a sound and goes down to the kitchen, and the Visitor is standing there. All because I wouldn't quit pushing, because I wouldn't give up.

"What aren't you telling me?" she asked, snapping me free of my thoughts. When I said nothing, she swore and paced at the foot of my bed. "You said you were being honest with me before."

"I was."

"But you aren't now."

"It's not lying if I don't say anything."

"Andy, I swear to God . . ."

"Sis, just . . . stop."

"Stop what?"

"Stop pushing. It's—" I gestured around. "It's not good. Nothing good will come of me telling you. Someday, okay? But not now. I can't do now."

She was winding up to take another swing at me when there was a knock at the door. It opened, and Cory stood in the gap. "Hey," he said.

I looked from him to Kel, who wouldn't meet my gaze. She'd called him. Of course. And I couldn't blame her. He deserved to know. "Hey," I said. "Come in."

Cory ambled over. As he neared, the damage I'd done to his face became more apparent while something inside me shrunk in congruence. "How you, uh, how you feeling?" he asked.

"Okay. Head hurts." I motioned to his face. "How about you?"

He touched his split lips. It looked like he'd been eating blueberry ice cream. "Fine, fine. Looks worse than it is."

Silence gathered in the room. Filled it up.

"Did you see Dad?" Kel asked.

"Yeah. He was sleeping so I didn't talk to him or anything, but the nurse said he was doing good. Heartbeat was strong and whatnot."

After another long pause, Kel said, "I'm gonna get a coffee. You guys want one?"

I shook my head, but Cory said sure. She left us alone, which I surmised was the entire purpose of getting coffee.

Dad's wishes from the day before were chyrons across this scene.

Brothers make amends amid family crisis.

Father's dying request realized by children.

Stop it.

"Cory—" I started, but he held up a hand.

"No, look. We don't have to do this. We don't like each other; that's the truth. It doesn't matter we're related. Brothers and sisters don't get

185

along all the time. It's okay. You don't need me, and I don't need you. We can leave it at that."

"I'm sorry," I said. It hurt a little to say it. He'd deserved the beating I'd laid on him, but I wasn't lying either. I was sorry. Sorry I cringed whenever I knew he was coming home. Sorry I couldn't talk to him like I could Kel. Sorry he felt the same way.

Cory blinked and looked out the window. "I didn't mean it how it came out. What I said about Emma. I always felt like I was on one side and you three were on the other. I know Emma looked up to you and Kel and didn't . . ." He shifted. "She didn't look at me the same way. Not like a big brother."

"Sometimes you didn't act like one," I said gently.

He sighed. "Yeah."

"Dad wants us to be good to each other. After—after he can't tell us that anymore."

"He makes it sound easy, doesn't he?" Cory smiled a little, and I relived a moment from when I was six and fell on some rocks in the woods where we were playing. Cory had inspected a cut on my knee and told me it wasn't bad at all. He smiled and said it would make me stronger. And in that instant I wanted to be, for him.

About then, Kel returned with coffee. She'd brought one for me even though I'd said no, but once again she knew me better than I knew myself, and I drank it down in a few long sips.

The three of us talked, really talked for what seemed like the first time in forever. What we would need to do for Dad in the coming days, months, years. Cory was mostly quiet, thoughtful, absorbing. It was a nice change.

When he left, he squeezed my shoulder once, not looking at me. "Get feeling better," he said and was gone. Kel took her leave a bit later—the girls were at a friend's, and she needed to pick them up. I assured her I'd call that night, and she said I wouldn't have to. That she'd be checking on me.

Dr. Johnson pronounced me fit to be discharged a little before six in the evening. I felt like a newborn calf for the first ten minutes on my feet, then steadied as I headed down the hall.

Dad's room was semiprivate, a solid partition in between his bed and another by the window. Whoever was in the next section over was either in a coma or deeply asleep, no sounds except the soft beep of Dad's heart monitor filling the room.

The man himself was out. Eyes closed and moving behind his lids. A tray picked clean of food sat at his bedside. At least his appetite was good.

A wave of grief and self-loathing washed over me.

All of this because I liked the sound of her laughter.

On the way out I told Dad I was sorry in my head. Didn't want to say it aloud and wake him. He needed his rest.

The front had passed on, leaving behind puddles and a clarity to the sky. The sun perched on the hills to the west, then fell beneath them as I pulled onto the Loop.

Dad's house was cool and quiet with a faint smell of gas lingering in the rooms. Whoever had come in and out—the fire department, the cops, other officials—they'd left the windows open, so the scent wasn't too bad, but it still turned my stomach.

For a few minutes I stood in the kitchen looking at the stove. Kel was right, we'd had it since Christ was a kid. I turned on a burner and it lit. Turned it off.

On again.

Off.

On.

They all lit the first time.

The floor had boot prints all over it. Scuffs, dirt, sand. I inspected all of them, walking slowly down the rear hallway to the back entry. The door wasn't locked. Hadn't been locked the night before either.

I locked it now and did the same to the front door after closing all the windows. The house had a sullen look to it with no lights on, no TV. It was only for a little while, until Dad came home, but it could've been permanent. Instead of the paramedics picking us off the lawn, they could've been rolling us out in body bags. Just like they had David.

Back at my place I didn't bother using the burner phone; I called HerringBone with my own cell.

"HerringBone."

"Speranza."

"Hold on."

The same pause, then the same gruff voice. I could almost smell cigar smoke. "Who's this?"

"Andy Drake, you piece of shit. I get it, you don't want me messing with your business, I understand that, but your issues are with me, not my dad. You want to kill me? Do it right. Come in and put one behind my ear—don't sneak around gassing innocent people while they sleep. Got me?" I was shaking, but my voice remained steady through the entire rant. Over my heaving breaths, the sound of a lighter flicking came through the phone.

"You done?"

"Yeah."

"Good." The line went dead.

I jerked the cell from my ear and looked at it, wound up to throw it. Set it down.

Paced.

A few minutes later my phone rang, and I didn't recognize the number on the caller ID. "Hello?"

"Andy. We gotta have a quick chat," the Visitor said.

27

"Is this connection okay? Can you hear me?"

"Yes," I said, turning to look out at the darkening neighborhood, wondering if he were watching me right now.

"Okay, that's good, because I want you to fully understand what I'm going to say about calling that number you must've memorized. I'll even put it in my own vernacular just to be clear—shit can't go on. Got me?"

"Was it you?"

"What, the gas thing? No. Sorry. Not my style."

"Bullshit."

"If you say so."

"Then who was it? Crane?"

"Ah, I see you're still barking up that tree. No, I'm afraid it wasn't your esteemed neighbor, since he was out of town last night until early this morning. A few of my associates have dealings with him. Actually part of the reason I'm still in the vicinity—that and curiosity killed the cat. Sorry to burst your little gumshoe bubble."

I settled into a chair. "My dad almost died."

"I'm aware, but I'm telling you I wasn't involved. Again, it would've gone a different way. Besides, you've been nudging around things that don't necessarily involve my interests. Our Venn diagrams aren't touching, so to speak. At least not enough to concern me. But what does concern me is you calling my employer. How do I put this . . . do not do it again."

There was a tangible menace in his voice I hadn't heard before. I could almost feel the cold press of a gun barrel on the back of my head.

When I didn't say anything, the Visitor continued. "Anyhoo, working on anything new?"

"Wh . . . what?"

"Anything new? Writing-wise. Got a novel going? I'm always jonesing for a good thrill."

"I, I mean, yeah. I just finished a new book."

"Ah, very good. When could I expect to see it in my local bookstore?"

"I don't . . . I have no idea."

"You know what? If you need an opinion, what do they call it, a beta reader? I'm your guy. You wanna send me the book early, I'll give you my take." He rattled off an email address, and I shook my head to clear it.

"Are you serious?"

"Andy, haven't you heard? Everyone's a critic."

Then he was gone.

Five days.

She and the boys had been gone five days. I knew the first forty-eight hours were the most crucial for finding a missing person. I'd done the research for the second Laird Holmes book. Those who were much better at finding missing people than I was knew this. I had no doubt that was the reason why Spanner had looked so drawn. David's and Rachel's parents were powerhouses of the community. They most likely had Spanner's number on speed dial and were using it. Probably hourly. He was working overtime to find Rachel and the boys, along with David's murderer.

And here I sat at my table in the dark. The same exact place where I'd studied the note left in my door lifetimes ago.

Endless circles.

Circles that didn't connect.

I knew what had happened. I knew when. I thought I knew why. I thought I knew how.

I didn't know who.

Who killed David and Ryan? Who chased me from Rachel's house? Who followed me to Mary Shelby's and then to the other parish? Because someone had. I knew that now. Not only from the creeping sense of being watched in her yard but because of waking up to the smell of propane in the morning.

I'd been getting closer to the truth, and someone didn't like it. Had been willing to risk sneaking into Dad's and turning on the gas. Had been willing to kill him as long as I was dead too.

Someone who knew about Dad's condition. Knew our deaths would be labeled as an accident caused by his disease.

I rolled that around a bit. How many people knew Dad was suffering from dementia?

A lot. Dozens? A hundred? Everyone in the neighborhood, that was for sure. The list went on and on.

My head ached.

From the start I thought everything would work out eventually, either by fate or the cops or my own intervention. Everything would be okay. I'd been telling Kel the same thing my whole life. I told Emma, too, but it hadn't been.

And it wasn't now. I'd tried my hardest to find Rachel and the boys, done everything I could think of, except one.

It was time to give the cops the note.

If there was even a shred of possibility it would somehow help the case, then I had to. I'd do it tomorrow after visiting Dad. I wanted to see him one last time before there was reinforced security glass between us. I could see how it would play out.

I'd hand Spanner the note, and he'd read it, look at me, and call me an unpleasant name. He'd find a reason to bring me in, keep me locked up after a round of questioning. I'd be suspect numero uno, because at some point you have to set romanticism aside and be realistic. People went to jail all the time for things they didn't do.

Maybe something new would come along to exonerate me. Maybe they'd find Rachel and the boys alive and well. Maybe they wouldn't.

Either way I'd be in prison. One of bars or of my own making.

I texted Kel good night and went to bed. Lay there for a few minutes, then got up and went across the street to Dad's and punched in the code to the gun safe. With the revolver tucked beneath my pillow back at home, I slept fitfully. Woke up coughing a few times. I dreamed.

The dreams were cruel. They were suggestions of Rachel's and my last time together, told in strange angles and sepia lighting.

Me kissing her shoulder blade. Her smiling.

Me thinking it was finally the right time to say something. To tell her. To ask.

Waking in the dim early hours, I thought of the words I'd said and wondered if they'd been the right ones. As a writer, you always wonder if the words you're using are good enough, if they'll find their way through a person's eyes and mind to their heart.

I could see mine had missed their mark that day.

Could see it in the way she looked past me. The way she rubbed the spot behind her ear.

Nervous, anxious, afraid.

That made two of us.

So I'd dropped it. Hadn't said anything more, and she hadn't brought it up again. But for that one second before she'd grown distant, I'd hoped.

The coffee tasted stale, and there wasn't much in the fridge to eat. I should've gone shopping. Maybe tomorrow if I was still a free man.

At the hospital I bought Dad's favorite candy bar from a vending machine and brought it to his room. He was awake, and his color was good.

"There he is," he said when I walked in. "Seen all three of my kids before noon on the same day. Gotta almost die more often to get attention, I guess."

"How you feeling?" I asked.

"Like someone took a chimney brush to my lungs. How about you?"

"Not quite that bad. I'm fine."

He gazed at me for a few drawn seconds. "I'm so sorry, Andy."

I shook my head. "It wasn't you, Dad."

"I must've gotten up to make something and . . ." He gestured angrily. "I don't fucking know. Left the burners on or some damn thing."

"I did it, not you."

He frowned. "What are you talking about?"

I told him.

Told him about what Mrs. Tross had seen. About going to Mary's and then talking to Jill. Told him my theory and that someone was following me. Someone wanting me to stop.

He was quiet for a time. "You can't know all that for sure."

"No. I can't. But I do."

"Spanner will use everything he can against you. He's gotta be desperate to pin this on someone."

"I'm sure he is. But I should've turned over the note days ago instead of trying to find them myself. It was selfish."

"Nothing wrong with not wanting to go to jail. Nothing wrong with being innocent."

I sighed and set the candy bar on his bedside table. "I'm sorry for all this." He looked at it, and while he was trying to come up with something to say, I hugged him. "Love you, Dad."

"You too," he said, voice husky.

I left a message for Kel on the way out of the hospital. Told her my plans. She'd have the same reaction as Dad. Wouldn't want me to hand the note over. Might as well be an admission of guilt. A written confession. Seth could write the headline.

Secret lover takes revenge on dutiful husband and community hero.

Maybe it wouldn't be that tabloidy, but still.

When I got home, I could hardly keep my head up. The caffeine had worn off, and my feet dragged up the front steps, each shoe a thousand pounds. I guess I was allowed to be tired. Hadn't slept really well in weeks. Almost died two nights ago. Excuses, excuses.

I took the note out of the rice and read it one last time, searching for some hidden clue that would blow the whole thing wide open. But that was for movies, for the books I used to write. Not real life. In real life, people got shot and died. They were taken in the middle of the night and never found. Innocent people spent their lives in prison.

I'd just sit down for a minute in the chair by the window. The sky was cloudy, and the wind had come up. It pried at the eaves, trying to find a way inside. The house creaked, and it was a comforting sound. It followed me down into sleep.

I woke to church bells.

Nothing new on the Loop. The church rang them Sundays and Wednesdays before Mass. It was Wednesday evening. I'd slept longer than I meant to. For that brief, beautiful moment coming out of sleep, I didn't remember. Those amnesia seconds, blissful and unaware. Then I recalled I would probably be locked in a cell tonight. Be spending hours on an uncomfortable mattress with the sounds of the county jail ringing in my ears instead of church bells.

Always something to look forward to.

For a bit I shuffled around the kitchen, doing anything to avoid the note and what I'd have to do next. Put some dishes away. Cleaned out the top shelf of the fridge. Took the garbage to the garage. All the while a part of me went to work on the rest.

You don't have to do this.

You can burn the note in the sink. Forget you ever saw it. Forget what happened up the street, forget what you had with her.

Move on.

It wasn't a novel idea. People did it every day. They pushed the uncomfortable things out of their heads, those pesky failures keeping them up at night. Why remember when all it caused was pain?

Take a page from Dad's book and forget.

Stop.

I picked the note up and folded it over so I couldn't read it anymore. It had nothing left to offer me. Maybe someone else could discern something I hadn't. I thought of Spanner and how much he disliked me, and knew the only thing he'd use the note for would be evidence for my incrimination. Unlike Sergeant Michael O'Rourke—the detective I'd shadowed in the city—Spanner wouldn't pay attention to details. He'd take the first bit of evidence he could get and hang it around my neck.

I thought about where everything had started and knew O'Rourke had been so right, especially about how cases never moved in a straight line. They zigged and zagged, twisted and turned like an amusement park ride, always ending up in the last place you expected.

The last place.

I sat stock still, both hands on the tabletop. It felt like all the air had been sucked out of the room. Nothing but me and an idea unfurling like a flower, one horrifying petal at a time.

With each passing second my core tightened, my center drawing in on itself. I'd collapse soon, be nothing but a black hole, a void where a stupid, stupid man had once been.

How had I missed it? It had been right there the whole time.

And there was one way to prove it.

I stumbled into the living room and grabbed my phone from where it lay on the windowsill. Pulled up the browser and typed. Hit the phone number that appeared on the screen. I glanced at the clock. Had she already gone home? Please, please, please pick up.

The ringing on the other end stopped, and Jill's voice came through the line. I cut her off before she could say the church's full name.

"Jill, it's Andy. I need a favor from you." I was still collapsing, condensing with each word. Getting slower and heavier. "The spreadsheet Mary left behind—can you look at it for me?"

"Andy, how are you? I heard about you and your dad. Are you guys okay?"

"Yeah, we're fine. The spreadsheet, Jill—can you find it?"

A pause. "Well, I was just heading out, and I'm late picking up Justin from day care."

"Jill, please." The desperation in my voice must've translated, because the next sound I heard from her end was the sliding of file drawers.

"Okay, hold on. Lemme look." More clacking and a few exasperated sighs, then she said, "All right, got it. What do you need?"

"You said the dates were sporadic for the donation amounts, right?"

"Yeah. They range over the last six or seven months, a few days here and there."

I took a breath. We were at the edge. Ready to go over. "Do any of those dates coordinate with Father Mathew filling in for Father Thomas?"

A drawn silence from her end, then the squeak of her office chair. I could see her settling back into her desk, turning on her monitor. God bless you, Jill. "I can look, I guess. All the schedules notate who does Mass on a particular day."

I passed from room to room, unaware of movement, of anything outside the sounds of Jill's keyboard, her mouse clicking.

"Well, that's weird," Jill finally said. "Yeah, you're right, Andy. All of these correspond with visiting sermons. Father Thomas has been gone ten times in the last six months, and they're all the dates on Mary's spreadsheet."

We went over the edge.

Falling.

"Andy? Did I lose you?"

"No," I managed. But I'd been lost. Lost in the weeds this whole time while the path was right there in front of me.

"What's this all about?"

"Thanks, Jill, I have to go."

"Andy—"

"I'll call you soon."

My thumb punched the little red button, and she was gone.

I was gone.

My collapse was complete. Only a void left. A paradox if there ever was one.

I slapped myself hard across the face, and everything came rushing back.

Everything.

All the layers peeled away. All the circles closed. Everything.

Because now it all made sense.

And I knew where Rachel and the boys were. I'd known all along.

28

At least a part of me had.

The part that woke up when I dreamed. The subconscious, where all the real work happened, where all the sausage got made. That's where I knew.

I'd been dreaming about endless stairways fading into darkness.

Of hands clawing at locked steel doors.

Oh symbolism, thou hast failed me.

It wasn't just subconscious mental alliteration. Somewhere, I'd known and had been screaming at myself to wake up and see. To think.

The day Rachel and the kids disappeared, she'd been seen around town. People had spotted her at the farmers market, the grocery, and lastly pulling into the church parking lot to pick up her boys from school.

What if they'd never left?

Nine-one-one? No, I needed to forgo the red tape and speak to someone on the same level. I found the number for the police department and stuttered that I needed to speak to Detective Spanner. A bit of hold music, and then Spanner was saying hello, and I was already talking over him.

"They're in the church basement. Father Mathew's keeping them there. He's behind it all. He's been taking money from the church donations. He's the one who tried gassing us."

"Drake? What the fuck are you on about?"

"Mary Shelby, before she died—was murdered—she noticed the church's donations declining. She went to David since he was the chair of the board, but he must've been in on it somehow, I don't know. Father Mathew killed Mary and made it look like an accident. Rachel must've figured it out. The day she disappeared, he took her and the boys hostage; he's got them in the church basement right now."

I ran out of wind. Backtracked through what I'd said and realized how wild it sounded.

"Are you high, Drake? You still huffing gas?"

"No, listen to me. There's documents—spreadsheets Mary made up tracking the money being skimmed off donations. David Barren and Ryan Vallance owed money to someone, and I think they were getting cash from Father Mathew."

The more I talked, the crazier it sounded, and the more I felt I was right. The pieces fit. The whole picture wasn't there yet, but it would be. I knew it.

"Pardon my French, but you're a fucking loon. Do you know how batshit you sound? Seriously." He paused, and I could almost hear him reloading more insults. "But now that I think of it, none of this shit started until you moved back here. Is that a coincidence? I get a real funny feeling about you, Drake, whenever I see your face. You know things and you're not saying. You and that sister of yours. Probably your old man too, who knows?"

"Detective, please. Just hear me out."

"I've heard enough. You think you're some kind of quasi cop because you write that shit? You don't know anything about the job. Nothing. Now leave this to the professionals or I swear to God I'll have you brought in for interfering in an ongoing investigation."

"At least check the basement. Please." But I was talking to myself. Spanner was gone.

———

Decisions, decisions.

Not really. There was only one path. I saw that now.

If you looked back over your shoulder at the days before, you'd see it, the road that brought you here, and you'd think to yourself that the path was paved with your decisions, your choices. And that's what made the path meander to the left or right or go straight. Ahead you wouldn't be able to see too far because you're not God, but the kicker is he can't see where it goes either. He doesn't know, and neither do you, but each paver stone laid down, each decision is what it was always going to be. There was never any choice; it was always going to happen this way—the decisions are already made way before they need to be.

I walked up the street, past Rachel's, past Crane/DeMarco's, moving with a purpose I hadn't felt in a while. Crane himself was on his porch smoking a cigarette. Tosca yapped twice at me, then sat down and panted, his tail wagging a little bit. I gave Crane a small wave, and he barely nodded. I'd have to apologize to him when this was all done. Because he wasn't involved at all, just a former mob connection in the wrong place at the wrong time. Maybe I could bake him something.

I left the sidewalk and walked on the grass up the hill toward the church. The sun drifted lower in the sky, throwing long shadows. The shade of the church steeple and its coolness washed over me. The parking lot had few cars in it, but it would fill up soon for Wednesday-evening Mass. Father Mathew would be preparing for the sermon, and the lower level would be quiet and empty.

Inside the back entry, air whispered in ducts, and the door's pneumatic hinge closed quietly behind me. There wasn't a soul visible in the hallway ahead, only a view out into the atrium, the doors to the sanctuary propped open to welcome parishioners. I took one step into the hall, and Father Mathew walked out of his office a few feet away.

He was in a hurry, already wearing his ceremonial gown, and he didn't so much as glance in my direction. I stood there, emulating a statue as best I could, hoping he hadn't forgotten anything in his office and would suddenly turn around. When he was a dozen paces away, I took two steps and left the hall for the stairway landing.

The stairs stretched down into the bowels of the building, a single overhead lamp at the top landing cutting only some of the darkness away.

I was seven again, not wanting to go down there but knowing I had to.

I could see the scene a week ago. Rachel coming here to pick up Asher and Joey and finding Father Mathew waiting for her instead.

My feet made dry rasping sounds on the treads, like a dying man taking his last few breaths.

He'd lured her down here with some promise. What had he said to get her to come with him? She must have already known about the money, known he was involved somehow. If I was a betting man, she would've been leery of him, so whatever he'd told her must've been persuasive.

At the bottom of the stairs, a short corridor branched left and right. To the left was an exit leading into a walk-out alley where the dumpsters were kept. To the right, the door to the old part of the church basement.

The light from the stairwell bled weakly across the floor before it was overtaken by darkness. I found a switch on the wall and was about to flip it but reconsidered. Someone passing by upstairs might see it on and come to investigate. Instead I let my eyes adjust for a second, pressed one hand against the wall, and moved forward.

A doorjamb met my fingers, and I jerked at the unexpected contact. The boiler/maintenance room. When the church had employed a full-time handyman, this doorway had always been open. Now it was shut. My hand grazed the knob, but I didn't turn it. They wouldn't be inside this room, not that close to the bottom of the stairs.

Another few steps and I was completely blind. Nothing but empty air in front of me, groping for the door I knew was there, lost in the abyss.

As I was digging for my cell to light the way, my fingertips brushed something, and the door materialized before me. Just a tall rectangle of deeper darkness. Hand on the knob. Turn.

It wasn't locked, but the door wouldn't move either. Something was blocking it.

I saw Rachel's and the boys' bodies piled up against the other side, and my stomach lurched. No, wait. There was a hasp built into the doorjamb above the knob. My hand traced the shape of a padlock.

Oh God.

For a few seconds my mind freewheeled. Thoughts of going back upstairs and searching for the key in Father Mathew's office came and just as quickly went. I needed something to get the lock open swiftly and quietly.

Backtracking to the boiler room, I turned the knob and sent up a silent thanks that it wasn't locked. Inside I closed the door and flipped on the light, wincing at the sudden brightness.

A simple room, long and low. Huge boiler in the corner along with snaking pipes coating the ceiling. And at the very back, exactly what I was looking for.

The rack of tools was neat and organized. Hammers in one section, wrenches and pliers in the next. My eyes traveled over everything before landing on something hanging near the bottom.

Bolt cutters. Bingo.

Back in the hall to the door. Two tries to line the cutters up with the padlock, then it was pinched between the jaws. I set my feet, clenched my teeth, and pulled the handles together.

Snick.

Almost too easy.

I set the bolt cutters down and twisted the snipped lock from the hasp. Put it in my pocket. Opened the door.

The worst thing that could've happened next would've been feeling the drag of a body pressed against the door. Or smelling the terrible scent of decomposition. There was neither.

When the door was closed behind me, I reached out and swept a hand along the wall. Spiderwebs, dust, grime, bank of switches. I flipped the first one up.

A naked bulb came on a dozen feet away and sprayed wan yellow light. The entry to the basement was just the same as when I'd been locked down here nearly twenty-seven years ago. A wide hallway partially filled with cardboard boxes. Doorways on opposite sides before the corridor made a T. I flipped the next switch in the bank, and light spilled around the corner to the left. The last switch did nothing. I toggled it up and down. Dead.

"Rachel?" I whispered, heart slamming hard against my ribs, longing for a reply. None came. I said her name along with the boys' a few more times a little louder, then moved deeper into the basement.

The first two rooms were piled full of storage. Boxes, chairs, tables, a few ancient desk lamps. The floor hall was scuffed with decades of use, but I couldn't tell if someone had walked through recently.

At the entry's junction, I paused. Left—another single bulb glowed. Right—darkness.

Left.

My footsteps were loud in the hanging silence. Any and all sound down here was dampened by layers upon layers of concrete in all directions. It was why I'd been able to scream my lungs out when I was a kid and no one had come. Even during Mass, someone could be calling out for help down here and no one would ever hear them.

A series of rooms opened up ahead. One after the other, all connected by doorways. Here were stacked desks, feet pointing at the sky like a mound of dead bugs. There a line of old file cabinets with some of the drawers missing or placed on the floor beside them. The next room had a switch, and I flipped it. Cases of wine and wafers. The next room—boxes of old toys and musty clothing donated and never dispersed.

Then I was at a blank wall.

A hint of uncertainty wound through me. Up above in the world of light and sound, my theory had been rock solid. All the pieces coming together to form the whole. Circles all closing.

Down here I wasn't sure.

But would Father Mathew have put them in the areas that had light and were actually used from time to time?

I turned around and headed back, shutting switches off as I went. At the entry junction I stopped, staring ahead. I said Rachel's name again and heard something deeper in the darkness.

A subtle shift of clothing. A soft exhale.

I moved forward slowly, dragging fingertips against the wall, searching for a light switch.

My hand met empty air. I'd come to a new room.

No switches, only rough concrete. I dug my cell free and turned its flashlight on. As bright as it had always seemed before, it was dismal down here. Shadows danced out of the beam's meager reach. Leaving the touch of the wall felt like stepping from dry land into a drop-off. I was adrift in the semidark.

One step.

Two.

Something brushed against my face.

I let out a choked cry and batted whatever it was away. It came right back, bumping my forehead. A string hanging in the air.

I found its swaying length and tugged it. The light it was attached to came on.

The room was oblong and held stacks of shelving and a row of bookcases along with a painting of the crucifixion. Christ's eyes gazed upward, searching for salvation, as his blood rained down on a soldier stabbing him in the side with a spear.

Another doorway yawned across the room, looking like it had been cut from black cloth.

"Rachel?" I said.

No answer.

Inside the next room the wall was smooth, and I guessed this was some of the oldest construction. No switches here, just interspersed lights with pull chains hanging down. Quaint.

Easing into the space with only the glow of my cell to go by, my foot struck something, and it rolled away. A low cart of some kind. As it stopped, a muted scraping sound came from a few steps away, and I froze, searching the darkness.

Something long and low was draped by a tarp in the far corner. I imagined a cage under there, well constructed and large enough to hold a woman and two children.

That same confidence overcame me as when I'd talked to Spanner. I *knew* Rachel and the boys were under that tarp.

Three steps and I was there. Finding the edge and yanking it back. Pulling. Dragging. Already saying her name. Hearing her weak reply.

It took several seconds for my eyes to register what lay beneath the tarp. A few more for my mind to accept it.

An old pool table, felt scuffed and torn. The one that had been in the activity room upstairs years and years ago.

No cage. No Rachel. No boys.

I backed away from it and stood there dumbly, wondering what I'd been hearing in the dark.

Hurried footsteps came out of the next room toward me. Fast.

No time to turn or dodge, just blindsiding pain, then I was airborne, landing hard on the concrete. Rolling.

As I tried pushing myself up, something struck my temple. Neon stars shifted at the edges of my vision, pulsing and blending with shadows. As they burned themselves out, a shape loomed over me.

There was a click and a light came on.

29

Father Mathew in all his glory.

Gown billowing, brow red and sweaty, fists clenched.

We stayed that way for a beat, me lying prone, head swimming and ears ringing from the kick he'd delivered, him standing above me, breathing hard. We could've been another painting like the one of Christ in the next room.

Then he leaped into motion and kicked me again.

Low in the stomach, his sharp-toed shoe digging in like a blunt dagger. Reflexively I caught hold of his leg as he tried yanking away, but I held fast, and he started to hop as I climbed to my knees and grabbed him around the waist.

His fist crashed down on the back of my neck like the fury of God himself, and I went flat again. Amid the waves of pain, I rolled away, knowing another kick was coming. It was, and when it landed, it glanced off my lower back instead of my stomach.

Dust flew up, invading my nostrils, and one of my palms abraded on the cement. Father Mathew's shoes scuffed in the half-light, and his hands latched on to my shirt collar as I made it to my feet.

He ran me across the room, all his weight and strength from work-outs evident as I slammed into a heavy table and slid across its top. A band of fire bloomed on my thighs where they'd met the table's edge, but it was quickly overshadowed by my head and right shoulder taking the brunt of my weight as I landed on the floor.

He's going to kill me, I thought absently. I was right about him and his involvement, and this man of the cloth was going to end me down here in the basement where I'd known real fear for the first time.

For some reason the thought angered me. It wasn't just the poetic injustice of it—it was everything.

Emma lying in her coffin, forever fifteen.

My mother's cold indifference.

Dad's disease.

Rachel's absence.

It wasn't fucking fair. None of it. And this man of faith was going to beat me to death, and that wasn't fair either. The strong won, and the weak put up with it.

My hand wrapped around something lying under the table, and I came up off the floor with all the speed and power I had left in my body.

He was rounding the end of the table when I popped up like a jack-in-the-box and lashed him across the face with the top half of a pool cue.

It caught him on the bridge of the nose with a sound like a cabinet door snapping shut. Father Mathew staggered back a couple steps and blinked. He brought his hands up to his face, and they promptly filled with blood. Gore ran in rivulets down either side of his nose and formed a red goatee on his chin. He stared dumbly at the blood; then his knees unlocked, and he sat down hard.

Our inhales and exhales were the loudest sound in the world. The only sound. We'd reversed positions, and now I stood over him, the cue wavering slightly in my grip.

He sat there bleeding, looking up at me, and after what seemed like hours said, "What are you doing, Andy?"

"Where are they?" I asked, taking a half step toward him.

He shrank back. "Who?"

"Rachel and the boys. You did something with them. This was the last place anyone saw Rachel. Where are they?"

"Andy, you need to calm down. I don't know what you're talking about. I heard someone down here and came to look. You surprised me. I didn't know it was you."

"Don't bullshit me. You know exactly why I'm here."

"I don't, I really don't."

"I saw Mary's spreadsheets. She had one at her house and made another one over in Brighton. She was onto you and David."

He blanched at that, the half of his face visible in the low light growing whiter amid the blood. "No, see, you've got it wrong. I—"

I hit him again. A hard rap on the top of the head with the thicker end of the cue.

He cried out and covered his head with his hands. "Stop! Don't hit me anymore. Please."

"Rachel found out, didn't she? That's why you took them. After Mary and Ryan were out of the picture, David must've told her about your little secret." I pushed the cue into his shoulder hard, and Father Mathew's eyes widened as he stared up at me. "She knew, didn't she? Didn't she?" I yelled the last words, and spittle flew from my mouth. I must've looked all of the psycho I felt, because something changed in him then. His bloodied face clenched, and he began to cry, tears mixing with blood.

"It was only the once," he whispered, chest beginning to heave. He slid himself back a few inches and leaned against the wall, breath hitching. I was about to contradict him. Tell him no, it was most certainly not just once, he'd been skimming money for months and months, when he continued. "I couldn't help it. I tried. You have to believe me. I tried to resist, but I couldn't help it. I'm not well. It was just the one time with Joey, never before, never since."

Adrift.

No longer a void—a supernova, my thoughts exploding outward and tumbling chaotic over one another. Slowly they coalesced, landing on what he meant, absorbing it.

Oh God.

I thought of little Joey, so much like his mother, anxious and quiet. How Rachel had said he'd become more detached and resistant to going to school over the last year. Now I knew why.

"You . . . you were . . ." I couldn't get myself to say the words, nausea forcing my throat shut.

"It was just the once!" He was pleading now. "David saw us and . . . and he was the one who set up the agreement. I gave him the money."

Scales falling from eyes. Everything laid bare. All circles closing.

David had caught Father Mathew molesting his son, and instead of outing him and pressing charges, he'd seen an opportunity. An opportunity to save his business from a bad investment by an unruly business partner.

"Mary found out about the money, and David killed her," I said quietly. His jaw quivered, and he looked around the room as if searching for salvation. I saw a flicker of something else in his eyes. "No. You killed her," I said, and his gaze snapped back to me. "It wasn't David, it was you."

He squirmed, shoving himself closer to the wall, and at that moment if he'd tried standing, I would've beaten him to death. This man. This monster.

"I tried to talk to her," he said. "I asked for more time."

"You made it look like her horse kicked her." The scene in Mary's stable played out in my head, this time with all the gaps filled in. The director's cut. I could see Father Mathew crouched there in the shadows, waiting for Mary to go riding. Springing out and hitting her with something hard in the face. Hitting her with all the muscle he'd built up over the years. Letting Hocus out of his stanchion and leaving the perfectly staged crime.

"Please," he whispered.

"Why did you kill Ryan?"

"I didn't."

"Yes, you fucking did; why lie about it now?"

"It was David," he choked out. Blood sputtered from his mouth and spilled down the front of his gown like communion wine. "He did it."

"Why?"

Father Mathew muttered something.

"What?"

"Because Ryan found out. About the arrangement. David let it slip one night when they were drinking, and Ryan came to me. Tried making me pay him on the side without David knowing."

Ryan's sure thing. The way he was going to make good on what he owed to HerringBone. He'd homed in on David's illicit agreement and tried getting a cut of his own.

Father Mathew was crying again. "David got him drunk, and when he passed out, he . . ."

I imagined David's hand laced over Ryan's, holding the gun up to his friend's head. Pulling the trigger.

"Jesus," I said.

"Please. Please, Andy . . ."

"Shut up." I looked to the left out toward the entry. Could've sworn I heard something.

Father Mathew lunged up from where he sat, and I kicked him in the chest. Hard.

He settled back down with an oof, lungs emptying. "Don't move," I said, starting to shake again. Could I do it? Could I hurt another human being very badly if I had to? I thought of little Joey, of Mary, of Emma and knew the answer.

"Where are they?" I asked. There was a coldness in my voice I didn't recognize, but it steadied me. "Where are Rachel and the boys?"

"I don't know."

"You came back to get the business card from David's desk to cover your tracks. You were there that night. You chased me out of the house."

"No, it was me," a soft voice said from my left.

30

Someone stood in the doorway, backlit enough to shade who they were. But I knew the voice.

"Elliot?" I said.

Elliot took a step into the room and raised his arm. I studied the pistol at the end of it. "Put that down, Andy."

"What are you doing?"

"He's crazy, Elliot," Father Mathew said. "He ambushed me. He tried to kill me."

"Shut up," I said without looking at him. I was more interested in Elliot's weapon and how he continued to train it on me. I kept my voice low and calm. "Elliot, what are you doing here?"

"I told you he was in on it," Father Mathew said. "Why else was he in David's house that night?"

"Is that true, Andy?" Elliot said. His voice wavered a little, and his pale face seemed to float in the gloom. "You were working with David Barren?"

"What? No."

"He's lying," Father Mathew said. "That's why he was out at Mary's house. Why he went to Brighton. He was in on it with all of them."

"Why were *you* in David and Rachel's house that night?" I asked. Mostly to keep him talking but partly because I was still trying to add up Elliot's appearance here.

Elliot shifted slightly, and I imagined how the muzzle flash would light the room up, how the burned gunpowder would hang thick in the air. How the bullet would feel tearing through my body. "I was looking for the lies David was holding over Father. I thought you were one of the men he owed money to. That's why I chased you into the woods. I thought you might've been David's killer." He brought his other hand up to brace the pistol. "Maybe you are."

My instinct was to dodge away, but I stayed frozen, trying to maintain a calm I didn't have. "I don't know what he told you, Elliot, but I wasn't involved in any of this." I gestured at Father Mathew. "He was molesting Joey Barren. David found out and blackmailed him."

Elliot shook his head. "No, no, no. Father told me the truth. I overheard him and David talking, and he told me what was really going on. David made up the story because he owed money to bad people."

"He just confessed to me, Elliot," I said. "He just told me the truth. He killed Mary and made it look like an accident."

"He's a liar," Father Mathew said, starting to inch sideways along the wall. I shot a look at him, and he quit moving.

Elliot took another tentative step forward. "Put the cue down, Andy. You're going to jail."

"He's been lying to you," I said, and all at once I realized why it had been Elliot in the Barrens' house that night and not Father Mathew himself. "He's setting you up to be a fall guy, Elliot. You're an usher. You have access to the donations too."

Elliot's eyes flicked to where Father Mathew sat, then back to me.

"He's full of lies," Father Mathew said. "Shoot him." His teeth were bared, blood lining the spaces between them. "Shoot him!"

Elliot licked his lips, starting to whisper something under his breath.

"Elliot, give me the gun. We can go upstairs and call the police. We'll talk to them together," I said.

"Don't give him the gun—he'll kill us both. Then he can tell all the lies he wants."

More whispering.

"No one has to get hurt. We can sort this all out."

"Shoot him! Shoot him, Elliot!"

I could finally hear what Elliot was whispering over the thunder of my heart.

"Save me, Lord, from lying lips and deceitful tongues. Thou shalt not kill. Save me, Lord, from lying lips and deceitful tongues. Thou shalt not kill."

Elliot's hand tightened on his gun.

"Elliot, please. Don't."

"Shoot!"

All the tension went out of Elliot's body, and he dropped the gun to his side. His head drooped forward. I let out a long sigh, waiting for Elliot to make another move. When he didn't, I nudged Father Mathew with my foot. "Get up."

Father Mathew stared at Elliot for another second, then climbed to his feet. I held the cue ready just in case, but the fight seemed to have left him.

"I don't know what to believe," Elliot said quietly, still looking at the floor. He sidled out of the way as Father Mathew made to pass him.

Those moments in life that border on precognition. When you can feel the electricity in the air the second before you see the lightning. That plunging sensation when you know you're going to kiss the person next to you for the first time.

I saw what was going to happen before it did.

I saw Father Mathew lunging, snagging the gun from Elliot's loose hand. Saw him spinning and training the sights on me as I stood there, stunned into deadly stillness. An easy target. Heard the shot rip apart the close silence of the basement. Felt it tear through my chest.

Father Mathew launched himself at Elliot. The two men jostled. I had time to take a half step forward and raise the cue.

The gun went off.

The muzzle blast lit the room in a flash of yellow, Elliot's and Father Mathew's faces highlighted in matching grimaces of struggle. They froze, standing as if ready to embrace each other. Then Elliot staggered backward and hit the wall, a dark stain spreading rapidly down the front of his shirt. He looked up at me with a dreadful pleading and sat down, clutching at the weeping hole in his chest.

Something clattered to the floor. Father Mathew looked down to where he'd dropped the gun and made to pick it back up, but he moved in slow motion. Like he was caught in a dream. I stepped forward and kicked the pistol away. He watched it spin into the darkness.

Elliot made a brief gurgling sound, and his hands fell from the wound. His body relaxed, and he slumped to his side, lying like a tired child at nap time. His leg jerked once, and he was still.

Father Mathew stared down at Elliot's body. I couldn't move. Couldn't think.

"Walk," I finally said weakly. When he didn't move, I kicked his fancy dress shoe.

We made our way past Elliot's body, stepping around the spreading pool of blood. The shock of it all—the fight, the confrontation, the sudden and irreversible death—was like some tainted drug mainlined into my system. I was drunk with sensory overload.

We made it to the basement entry before the cops stormed in.

Shouts, pistols, wide eyes.

I followed directions, dropping the cue and wondering at the absurdity of how I must've looked holding it in the first place.

Then I was thrown to the floor, cheek and chin scraping against the concrete. Hands behind my back, cuffed. Then onto my feet, being led out into the downstairs corridor, the only solace seeing Father Mathew's hands secured behind his back as well. At some point his stupor wore off, and he started talking. Saying I was crazy, saying I'd attacked him and had tried to kill him. Saying I'd killed Elliot. I didn't try to refute him. Didn't have the energy.

Because I knew I'd been wrong about one thing—the most important thing. Rachel and the boys weren't in the basement. They might've been there at one time, but they weren't there now. I didn't know where he'd taken them, where he'd put them.

He'd eventually break, just like he had in the basement. Because he wasn't used to being held accountable for anything. Not for a young girl's suicide and not for the tangled web he'd woven for himself by giving in to his illicit desires. Soon he'd tell them where Rachel and the boys were, and the waiting and wondering and guessing would be over. For now he simply lied.

"He and Elliot Wyman were in on it together," Father Mathew said to the cops leading us out through the church. "They planned everything. They've been taking money from the church donations, and David Barren finally caught on to them."

I raised my head from looking at the floor. We were nearing the sanctuary, and something strange was happening. A few dozen people milled around in the atrium, parishioners here for their Wednesday night worship, which should have started a while ago. There was a weird reverberation in the air, and for a moment I couldn't figure out what it was. I was hearing Father Mathew's continued liturgy of lies both from him and from somewhere else ahead. From the sanctuary speakers.

He sputtered out a few more words, then realized he was hearing it, too, and slowly quieted.

My eyes went down to his waist, to the microphone pack he wore there for Mass, to the little green light glowing beneath his gown.

It must've gotten turned on during our initial scuffle.

Though the police kept us moving, it felt like we were wading through amber. Everything slowed down.

The parishioners stood watching us being led out, arms crossed over chests, expressions aghast at what they'd heard. Their eyes were pinpoints, focused on the father as he was escorted past. He tried saying something but stopped as some people turned their backs. Others murmured to themselves.

None of them spared me a glance.

Outside, the parking lot was alive with red-and-blue lights. Police cruisers were parked askew of each other, doors still flung open, radios chattering away. The cops holding my elbows guided me over to one of the cars and put me in the back. The seat was hard plastic and uncomfortable. Two cars away Father Mathew was placed in the back seat of another cruiser. I could only see the crown of his crew cut. I wondered if he was praying.

Sometime later, could've been two minutes or twenty, Spanner rolled into the lot and climbed out of his sedan. He stood talking to several uniforms, and one of them gestured at the church, then at the cars where Father Mathew and I sat. Spanner threw me a look, then turned and went inside the church. He came back maybe fifteen minutes later and opened the door beside me.

I looked out at him through one eye. My other was swelling shut. We sat that way for a few seconds, just studying one another. Then he shook his head and told me I was going to the station. I didn't say anything; it could and would be held against me and all that. He shut the door, and a uniformed cop eventually climbed in the front seat, and we drove away.

The church and the Loop receded from view. The last evening light snagged on the church's steeple, and I thought of a day a million years ago when I'd told Rachel I loved her. Asked if we could be together someday. Even though she hadn't said it back, I'd held on to hope, all the way from then until now.

They found her and the boys the next morning.

31

I was in lockup when it happened, so I didn't hear about it until later.

But it went something like this:

Around ten in the morning, about the same time I was listening to Kel berate the city jail officer regarding my bail, Rachel's car pulled onto the Loop and glided to a stop in the Barrens' driveway. It sat there idling for a few minutes, then Rachel climbed out and looked at the house. Asher and Joey tried getting out from the back seat, but Rachel said something to them and they got back inside and shut the doors. She made her way slowly up the front steps, stopping to look at the broken window in the door, which had been covered over with a piece of cardboard. Then she went inside.

Mrs. Tross, unsurprisingly, was on her front porch with her binoculars and witnessed this new development in the development. She immediately called the police. So did Mrs. Pell across the street. All in all, the Sandford PD received no fewer than ten calls that morning regarding the woman and children who had been missing for a week.

By the time the first cruiser rolled onto the Loop and came to a stop before the Barrens', Rachel had exited the house and was standing in the driveway as if she were lost. The responding officer came up to her, and they spoke. Several people said later that Rachel pointed at the house and shook her head. Then her voice rose loud enough for most listening out of open windows or gawking from porches to hear. Only one word, but it conveyed plenty. *What?*

She wobbled a little, and the officer helped her over to the hood of her car, and she leaned against it. She stayed that way as more and more police showed up. Asher and Joey tried exiting the back seat again and were banished for a second time.

After a half hour of spectacle, Rachel climbed into her car and backed out of the driveway and followed a single cruiser out of the neighborhood while several others trailed behind. Then they were gone, and all was quiet again on the Loop.

That was how Rachel Barren and her boys were found, and how she learned her husband had been murdered.

———

They always say what you're trying to find is in the last place you look. Well, it was doubly true with Rachel and the boys, since no one under the sun had thought to look at Sadie Gardner's house out in the foothills.

It made total sense later when I thought about it. I'd seen the two women talking at the farmers market the day Rachel and the boys vanished. Sadie, the no-nonsense woman who'd finally had enough of getting beaten by her husband and put him in the emergency room. Sadie, who owned a farm completely off the grid with no real means of communication with the outside world. Someone Rachel knew well enough to ask for a favor but not well enough for anyone to check with when Rachel and the boys went missing. Rachel also knew that given what she was dealing with at home, Sadie Gardner couldn't very well turn her away.

The rift in the Barren household became a gaping chasm the night before Rachel and Sadie made their agreement, when Joey came home and told her what Father Mathew had made him do that day in his office. Rachel told the police she'd been completely blindsided and devastated when she finally understood what her son was trying to explain, what he'd been holding in for months. All of the boy's anxiety and behavioral problems suddenly made sense. When she went to David with the news and the declaration she would be calling the police, everything had fallen apart.

Because, of course, David already knew what was happening up at the school on the hill. He'd helped engineer it in a way. Maybe he actually believed Father Mathew hadn't touched his son again after the day he'd caught them together and begun his blackmail scheme, but if he did, it was a blind belief. It was looking the other way while pretending everything was okay.

David told Rachel that she most certainly wouldn't be going to the police, and if she did, who did she think the authorities would believe? A troubled little boy and his anxiety-stricken mother? Or a well-respected business owner and a prominent man of faith? Would they listen to the woman who got a little too tipsy at some of the community functions? Someone who had fallen into a drug-addled sleep in her yard while she was supposed to be watching her sons? Who had let her two-year-old almost get hit by a car in front of the entire neighborhood?

David had told her that nothing was going to change, unless she never wanted to see the boys again. Because he could do that. He could make sure he gained full custody, make sure she became a pariah in the community. His parents would back him up, and he was pretty sure hers would as well.

He'd assured her everything would work out now since their loan agency would be saved by Ryan's untimely death. David would be receiving a large sum from the insurance company, and things would be fine again.

Unless she went around shooting her mouth off, then her world would come crashing down. And she didn't want that. Did she?

No. No, of course not. That's what she'd told him.

That night she'd formulated a plan to get away, create some space between her and the boys and David. She'd known Sadie's story, known she would probably have a soft spot for an abused woman and her children. Would open her home as a refuge where they could hide away for a time without the interference from the outside world. Away from corrupt husbands and chiding parents. Away from the news about what was happening on the Loop in their absence.

So that's what she'd done. After I'd spoken with her at the farmers market, she'd gone grocery shopping, picked up the boys from school without incident, and never gone back home. Instead she'd driven straight to Sadie's house, where they'd stayed for over a week. Enough time for Rachel to decompress and formulate a plan to confront David, to ask for a divorce. Because there was no way she was continuing to put her son through the hell he'd been enduring for months on end. No way the sick charade David had concocted would continue.

But when she arrived home, the house had been empty. David had been dead for a week, and the whereabouts of her and the boys were the great concern of the community as well as one heartsick fool who lived down the street.

Of course, I learned all this later after spending almost two days bouncing back and forth from a cell to an interrogation room where I answered questions. Lots and lots of questions. The only highlight of this being none of them were asked by Detective Spanner. It seemed his outright dismissal of my call of alarm prior to going up to the church and his refusal to follow up on it didn't sit well with the powers that be. Not well at all. I saw him once during those two days of questioning. He looked even worse than he had at the hospital, and that was saying something. I had trouble gathering much sympathy.

Regardless, I was put through the crucible. How had I come to know about Father Mathew and David's scheme? How had I known Mary Shelby's death hadn't been an accident? I was again in the middle of a minefield. Each and every step could create an explosion that would destroy my chances at seeing anything other than the inside of a cell for the foreseeable future.

So I told them the truth. Or at least as much of it as they needed.

I said I'd never believed Mary's death had been an accident (I hadn't).

I said I'd gone to her house to gather some pictures out of sentimentality and gotten curious, then searched through her computer (I had).

I told them that the discovery of the spreadsheets had led me to question Jill Abernathy (it had), which in turn led me to deduce that Father Mathew was involved somehow with the diminishing payments and ultimately Mary's demise (he had been). I also said I'd heard rumors that David and Ryan's business had been floundering and theorized their deaths had tied into the church donations after speaking with one Mrs. Tross, who had told me she'd seen Mary Shelby meeting with David shortly before her death.

I learned something else, too, as I was interrogated—cops did not like being one-upped. Especially in an investigation where they'd been stymied. I tried downplaying my involvement to the very basics, telling them I was simply concerned about Rachel and the boys since they were my friends.

"Friends, huh?" a detective by the name of Daern said in one of the longer questioning periods. He had removed his jacket, and there were little half-moons of perspiration in the armpits of his shirt. "That it?"

"That's it," I said. "My nieces play with her boys pretty often. She checks in on my dad from time to time. Neighbor stuff."

"Neighbor stuff," Daern repeated, and looked at me like I was a pane of glass. But that was all that was said.

The central issue the authorities were concerned with was Elliot Wyman's death.

Just like I'd guessed, Father Mathew had cracked with a little pressure and the fact that over two dozen members of the church had heard his confession through the sanctuary's speaker system. He'd spilled his guts about everything—Joey's molestation, David's blackmail, Mary and Ryan's murders, Elliot's accidental involvement and how he'd used the impressionable man to do his bidding, including but not limited to following me after I'd asked Father Mathew about his phone call with Ryan Vallance. In regard to Elliot's death, he eventually confessed about the struggle and the gun going off. He hadn't meant for Elliot to die, just like he hadn't meant for any of the other things to happen. Even after admitting to them, he still couldn't take responsibility for his actions. I wasn't surprised.

Though they couldn't hang any of the deaths on me, I was formally charged with assault, breaking and entering, interfering with a criminal case, and several other crimes that escape me now. I was allowed bail since my record was clean other than the vandalization charge from when I'd broken the church's window, which had ultimately been dropped anyway.

When I was released, Kel picked me up outside city hall, where the jail was located, hugging me hard, then punching me even harder in the shoulder. She said I was a stupid, stupid person and she loved me very much. Dad said about the same when I got home and visited him—he'd been discharged from the hospital the day before and had been issued a canister of oxygen—but all in all, they understood better than anyone why I'd done what I'd done.

I sat alone by the big windows that first night back in my house. Sat looking up the street at the darkened shape of Rachel's home. I'd heard she and the boys were staying at a hotel and thought it very telling they weren't at her parents' house. I thought maybe a reckoning was taking place within the Barren and Worth households. The allegiance between the two power families was suddenly and rapidly dissolving, and I wondered how everything would wash out. In any case Rachel and the boys were safe now, and that was all that mattered to me.

What my mind kept coming back to, like a tongue probing the place where a tooth used to be, was David's murder. As hesitant as Elliot had been to shoot me, I couldn't see him killing David in cold blood—even if he'd been willing to search his house for any blackmail David had been holding over Father Mathew, who would be the next most likely candidate. For a moment I questioned why, if Father Mathew had killed David, he hadn't done it sooner. Instead of going to the lengths he did, why not nip it in the proverbial bud? But just as quickly, I realized it was calculated risk. Skimming from the church's donations was less dicey than killing a prominent businessman with a family. Even when he was pushed to the extreme and forced to kill Mary to keep the secret, he'd hedged his bets. Mary lived alone and had horses, which could be dangerous at times.

But really the suspect who made the most sense was the Visitor. My first ideation of David's death was probably the most accurate—a loan shark's collection agent makes a nighttime visit, things get out of hand, and bam, Occam's razor and all that. But there was one thing that kept throwing that scenario off. One glaring detail that gave me pause and wouldn't let my mind rest. I set it aside for later, knowing I'd revisit it soon enough.

In the pantry I took out the note from where I'd replaced it in the rice (the police had searched my house, but thankfully no one had thought to dig through my dry goods) and read it one last time before lighting it on fire in the kitchen. It burned quickly, and I rinsed the ashes down the sink. Then I went to bed, and in the morning Dad told me Rachel had called and asked if I could meet her for a picnic.

———

The pull-off was deserted just like the last time we'd met at the hiking trail in the mountains. I thought maybe she'd gotten a ride from an Uber or Lyft as I made my way up the path, my assumptions proving out when I rounded a bend and spotted her sitting on a large boulder just off the trail.

I tried not to run but still broke out into a little jog when I saw her. She climbed down, and I attempted interpreting her expression as I got closer, but then she was in my arms, her hair brushing my face, and I was lost and found all at once.

We stayed that way for a time, and when we released one another, I let her be the guide as to what came next. She didn't lean in for a kiss, only stood back a little and looked at me. I tried to find words (it's kinda my thing), but there were none, so I just waited.

She took my hand and led me to the rock, which was pleasantly warm from the sun cresting over the nearest mountain. There was birdsong and the chitter of insects waking up for the day. And my heart, aching and beating furiously over all of it.

"Are you okay?" I asked finally.

She nodded. "As well as I can be."

"How are the boys?"

"They're . . . not great. Joey's been quiet ever since we left home, hasn't said more than a few words in a row. Asher has been crying almost nonstop since we got back and found . . . found out. My mother's watching them this morning. I said I had to get away, clear my head. Didn't think it would be a great idea to be seen together."

"No, probably not." I picked at some flakes of rock. "I thought you were—I was really worried."

"I know. I heard what you did." She reached up and touched the cuts and bruises on my face. Most were healing well, but the sensation of her fingers set them all alight again. "Thank you."

Right then, I wanted to tell her everything. Wanted to blurt out I'd been in her house, found out about HerringBone, everything. But I couldn't. Not yet at least.

She asked about how my dad was doing after the gas incident. I told her he was recovering fine and that the doctors didn't think there was any permanent brain damage. She laughed when I said he'd asked how the hell they'd tell the difference at this point.

God, I'd missed her laugh.

"You think Father Mathew tried to gas you?" she asked.

I shrugged. "He hasn't confessed, but why add on another fifty years to his sentence? I don't think Elliot was capable of it. Not given how hesitant he was to shoot me."

I could see the look in Elliot's eyes again, had seen it most nights before dropping off to sleep, and wondered how many foot-pounds of pressure had been left on the trigger before he'd lowered the gun. Everyone has their breaking point, and I didn't know how close Elliot had come to reaching his. Maybe it was better not to know.

Almost echoing my thoughts, Rachel said, "You never know what people are capable of, do you? What's really hiding underneath. David was always . . . intense. But he became so much worse once the business started going downhill. He . . ."

I waited, an intuition of what was coming keeping me quiet for nearly a minute while she struggled.

"He never hit me, but he threatened to. He said things . . . that really frightened me. That's why I left my cell behind when we went to Sadie's. I was afraid he'd track us somehow." She grimaced and took a deep breath. "Sometimes I could feel the anger coming off him like heat, and I was afraid for me and the kids. I don't know why I didn't tell you. It was like if I didn't say it, it wouldn't really be real. It was like a nightmare: if you can get enough distance from it, then it fades more and more." A tear slipped free of her eye and slid down the side of her nose. She swiped it away. "Oh God, I should've done something sooner. If I would've left him, Joey would've never—"

"He would've gotten custody," I said quietly. "He would've used all his power and carried on just like he wanted to. People like David usually do. Don't blame yourself. You're going to hear this a lot in the next year or so, but I mean it. This wasn't your fault."

She leaned into me then, and I put an arm around her. When she finally sat back, her face was blotchy and tear streaked, but a clarity had entered her gaze. "I wasn't ready."

I nodded. "I know."

"You . . . you were everything I needed, everything David wasn't, and it scared the hell out of me. When you said . . . that . . . when you told me and asked if we could be together, it terrified me, Andy. It scared me because of how much I wanted to say it back. How much I wanted to say yes."

My heart surged. A thousand suns flaring. I waited until I knew my voice would be steady, then said, "That's why you left the note in my door."

Her eyes flashed up to mine, and I could almost see the shock wave roll through her. "How did you . . . when did you . . ."

"Last night. I was at home thinking about everything. Taking it all apart and putting it back together. I'd thought the note had been the catalyst for everything that came after. I thought I was the reason you were missing, but it was just a coincidence. Bad timing, I guess."

She uttered a shaky laugh. "I didn't know what else to do. I didn't have it in me to tell you I didn't want to see you anymore, mostly because it wasn't the truth. So I took the coward's way out and left you the note one night when I knew you were at your dad's. It was easier than breaking your heart. Easier than breaking mine."

I took her hand and kissed it, held it to my chest. "Not broken." She smiled. "But there is one thing I have to tell you."

"What's that?"

"The next time you write a semi-threatening blackmail note, let me read it over first. It was a little melodramatic."

She laughed again. Music to my ears.

32

You fall back into a routine, the old adage that people can get used to anything proving true once again.

You get up in the morning, work on the edits of the book that was bought for a very nice advance from a new publisher you've never placed anything with before. You make lunch for your father and note a few more idiosyncrasies in his behavior, the scoreboard ticking another span of points for the disease that will eventually win the game. The way things are progressing, you're almost certain it won't go into overtime.

You while away most afternoons tinkering with a new idea that may or may not become a novel. Maybe a short story—no, a novel. Who knows? You make dinner and spend the evening watching some television, maybe sitting outside under the stars and sipping a beer with your old man. Sometimes your sister and her kids come over too. The girls' laughter is good for you.

You keep in regular correspondence with your brother, who is still—to be honest—kind of a dick. But you can talk to him now for more than a few minutes without wanting a drink or to hit something, and that's progress, as they say.

You take long walks before bed, leaving the Loop behind and traveling around the pond in the nearby park. You like the way the last light holds on the water until it's gone, as if the sun left a little bit of itself there and won't pick it back up until morning. Then you go home and get in bed and think until sleep finally pulls you under.

You do this all summer.

———

I don't know who organized the event. It was something Mary would've typically done for a church function, but of course Mary was no longer here, and the church had been in a period of upheaval for months.

A new father was coming in a few weeks to take over the disgraced helm left by Father Mathew, who was awaiting sentencing in a county jail north of New York City. He never did confess to sneaking into Dad's place and turning on the gas burners, but I'm sure he did it. He could keep that secret if he wanted. We all hid one thing or another in the end.

I walked with Dad, Kel, and the girls to the park where the community cookout was taking place. It was late September and had that perfect tone of so many fall days—warm sun, cool breeze. The kind that was made for the smell of hot charcoal and the last of a cold beer sliding over your tongue with another waiting for you in some ice nearby.

Most everyone from the Loop was there. Mrs. Tross, now in a wheelchair, sat gabbing with Mr. Allen Crane like they were ancient friends. He and I nodded at one another as we passed. It was amazing what a cheesecake and an apology would do.

Mrs. Pell and her husband had brought their smoker down the day before and had been here since sunup, a whole pig turning slowly and issuing a most delicious scent on the breeze. A few dozen other couples and people I only recognized from church were there too.

And Rachel and her boys.

They were at a picnic table at the far end of the park, only a little removed from the rest of the group, but I noticed the polite gap between them and everyone else. It was a visual representation of the feeling within the neighborhood, but I was glad to see a couple of the other young mothers standing with Rachel, trying to include her even though she no longer lived on the Loop.

She'd sold the house up the street a few weeks after reappearing. Too many memories, she told me at one of our few meetings up on the hiking trail. It was really the only place we felt safe being in one another's company, neither of us wanting to throw any morsels to the gossip crowd, which was still hungry even though the initial furor had died down following Rachel and the boys' sudden return.

We were taking it slow. Nothing physical other than a gentle kiss here and there. That was more than fine by me. I was happy enough being in her company, listening to her voice, making her laugh if I could. She was laughing more often now, and I thought that was a very good sign. I wondered if she was singing again.

To be honest I'd been deeply afraid she and the boys would move completely out of Sandford. It wouldn't have surprised anyone. Word about David and Father Mathew had gotten around the entire town so quickly you would've thought it had been planted in the collective consciousness overnight. Not that I'd heard anyone say anything against Rachel, but there was an undercurrent to how people spoke of her. Almost as if when they said it was a tragedy and what a horrible situation she'd been put in, they were also saying she should've done something different. I guessed a few of them, though they'd never admit it, wished she would've kept everything to herself. Then the nasty underbelly could've stayed hidden and no one would've been inconvenienced with the knowledge.

Overall, things seemed to be healing, and Rachel hadn't said anything about moving farther than the little two story she'd purchased on the south side of town.

I watched Alicia and Emmy race over to Asher and Joey, smiled at how the boys' faces lit up when they saw them. The children struck up an immediate game of tag and flew over to the playground to continue it among the jungle gym and slides. Both Asher and Joey were in therapy, and Rachel said they were doing a little better, but it would take years. Children were resilient, nothing short of miracles really, and I hoped someday they would both be able to come to terms with what had happened. I hoped I'd be able to help.

"You think Cory will make it today?" Dad asked as we sidled up to the table where a dozen or more dishes were laid out. Kel and I shared a look as she added an apple pie she'd baked to the soiree of food.

"Don't think so, Dad," I said, helping him with a plate. "Maybe next week, though." He seemed to accept this and spooned some potato salad beside a chunk of steak. I was dreading when he started to ask about Emma or our mother. For now I counted every relatively good day as a blessing.

And as blessings went, the news I'd received two days before definitely counted. All charges against me had been officially dropped by the Sandford district attorney. Not that they hadn't tried to make them stick, mind you. I had been called back into the station no fewer than four times throughout the summer to answer questions, but with each session it became more and more apparent they were only treading water, not making any real headway. It was because there was nothing tying me to anything beyond what I'd already admitted. No incriminating evidence, nothing a jury or judge would deem worthy of hard time.

The very last day I'd sat in the interrogation room with Detective Daern, he'd tapped a number printed on a sheet of paper I recognized as one of my phone statements. I'd handed them over the month before, no subpoena necessary.

"What's this?" he said, pointing to the number the Visitor had called me from. I knew they'd eventually get to that since he'd rung my regular cell instead of the burner.

"Not sure. Must've been a wrong number," I said.

"You don't remember?"

"I guess not."

"You talked for a couple minutes. Kinda long for a wrong number."

"Maybe we struck up a conversation. I'm always looking for material for my books; it's funny where you find inspiration." I said all this with a straight face, looking directly at Daern.

He watched me for a second, then nodded to his partner. "Go ahead and show Mr. Drake out."

"It's okay," I said, standing. "I know the way."

The day after my agent let me know the good news about my manuscript, I sent it off to the email address the Visitor had given me. I got no reply initially but received a postcard in the mail about a week later, a gorgeous sunset going down behind an island that might've been in Polynesia somewhere. On the back, typed, was this:

> Taut. Good characters. Too many metaphors. Liked the
> happy ending.

So did I. So did I.

I caught Rachel's eye as we settled into a table kitty-corner to hers. She was still talking with the other mothers and flashed me a brief smile. She was holding a beer, and when she laughed at something one of the women said, it sounded genuine. I was glad.

The pork was delicious and the beer was cold and the day was perfect, but as it wore on, I felt myself falling back into a groove I normally wore deeper at night. My thinking time. I'd taken to lying awake for hours in the dark, my mind treading and retreading the events from the months before.

Really it was one thing that kept coming back to me. Something innocuous, but glaring whenever I thought about it.

The broken window in the Barrens' front door.

I'd tried accepting that the Visitor was responsible, since Father Mathew to this day still denied he'd killed David, but the broken window kept getting in the way. The Visitor was a pro. He'd gained access to my house with barely a sound, no jimmied lock, and no broken glass. What had he said when I'd accused him of trying to gas me and my dad? *Not my style.* And neither was the broken window. It had almost been like an afterthought. A stark and undeniable clue pointing to someone breaking in. Someone outlining in neon that **THIS WAS A ROBBERY GONE WRONG.**

In other words, a little melodramatic.

I looked at Rachel again. She was watching her boys and Kel's girls playing. I thought of what David had told her the night she realized what Joey was being subjected to. I thought of the summer storm behind her eyes that thrilled, and if I was honest, frightened me a little at times. An intensity like a flash of lightning over a raging sea.

I could see her that night, lying in bed planning what she was going to do. The conversation with Sadie, the rest of the day while she went about her errands, then picking up the boys to leave town.

But what kept me awake in those hours before sleep finally dragged me under was what happened after that. If I wrote the scene, it would go something like this:

Around one in the morning, Rachel gets up from the spare bedroom Sadie made up for her and the boys. She looks at her children and silently leaves them where they sleep. Maybe she finds a gun never registered by Sadie or her ex-husband in a closet or basement. When she has it, she leaves the house and drives the twenty miles back into Sandford. She shuts her lights off as she enters the Loop, but it's probably needless—the street is silent and motionless, almost everyone sleeping. Almost.

She parks at the far end of the turnaround and walks the short distance to her house, making sure to keep out of the streetlamps. She still has her keys, and David's forgotten to arm the alarm like he usually does.

She doesn't try to hide the sound of her entry, makes enough noise to rouse her husband and simply waits in the hall where there is nowhere to hide and chances of missing go down considerably. David steps out of their room to investigate the sound, makes it almost to the kitchen before a single shot lights up the dark. Enough for him to see her face in the muzzle flash, maybe see the way her eyes burn.

She tears through their room, snagging some cash and jewelry, then leaves, stopping on the front steps to knock a single pane of glass from the door with the butt of the gun before hurrying back to her car. She drives away, not seeing the old man two houses down from hers standing in the dark of his living room, awake and watching.

In the morning Dad remembered the only connection his failing neurons could make, saying he'd seen George Nell, who had been dead for years. At the time I'd brushed it off as confusion, but it hadn't been. In a strange way it made perfect sense.

Because when George Nell had been alive, he'd lived in Rachel and David's house.

I came back to myself and realized Rachel was staring at me. The other women had rejoined their families, and she was standing alone, clutching the empty beer bottle to her chest, knuckles white. The look was in her eyes now, the one that could send a little ripple of unease through me, one that spoke of a well of strength with no bottom.

Everyone has a breaking point, and I knew Rachel had reached hers that night.

We continued to look at one another, something passing between us—unspoken knowledge leading to a precipice. A divide. Before and after.

After a breathless moment, I gave her a smile. Slowly she returned it.

Somewhere, I felt that everything was going to be all right.

See, my problem is I'm a romantic.

RESOURCES

The National Suicide Prevention Lifeline is a national network of local crisis centers that provides free and confidential emotional support to people in suicidal crisis or emotional distress 24 hours a day, 7 days a week. They are committed to improving crisis services and advancing suicide prevention by empowering individuals, advancing professional best practices, and building awareness.

Call 1-800-273-8255 or visit https://suicidepreventionlifeline.org/

The Trevor Project is the world's largest suicide prevention and crisis intervention organization for LGBTQ (lesbian, gay, bisexual, transgender, queer, and questioning) young people. Visit https://www.thetrevorproject.org/

The Human Rights Campaign has resources to help you come out and live openly at home, at work, and in your community. Visit https://www.hrc.org/resources/coming-out

ACKNOWLEDGMENTS

Thanks goes out to my family as always—I couldn't do any of this without you. Thanks to my agent, Laura Rennert—I'm beyond grateful to have someone so dedicated and supportive in my corner. Thanks to my editor, Liz Pearsons, for truly believing in me and the book. Thanks to Jacque Ben-Zekry, who continually pushes me to be a better writer. Thanks to Matt Iden, Blake Crouch, Matt FitzSimmons, Dori Pulley, Richard Brown, and Steven Konkoly—I'm beyond privileged to count you as friends and am so grateful for your generosity and insight. Thanks to the Thomas & Mercer team for believing in stories while helping bring them to life. And thanks to all the readers who continue to make what I do possible; the books are nothing without you.

ABOUT THE AUTHOR

Photo © 2019 Jade Hart

Joe Hart is the *Wall Street Journal* bestselling author of fourteen novels, including *The River Is Dark*, *Obscura*, *The Last Girl*, and *We Sang in the Dark*. When not writing, he enjoys reading, exercising, exploring the great outdoors, and watching movies with his family. For more information on his upcoming novels and access to his blog, visit www.joehartbooks.com.